EVENING CODE

A NOVEL

STUART FABE

Author's Note

IT'S HARD TO imagine a time when there were no such things as photographs or when instant communication was just pure fantasy.

And yet, less than two hundred years ago there were no accurate visual images until Louis-Jacques-Mandé Daguerre created the first photographs in 1839. His daguerreotype images were of such pristine quality that they became affectionately known as "the mirror with a memory."

Similarly, it wasn't until Samuel Finley Breese Morse invented the telegraph that real-time communication became possible. The years prior to Morse's invention came to be known as the "great hush." His first transmitted message from Washington DC to Baltimore in 1844 was both haunting and prophetic:

"What Hath God Wrought?"

Evening Code is a work of fiction, and I wrote it purely as entertainment. While many of the references in the story are historically accurate, I have taken certain literary liberties with others. I'm a storyteller, after all.

This is the third novel in the Clay Arnold series, and past readers will recognize some familiar characters. I hope you enjoy reading *Evening Code* as much as I enjoyed researching and crafting the story!

Stuart Fabe

Dedication

In Fond Memory of Louis Daniel Brodsky,
Forever Friend and Mentor.

Chapter 1

COULDN'T HELP BUT SMILE at my good fortune. I woke up early on this brisk mid-November morning with soft moonlight cascading through my bedroom skylights. It's just before six thirty, and my eyes are still adjusting to the darkness. Despite the low light, I can make out several features in the room: my grandfather's chair, my favorite antique camera, a well-occupied bookshelf, several of my large photographs, and beside me, the peacefully sleeping form of the woman I love, Maggie Bodine.

In the moonlit darkness, I can make out the shimmer of her auburn hair as photons of light coalesce into an auric corona. Maggie's head is resting on a pillow, and her face is turned toward me. Eyes closed, she breathes evenly, away somewhere in secure sleep. Beneath her blanket, I can see the rounding shape of her heretofore trim belly, and I stifle a gasp at the thought of what we are creating, and how our lives will be unpredictably different. In many ways I have lived a very fulfilling existence during my thirty-six years, but at the heart of it, Maggie and our baby will forever be my very best good fortune.

Maggie is four months along in her pregnancy now, and I don't want to disturb her sleep. All of our friends tell us to get the sleep now because there may be precious little of it once the baby comes. I quietly slip out of my side of the bed and put on my robe and socks. The moonlight is waning now, and I feel my way through the shaded room to the sliding glass doors leading to my rooftop deck. The distant glow of the eastern sky gives colorful hints that the sun is rising, and the morning chill welcomes me to a new day as I step outside.

My name is Clay Arnold, and I'm a professional photographer who has enjoyed a prosperous career traveling the world on photographic assignments that I find personally appealing. In many ways my professional career has been ideal. I've made a lot of money doing what I love, and I've been generously recognized by the art and academic worlds for my efforts. But, I've also learned that no one is immune from the vagaries of life, and I've known my share of heartache, too.

I look out over the renovated nineteenth-century beer brewery complex that I own. Across the cobblestone courtyard, I can see that there are no lights on yet at the original farmhouse where my lifelong friends Tori and Weed Rawlins live. The farmhouse was built in 1855 when the Block brothers emigrated to America from Bavaria and opened their beer brewery here along the White River a few miles above Indianapolis, Indiana. I do, however, see faint illumination inside the original brewery power plant where my wise old friend, Mace Davis, lives along with our young former street urchin, Rennie Cotton, who came to work for us a few years ago and earned his way into our close family of friends.

I'm not surprised that Mace is awake. At age seventy-two, he's lived as the caretaker of the brewery complex ever since he moved here looking for work as a destitute, skinny, fourteen-year-old kid from Freeport in the Bahamas. The Block Brothers Brewery had closed several years before and was now the location of the Jeffries Woodworking Mill when Mace showed up looking like a stray. Fifty-eight years have passed, and he's still here keeping the entire property in excellent shape. In fact, when I bought the brewery complex several years ago, Mr. Jeffries sold it to me on one indelible condition: that Mace Davis be permitted to live in the power plant as long as he wished. I agreed, and it was a decision that I've never regretted. I respect Mace's knowledge and skills and treasure his friendship.

Thinking about our newest family member, Rennie Cotton, always brings a smile to my face. Rennie is about fifteen years old and resides in the power plant with Mace and our three-legged black labrador, Lex. The story of how Rennie came to live with us is a bit long. Let's suffice it to say that some eight years ago I was shooting a series of inner-city street scenes in Indy when I shot an image of a lonely black kid sitting in a tenement doorway. It became one of my favorite photos ever, and three years ago, I asked Mace to help me find him. We did, and after some rough days of his adjusting to working for us and living here in more appealing surroundings than the shack he'd been subsisting in, Rennie finally settled in.

Shortly after he arrived, he and Tori, who is Weed's blind sister, were walking on a path along the White River when they were attacked by two men. Rennie saved Tori's life and Lex's, too when the dog was shot by Newt Hacker. Rennie is one of us now, and we all make certain he has our support, instruction, and guidance. Besides that, he's a darn smart and fun kid.

With each moment that passes, the eastern sky continues to brighten. A few stars are still visible, and before long our closest star, the sun, will provide life-giving warmth and light to our planet's flora and fauna. I admit that I am not a man of God, at least not in the traditional sense, but looking into the vastness of space creates mysteries for me that border on the theological. The creation of life itself, and the awareness that in a few short months Maggie will deliver a new sentient being to our universe is another mystery that exceeds my ability to fully comprehend.

Another moment passes, and I am joined on the deck by my buddy, Satchmo, who is the largest darn Maine Coon cat that you ever saw. Satchmo snuffles a greeting to me and proceeds to offer his human a lifeless chipmunk by my feet.

"Oh gee, thanks, Satchmo," I offer in sarcastic response to his generosity. "I'm surprised you haven't wiped out the entire rodent population around here by now." Satchmo rubs his furry flank against my leg, offers another audible snuffle, and is gone an instant later to continue his clandestine rounds of the brewery complex.

Alone again, I can't help but think back on the events over the past couple of years that affected the lives of everyone in our close family of friends.

About three years ago I lost my fiancée, Dr. Jennifer Skyler, to a domestic terrorist bombing of the Planned Parenthood Center where she worked in Broadripple. Her murder set me on a path as an avenging vigilante that saw the dark side of my personality take over to even the score for those among us who couldn't protect themselves. My mantra became, "evening comes." Both Weed and Mace helped me with my "self-anointed judgments" by creating clandestine weapons for executing people that I deemed deserved it. I'm not especially proud of my avenging behavior, but on the other hand, I really don't lose any sleep over it either. Just saying.

Then, just two months ago when I was receiving an honorary doctorate at Kissinger College in Greencastle, Indiana, a particularly pissy cuss named Dr. Mortimer Chestnut kidnapped Maggie's niece, Laura, and created a lot of turmoil, including my finally coming clean with Maggie about my alter-ego as an avenging vigilante.

Fortunately, we were able to rescue Laura and apprehend Mortimer Chestnut without anyone getting really hurt. My blood still boils with anger though when I see or read about ugly behavior and mean-spirited bigotry. Happily, with the loving presence of Maggie in my life, and now with our baby on the way, it's helped calm the savage beast that, while dormant, still resides within me.

In a flash I'm brought back to the present as Satchmo leaps up to the handrail near my elbow with yet another rodent hanging limply from his whiskered maw.

"I swear, Satchmo, you're like a gray ghost that just appears from out of nowhere. And what's with the dead rodent? You look like you have a huge walrus mustache with that thing hanging there."

Satchmo replies to my snarky comments by dropping his trophy on the handrail and rubbing his forehead against mine and nuzzling my nose. It's hard not to smile at moments like this. But our "moment" is short-lived as he delivers a parting snuffle and bounds away to begin a new adventure. And I'm alone again with a dawning day, a dead rodent, and the streaming of my thoughts.

And then I feel a presence press behind me, and two soft arms reach around to my chest and pull me close. I feel her breasts nestle my back, and her thighs lean into the rear of mine. She places her mouth by my ear and whispers what every man yearns to hear, "Meow!"

Maggie's awake! "Good morning, Clay!" she says as she slips in between me and the hand rail.

"I saw you having a moment with Satchmo and didn't want to miss out on all of the fun."

"Good morning to you, too, sweetheart. I woke up early and didn't want to disturb you so I thought I'd come out here and watch the sun come up. And don't worry about missing out on any fun. Satchmo doesn't hang around very long, especially if there are chubby chipmunks to be found."

We held each other close and kissed for some long, very pleasant moments, and in the morning chill, Maggie whispered the words that every man really wants to hear, "Let's get back in bed!" And so we did.

Twenty minutes later we lay in a heap amid a tangle of bedsheets and arms and legs. Maggie's head rests on my chest, and I lightly stroke her auburn hair. The moon glow is long gone from the skylights, replaced by streaks of sunlight. We lay there for a few minutes enjoying each other's warmth and the security of knowing that we are committed to one another.

"So, Mr. Arnold," Maggie began, "any chance I'll see a wedding ring on my finger anytime soon?! It might be nice if we legalized our partnership so that little Sputnik here gets a proper welcome."

"Oh, I think we might be able to make that happen," I toyed with her. "Just tell me when and where you want to have a wedding ceremony, and I promise I'll do my very best to be there."

My playful reply earned me a gentle jab in the ribs from Maggie, and then we did what seemed like a really very good, terrific idea, and we made love again. About eight thirty we finally returned to full control of our senses and lay in each others' arms talking about a wedding and a number of other things that both of us needed to do before the rigors of pregnancy got too tiring for Maggie.

"Spending the past two months here with you and everyone at the brewery complex has been terrific," Maggie cooed. "After living in Santa Fe these past several years, I never thought I'd be happy living anywhere else, but this feels like home, and getting to know Tori and Weed, Mace and Rennie confirms that this is my home now."

"Well, I'd be less than honest if I didn't say that I was concerned about how you'd feel living in the Midwest," Clay admitted. "Aside from the occasional bombings, kidnappings, and murders we have a good life here," I said only half in jest. "And actually," I continued, "I don't see any reason why we shouldn't keep your home in Santa Fe, too. I think we can afford it, and keeping your home will give us a great place for getaways, and you won't have to feel like you've given up everything to be with me."

"I think I'd like that," Maggie replied. "And, you know all of our friends here, plus my sister's family would always be welcome to vacation there, too."

"And speaking of Santa Fe," Maggie continued. "I think it's about time that I went back to look after my home and some work responsibilities that I've let slide a bit. My public relations business has continued to grow, and I don't see why I can't fly to various locations as needed in the future and handle most other things by phone or from my computer."

"When do you think you'll head back?" I asked.

"Well, probably day after tomorrow," Maggie said as she inched even closer to me. "Thanksgiving is next week, too, and I'm thinking this may be the last family holiday that I'm able to spend with Rita, Tom, and Laura before the baby arrives. Are you okay with that?"

"Of course, but you know I'll miss you horribly," I replied. "And, Weed and I have been talking about going to Chicago to attend an auction of some very rare art and early photographic ephemera. There's one camera in particular that is about as rare as they come, and I've been thinking about trying to get it for our antique camera museum."

"So how rare is it?" Maggie asked. "By rare, I assume it's also pretty expensive, too."

"Uh, yeah," I gulped. "You see that wooden daguerreotype camera on the studio stand over there?" I pointed. "Well, that's a camera from the 1840s that Mathew Brady used. He got it from Samuel Morse who is best known as a painter and the father of the telegraph, but prior to that, he introduced photography to America. Brady was one of Morse's students in New York and earned fame taking pictures of the Civil War."

"The camera I'm interested in has never been sold at auction before. It's the daguerreotype camera that Louis Daguerre gave to Samuel Morse in 1839, the year that Daguerre invented photography. The only other example is in the permanent collection of the Eastman Kodak Museum in Rochester, New York, and it will never come up for auction."

"So, if you don't mind my asking, Clay, how much could it be?" Maggie inquired cautiously.

I cringed and said, "Well, it's an auction so it all depends on how much interest there is in it. Given it's rarity and condition and its excellent provenance, it should garner a lot of attention from a few serious collectors."

"So, how much do you think?" Maggie tried again.

"Uh, it'll probably start around half a million and could go for well over a million dollars."

Maggie bolted upright in bed and looked at me as if I'd hit my head on something. "You're kidding!" she managed to say. "And you can afford that, Clay?"

I nodded affirmatively. "Yeah, I can afford it, and it'll be the capstone to the camera collection that I've been building for years. This camera that Louis Daguerre gave to Samuel Morse in 1839 is about as rare as they come, and I have just one shot at owning it. Weed has offered to join me for the auction next week, and it's something I really want to do."

Now it was Maggie's turn to gulp. "My goodness, Clay Arnold, you're full of surprises, aren't you?! Just promise me that we'll be okay financially, and I hope you know that I love you no matter what."

"Don't worry, Maggie, we're fine. I've never discussed my assets with you before because I didn't want my resources to sway your thinking about us. Please just trust me, and I promise you we'll go over all of my financial accounts when you return after Thanksgiving, okay?"

Maggie looked at me with an amused expression on her face and shook her head in amazement. "My goodness!" she laughed. "I've got me one heck of a stud for a husband, and he's rich and famous, too!"

She couldn't help but smile at her good fortune.

Chapter 2

L UCRETIA LAND STARED far into the distance across Lake Michigan from the garden of her family's home on Chicago's Gold Coast. She often did her clearest thinking when she let her mind wander past what her eyes could see. Looking eastwardly across the great lake gave her time and space to think; to think about her life now that her famous father, Ralston Land, had died, and to ponder her next steps to counter her brother's unceremoniously tossing her off of the Land Foundation's board of trustees and robbing her of her rightful inheritance. She was in shock from both.

Lucretia's home was, indeed, very special to her because it was where she grew up and enjoyed the privileges of being born into a well-to-do family. As a young girl Lucretia loved exploring their Victorian-era house with its large rooms and a huge attic boasting several closets and crawl spaces. One closet in particular was more like a small walk-in cedar room that her father often referred to dramatically as the Cedars of Lebanon. She and her father frequently played in this aromatic cedar closet, and they pretended that this was their secure sanctuary from pirates and robbers. Even to this day, she remembers the fun they'd had and still senses that the house holds certain secrets that might someday be revealed.

Growing up, Lucretia was also blessed with having loving parents who made certain their daughter, and her annoying brother, Malcolm, were well-educated and exposed to the art world. Indeed, in her parents' home, the discourse about art was paramount, as was the continual hunt by Ralston and Miriam Land for important paintings to acquire for the family's collection. And acquire they did. Their only self-imposed condition on collecting was that it had to be American art. Over the course of some thirty years, Ralston and Miriam collected scores of important paintings, sculptures, prints, and photographs and had them safely stored away awaiting their formal presentation to the art world. Alas, their dream of building a world-class museum to display their art trove faded away with Lucretia's mother dying a year ago and now with her father's surprise death just last week. Until further notice, all of the family's art now rested very securely in an antiseptically clean, climate-controlled warehouse six blocks away from her home.

Sadly, the Land family home was very important to Lucretia for another heart-wrenching reason. She learned late last night from her attorney that it was the only asset that her father's new will stated she was entitled to. Heretofore, Benton Pettengill drafted all wills and legal papers for the Land family. Apparently, Malcolm had retained another attorney, a shady looking chap named Ernst Kline, to rewrite Ralston's will. Then, he must've somehow convinced his dying father to sign it. Malcolm had sent a photocopy of the will to Benton's office as a "courtesy" to him and his dear sister, Lucretia. Essentially, Lucretia had been cut out of the estate, kicked off of the foundation board, and neither her brother nor his attorney were returning their phone calls.

Lucretia walked along the stone path from her garden and returned to the house. Never in a million years would she have suspected that her brother would behave so greedily. She always felt that Malcolm was a bit of an odd duck, but surely their parents' estate had enough assets that each sibling would be very comfortably set for life.

Earlier that morning Lucretia left a phone message asking Benton to call her to discuss contesting the will, but she hadn't heard back from him yet. They had spoken only briefly the night before, and he said he would speak with her further in the morning. Right now amid the grandeur of the Land family home, she felt alone and scared, betrayed and angry.

Lucretia entered her living room and stared once again across the expanse of Lake Michigan. She looked at her watch and shook her head in frustration. "Where are you, Benton?"

She absently walked around the spacious living room looking at familiar paintings on the walls and touching various objets d'art that her parents had purchased on their many travels. A few minutes later, the phone finally rang, and Lucretia answered it on the second ring. "Benton, is that you?" she asked breathlessly.

"Lucretia, good morning, it's me, Drew. I hope I haven't called you too early."

"Oh, hello Drew, sorry for my abrupt greeting. I've been waiting for a phone call from Benton Pettengill."

Drew Thomas was the sort of faithful employee that all family businesses would be lucky to have. Well into his sixties now, Lucretia's father had hired him as a clerk forty years earlier, and he had risen through the ranks of employees to a position of trust. What he lacked in higher education and social connections, he more than made up for with a tireless work ethic and unwavering loyalty to the Land family. To Lucretia, he had always been "Uncle Drew" even though there was no real blood relationship. From her childhood on, he treated her with respect and kindness and dutifully watched over her from a distance.

Unfortunately, her brother, Malcolm, never embraced the guidance that such a valued employee could provide, and he regarded him merely as just one of the staff and a doddering old busybody at that. Now, with his father gone, Malcolm kept Drew around only because he knew the inner workings of the Land Company and its art collection as well as anyone, but Malcolm also knew that in the not-too-distant future Drew's services would no longer be required.

"Well, I won't keep you long, Lucretia, but I wanted to let you know about something that has come to my attention."

"Oh, what's going on, Uncle Drew?"

"Well, first, I've just learned that your brother somehow convinced the other trustees to "retire" you from the Land Foundation's board, and he has legal documents stating that your father changed his will a few days before his untimely death. I am utterly stunned by this turn of events, and knowing the love and devotion your father felt for you, I cannot comprehend a situation in which Ralston would cut you out of the estate."

"Thank you, Drew, I appreciate your consoling words. I'm still in shock, and I thought it was Benton Pettengill calling me back when the phone rang. Ben told me late last evening about my father's new will stating that all I get is our family home. He also mentioned something about a hastily scrawled notation on the last page of the will that was handwritten by my father. Benton said that it was crudely inscribed, and he wanted to examine it more closely. He said that he'd let me know if he thought it was anything significant."

"Fascinating indeed!" Drew voiced lowly. "Lucretia, the real reason for my call," Drew continued, "is to alert you that Malcolm is moving very quickly to liquidate some of your parents' art holdings in an effort to generate cash."

"You're kidding!" were the only words Lucretia could immediately find to express her surprise.

"Seems like Malcolm has dreams of fame and fortune beyond the Land Company's main business as a commercial real estate developer, and he wishes to use the sale of artwork as the way to fund them. Apparently, this is something he's been quietly planning for a while since he's already gotten a major auction house lined up to sell artwork next week. Rumor also has it that he's incurred some hefty gambling debts to some rather unsavory characters, and he's looking to repay them quickly."

There was dead silence on the phone, and Drew asked, "Are you still there, Lucretia?"

"Yes, I'm still here, Uncle Drew. I just can't believe this is happening. Do you know what he's looking to sell?"

"Well, the painting by Winslow Homer, another one by Albert Bierstadt, one of the two paintings by Georgia O'Keeffe, a few very early photographs, and a camera once owned by Samuel Morse."

"Oh no, not an O'Keeffe! My mother loved her art, and my father bought two works for her directly from Georgia herself. Any idea where the other O'Keeffe painting is?"

"I'm not sure, but I'll see if I can locate it." Drew continued, "I've learned that there's a very exclusive auction coming up next week here in Chicago at Snow Auctioneers, and that the items I just mentioned are all to be sold without reserve to the highest bidders."

Lucretia's silence was now replaced by muted sobs.

"I'm very sorry to be the bearer of bad news, Lucretia, but I thought you'd want to know. If you wish to go to the auction next week, I'm certainly willing to accompany you."

"That's very kind of you, Uncle Drew, and I would appreciate that. First, I'm hoping to hear back from Benton Pettengill to see if we can legally contest the will and block the sale. I'd also like to know more about the handwritten note he thinks my father left on the will. Can I let you know?"

"Of course, Lucretia, I can't imagine that your parents would ever want some of their favorite paintings to be sold, or to have you removed from the Land Foundation's board of trustees. I'll await your call about attending the auction, and I'll be happy to keep you informed of any other developments that I learn."

"Thank you, Uncle Drew, you've always been there for me. I hope you know I'm very grateful."

They ended the phone call, and Lucretia stared out her large picture window again at Lake Michigan. "Where are you, Benton Pettengill, and why haven't you called me back?"

Chapter 3

Maggie and I drove along I-70 in my silver Tacoma and took the exit for the Indianapolis International Airport. Her flight back to Santa Fe was scheduled to depart in about ninety minutes and that gave us a little more time together. We'd been together virtually every moment since she arrived eight weeks ago, and here we were hanging onto every last fragment of time before we had to say goodbye.

"I'll probably be gone for about ten days, Clay. I have a ton of work I need to handle, and my home needs some attention, too. And of course, I'm really looking forward to being with my sister's family

over Thanksgiving. It's hard to believe that the last time I saw them we were driving them to this very airport after we rescued Laura from that lunatic kidnapper, Dr. Mortimer Chestnut. I hope you know I'll miss you horribly, Clay."

I nodded my understanding. I know that our time apart from each other is important, too, but right now I felt like half of me was preparing to get on that plane. What had begun two months ago as just a visit for a few days to help celebrate my receiving an honorary doctorate, had turned into Maggie and me making the ultimate commitment to each other … with a baby on the way, talk about our wedding, and Maggie moving in with me here in Indiana. All really big stuff!

I parked the Tacoma in the airport lot, and we walked arm in arm to the security area. It was finally time to say goodbye, and I caught one final blown kiss as she exited security to go to her gate. I stayed for about a minute longer hoping that she might've changed her mind or forgotten something, but it wasn't meant to be. It helped knowing that her departure was only for ten days. I thought surely I could find something to occupy my time while Maggie was away, and then I remembered the upcoming auction in Chicago and started to get excited about that little adventure. Plus, it was going to be a lot of fun being on the road with my great friend, Weed Rawlins. It had been a while since we'd taken a trip together, and knowing Weed, it would be memorable!

I arrived back at the brewery complex about an hour later and took the home elevator up to my comfortable living quarters. I could still smell the faint scent of Maggie's perfume, and I lightly touched a sweater she'd left on a chair. My life was much different now than it had been just three years ago. Back then, I was crazed by Jennifer Skyler's murder, and took my anger out on mean-spirited bigots as a way to assuage my pain. I became an avenging vigilante, and I was eager to "even the score." Now, thanks to Maggie, I'm pretty much beyond that, and with our baby on the way, I'm relieved that those primal instincts are, at the very least, dormant.

I texted Weed and Mace to let them know that I was back home and suggested that they meet me in our antique camera museum when they were free. Each texted me back and said they'd be there shortly. My antique camera museum is a very special place to me. When I bought the brewery complex and renovated the old brew house where I live, I knew it was large enough to house my growing collection of rare antique cameras and early precinema devices. Fortunately, I had the financial resources to not only collect some of the best examples of each camera, but to also create an interesting and informative space to showcase my collection.

Upon completion of the renovation, I opened the museum to the public, and my friend, Mace, became knowledgeable enough about the cameras and the historic timeline of photography to provide tours for visitors and school groups. I'm very proud that the museum's reputation has grown in stature and delighted that Mace has taken such an active interest. So many collectors just become selfish hoarders. I always believed that sharing the history of photography was a good thing, and letting a kid or an adult actually hold a rare camera helped bring that history to life.

I walked down the steps to the museum and flipped on the lights. I felt like I was immediately greeted by old friends, and I slowly walked past each display case and recalled the details of each camera's significance and how it came into my possession. With Maggie here, it had been a little while since I spent time viewing the collection, and it felt really good to refresh my association with each item. A few minutes later Mace and Weed joined me in the museum.

"Did you get Maggie to the airport okay?" Weed asked.

"Yeah, she's on her way back to Santa Fe now," I replied.

"Clay, I hope you know we're all thrilled that she fits in so well with each of us here. I know that Tori and Rennie both think the world of her. We do, too, don't we Mace?"

"Yeah, she's pretty special," Mace added, "and the thought of us all having a little baby to dote on sure will change the tone of our family here."

"I'm excited as all get out," I said, "but I honestly don't have a clue what it'll be like to be a dad. Thank goodness Maggie and I will have all of you to help. Hint hint!"

"Don't worry, Clay, I have a feeling this kid will have plenty of supervision and guidance. Rennie has been asking me a lot of questions about babies, and I've confessed that this is a whole new experience for me, too." All three men grinned as they acknowledged that they were pretty clueless when it came to raising a kid.

We walked around the museum, and I asked Mace if anything in particular required attention.

"I think we're in pretty good shape," Mace said. Last week while you and Maggie were off in La La Land together, Weed and I changed the lighting around a bit to showcase some of the precinema pieces better. The Mutoscope now has a place of prominence that it deserves."

I couldn't help but smile that at age seventy-two, Mace Davis had found a genuine interest in learning about items that literally changed the way we see the world. He did an entertaining job in explaining old stuff to young audiences.

"So, Clay, tell us again what you hope to buy at this auction in Chicago," Weed said. "I know you mentioned that you've only got one shot at ever owning this particular camera, but I've forgotten its significance."

"Well, I'll try to keep this brief," Clay began, "but bear with me a little, okay? In 1839 a Frenchman named Louis Daguerre essentially invented photography. A lot of people had attempted to do so, but it wasn't until Daguerre invented the daguerreotype process that images taken with a camera became permanently fixed. Prior to that the only pictures and portraits were those made by an artist's hand. Daguerre made his invention available to the world for free, and the world has never been the same. That same year, Samuel F.B. Morse, the inventor of the telegraph and the Morse Code, traveled to Paris to meet Daguerre to learn the daguerreotype process. Once he felt secure in his knowledge of the process and the photographic equipment required, Morse returned home and introduced photography to America. As a parting gesture of the respect and friendship Daguerre and Morse had developed, Daguerre gave him his first daguerreotype camera that his brother-in-law had built for him. That, my friends, is the camera that I'm after."

"Whoa!," Weed exclaimed. "That's like the holy grail of the photographic world. Naturally, I understand your interest in it as a photographer and collector, but I also find its rarity and provenance pretty fascinating. How is it possible that it is even available for sale?"

"Damn good question, Weed! Apparently the camera has been in the possession of the Land Foundation in Chicago for many years. Who owned it prior to that, I'm not certain, but I understand from Gordon Snow, owner of the auction house, that the Land Foundation wishes to liquidate a few pieces from their collection to help generate cash. But again, I think your question is a darn good one, Weed."

Mace asked, "How much interest will there be in the Morse camera?"

"A ton!" I said. "However, the high bids will reduce the number of potential buyers a lot. It'll all come down to how badly two or three people really want it."

"I'm afraid to ask how much this camera could cost," Mace stated quietly.

"Me, too!" I laughed. "I know the opening bid is set at half a million dollars, and I expect the final hammer price will exceed a million bucks. Then, of course, there's the buyer's premium of 15 percent on top of that I'd have to pay to Snow Auctioneers. Not cheap!"

Both Weed and Mace began to laugh at the same time mainly because their friend, Clay Arnold, had the money to even contemplate such a purchase. They just found his unassuming manner about his wealth rather amusing.

"You know, Clay, if you hadn't been so generous with all of us all these years, I'd say you're out of your mind, but I say go for it. Have you told Maggie?"

"Of course I've told Maggie," I replied.

"And?" Mace queried.

"And, she reacted pretty much the same way you guys did. I told her not to worry about the dough, and she began laughing again. Look at it this way, Mace, you'll have the coolest camera ever to share with visitors here."

"Man-oh-man-oh-man!" was all that Mace could say.

"So, Weed, are you ready to head up to Chicago tomorrow afternoon?" I asked. "The auction is scheduled to begin at noon the following day, and we should be able to view the items up for sale tomorrow night at the auction preview. What say we drop by Snow's auction house, check things out, and then go to that Blues club you mentioned for dinner and entertainment."

"Sounds good to me," Weed affirmed, "Although I don't know if the Blue Wisp allows expectant fathers inside," he teased. "Yeah, I'll be ready to leave after lunch tomorrow, and that'll give me some time to help Tori with a few things in the morning. I think Rennie is going to bunk in the farmhouse while we're gone. Anything you need us to help with, Mace?"

"Naw, I think we may be able to survive without you guys for a couple of days. Have fun and let me know how the auction goes."

"Okay then," I said. "Weed, let's meet in the courtyard after lunch, say around one o'clock. I'm starting to get really excited about this trip. No telling where our little adventure might lead."

Chapter 4

I T WAS WELL PAST NOON, and Lucretia still hadn't heard from her attorney, Benton Pettengill. For the umpteenth time she stared out her living room window across Lake Michigan trying to understand everything that was happening, and with each passing minute, her frustration grew.

When the doorbell chimed, she thought finally it's Benton. Instead, it was a delivery service bringing her a large envelope marked "personal and confidential." It was from Benton. She tore open the envelope's seal, and saw that it was the photocopy of her father's new will, the one prepared by Malcolm's attorney, Ernst Kline. Benton also had attached a

note saying that he believed he was being followed by someone, and he wanted her to have the copy of the will for safekeeping. Nothing more.

Lucretia felt stunned looking at the documents and sat down to steady herself. She spent several minutes reading and rereading the will. Sure enough, the terms of the will called for her to receive the family home, but nothing more. And sadly, the will bore her father's signature. She wept. Then, Lucretia looked closely at the last page of the will and saw the confusing note that her father had scrawled there. It read, "LL cedarsleba". His penmanship failed at that point. Aside from believing that the LL referred to her, Lucretia Land, it otherwise made no sense to her at all. And finally, she wondered why Benton Pettengill would think someone was following him. Again, none of this made any sense to her.

By late afternoon Lucretia still hadn't heard from Benton Pettengill, and she called his cell phone. Again no answer, and again she left an urgent message on his voice mail asking him to call as soon as possible. After two hours with no reply, she picked up the phone and called Drew Thomas.

"Uncle Drew, hello it's me, Lucretia. I still haven't heard back from Benton Pettengill. I received a copy of father's new will from him this morning, along with a note saying that he thought he was being followed. Frankly, I'm very concerned. Can you please come over?"

"Hmm, very strange, indeed," Drew replied. "Of course, I'll be there in twenty minutes."

Lucretia spent the time awaiting Drew's arrival by trying her best to figure out what was happening to her world. Her father had recently died. Her jerk of a brother had her father's will changed cutting her out of the estate. She had been booted off the Land Foundation's board. Several cherished items from the Land family art collection were to be auctioned off. And, her attorney was missing in action. All in all, not a good time in Lucretia Land's otherwise idyllic life.

Drew arrived several minutes later and followed his late employer's daughter into the grand living room of the Land family home. Lucretia was distraught. Understandably so.

"No word from Benton?" Drew asked.

Lucretia closed her eyes and shook her head. "No".

The two of them just stared at each other. Drew spoke first. "I think it's time you considered retaining another attorney to protect your interests. This isn't like Benton Pettengill to be uncommunicative. He's either incapacitated in some way, scared, or for some inexplicable reason he's chosen not to communicate with you, other than sending you the new will, of course."

"Benton has been our family's attorney forever," Lucretia said softly. "I just don't understand his silence. It's not like him."

Together they vacantly stared out the window as the fading November light dimmed across Lake Michigan. The only sound in the room came from the handsome Chippendale grandfather clock that mechanically ticked the passage of time. Then, the somber quietude was dashed by the intrusive sound of the front doorbell.

Lucretia looked at Drew and made haste to answer the door in hopes of seeing Benton Pettengill in the doorway. Instead she opened the door to see a man she didn't recognize.

"Ms. Land? Ms. Lucretia Land?" came the steady voice from the man in the dark overcoat. He held up a badge for her to see. "I'm Detective Christopher Cioffi with the Chicago Police Department. I'm sorry to intrude on your privacy, but may I please come in? I'd like to ask you a few questions."

Both Lucretia and Drew had stunned looks of surprise on their faces. "Of course, Detective, this is my friend and associate, Drew Thomas. Please come in."

They walked into the living room and Lucretia asked the detective to have a seat. "How may we help you, Detective Cioffi?"

Christopher Cioffi had been with the Chicago Police Department for three decades and had been in a lot of homes, but he couldn't recall seeing a place as tastefully and artfully decorated as the home in which he now sat.

"Do you know an attorney named Benton Pettengill, Ms. Land?"

"Yes, of course, Benton has been our family's attorney for many years. He's also a dear friend. I've been expecting a phone call from him. Is there something wrong, Detective?"

"I'm sorry to report, Ms. Land, that Mr. Pettengill was found dead at his desk earlier today." He closely watched both Lucretia and Drew's reaction to this news.

Lucretia sagged in her chair. She pulled both hands to her face and cried. "I knew something had to be wrong, Detective Cioffi. Benton called me late last evening and said he'd get back to me this morning, but I never heard from him. What happened?"

"We're not sure yet, Ms. Land. We received a phone call from his housekeeper when she arrived at his home this morning. She found him in his home office. It appears that he had a heart attack at his desk, but that's just conjecture until the medical examiner has had a chance to perform an autopsy and we get the reports back from the lab. We should know the cause of death in a few hours."

"I can't believe this is all happening," Lucretia said to no one in particular. "Why did you think to contact me, Detective Cioffi?"

"We looked at his cell phone and saw what you just mentioned: that he had phoned your home last night. Can you tell me about the nature of your conversation?"

Lucretia looked at Drew for emotional support and then told the detective about her father's recent death and all of the upsetting developments with her brother and her parents' estate. Drew sat quietly by her side speaking only when either the detective or Lucretia required corroboration of details.

"Benton also told me that he thought he was being followed, and I assure you, Detective Cioffi, Benton Pettengill was not the sort of person to make hysterical claims." Drew nodded his agreement.

"I see," Christopher Cioffi said as he jotted a few notes in a small notepad he carried. "Do you have any reason to believe that someone may have wished to harm Mr. Pettengill, Ms. Land?"

"No, I do not, Detective." But then she paused and said, "Actually at this point with everything that's been happening, I'm not so sure. Benton was a dear, kind man, and I can't believe that he's dead."

The three of them sat quietly for a few minutes in the living room. Over the years Detective Cioffi had learned that silence was often its own reward.

Most people can't abide by silence, and he patiently waited for Lucretia or Drew to provide more details. None came.

"Well, I believe I have all of the information that I need right now. Of course, I may need to speak with you again, and please let me know if you hear anything further that can be helpful." He gave them each his business card. "I appreciate your cooperation, and again I'm very sorry to be the bearer of sad news." He took Lucretia and Drew's contact information and said he would be back in touch when the toxicology reports came back and as his investigation proceeded. He took a final look around the interior of the Land family home, raised his eyebrows in admiration, and then departed.

After he left, Lucretia slumped against Uncle Drew and sobbed.

"Let's go together to the auction preview tomorrow, Lucretia. Maybe we'll see that recalcitrant brother of yours or his new legal counsel. They both have a lot of explaining to do."

Chapter 5

WEED AND I CRUISED along I-90 in my Tacoma and saw the Chicago skyline in the distance. Situated alongside the big lake, the sprawling city glistened like a magical kingdom and beckoned us to experience what it had to offer.

"With any luck the traffic on the Dan Ryan Expressway will be flowing smoothly this time of day," I commented. Weed and I both knew that rush hour around here could turn a pleasant drive into a royal pain in the neck.

"Always better to approach Chicago with a full tank and an empty bladder," Weed added.

It was approaching three o'clock when we pulled into the entrance to the Viceroy Hotel in the upscale Historic Gold Coast District. Weed whistled his approval when he saw the sophisticated hotel in its Art Deco tower overlooking Lake Michigan.

"I need to travel with you more often," Weed said. "We be running with the big dogs now!"

"Yeah, it's pretty darn nice," I admitted. "I wanted a place that gave us a good view but that's also in easy walking distance to Snow Auctioneers. I hope you don't mind, Weed, but I booked us a suite so we can stretch out a little."

"You'll get no argument from me, my man!" he added.

I joined Weed by our large picture window, and we both looked up and down the lakeshore sites. I pointed to Navy Pier a mile or so south of our location and reminded Weed about my having "eliminated" a couple of ugly neo-Nazis that were harassing a Sikh professor. It was back in the day when I was in full pissed-off mode as an avenging vigilante. Weed and Mace had helped weaponize several of my antique detective cameras, and I used a ring-camera popularized by none other than the Russian KGB to poison this nasty couple. After taunting the turban-clad professor, they sipped their drinks that I had, uh doctored, and climbed aboard the ferris wheel. Alas, they were both quite dead when the ferris wheel returned from its scenic circuit.

Later that day, I met Maggie at the hotel where we were staying, but I never mentioned my assassination to her. Since then, I've been open with her about my "evening the score" with certain deserving elements of our society, but it's not a topic we dwell on. Seeing the ferris wheel in the distance brought back these memories, and I felt relieved that these violent episodes were now in my past. Maggie's love and the prospect of our being parents has kept my blood from boiling with self-righteous anger. Well, so far, anyway …

"We have a few hours before the auction house is open for preauction viewing," I said. "Anything in particular that you want to do, Weed?"

"You know, we haven't eaten lunch yet, and we'll probably end up having a late dinner. Why don't we head up to the hotel's roof terrace, grab a bite, check out the view, and then I'd be happy catching forty winks before we head over to the auction house."

"Sounds like a good plan," I said. "Instead of napping, though, I think I'll give Maggie a call and then get some exercise walking the streets in the historic district." And that's what we did.

After our late lunch Weed went down to our suite to get horizontal on his bed, and I called Maggie. The first three rings went unanswered, but

Maggie managed to breathlessly answer the phone before voice mail kicked in.

"There you are!" I said. "How are you, darling?"

"Whew, out of breath," Maggie declared. "I'm not used to carrying the extra weight around. But, I'm doing fine, Clay, and have you and Weed arrived in Chicago yet?"

"Yeah, we got here a couple of hours ago. I got us a suite at the Viceroy Hotel. After a late lunch, he decided to crash for a bit, and I wanted to get some exercise, so I'm touring around the Gold Coast."

"Hmmm, I'm envious about all of those things," Maggie teased. "Well, I've been up to my elbows in work stuff and straightening up things around the house. Actually, everything seems to be in pretty good shape. I've already booked some exciting corporate PR projects, and everyone seems to understand that I'll be having a baby in about five months. So, forewarned is forearmed. So, tell me, when is the auction again?"

"Well, there's the preauction viewing that'll start in about an hour, and the actual auction itself begins at noon tomorrow. After we hang up, I'll go back and meet Weed, and we'll head over to Snow Auctioneers."

"Are you excited?!" Maggie asked, already knowing the answer.

"Oh yeah, you could definitely say that. If this camera is everything that it's touted to be, it's beyond rare."

"Clay, I'm really excited for you, too. I hope it's the camera of your dreams. Just promise me that if you get it, you won't bring it into bed with us!" She teased.

"I promise! I miss you, Maggie! I wish we were together now."

"Me, too, Clay. I'm glad I'm so busy around here that it keeps me from thinking about you and the baby all the time. But soon! Now, you and Weed go have a terrific time, and let me know how things go!" We each did a mushy goodbye and then hung up.

After we said goodbye, I took the elevator down to the main lobby and exited the hotel. It was still sunny outside, but the mid-November sun was getting lower in the sky. I crossed over N. State Street and walked east toward E. Cedar. Virtually all of the leaves were off the trees at this point, and my photographer's eye enjoyed framing the shadows of the bare tree limbs as they cast their presence on the pavement before me. Great light. Great homes and subject matter everywhere I turned. I walked down to Lake Shore Drive and then turned west on E. Elm Street. I turned my back against a sudden stiff Chicago wind and noticed a figure about a block away looking at me. There were a fair number of people on the street so I didn't give it much thought, but as a former vigilante, being aware of my surroundings is something I do instinctually.

I strolled along E. Elm and then N. Dearborn Street and was preparing to head back to the Viceroy when I thought I spotted the same individual as I did before. My defense senses went on alert, and I ducked behind a large planter and waited to see if I was, indeed, being followed. I watched for reflected motion from a nearby shop window, but nothing unusual occurred. Thirty seconds later I peered around the corner of the planter to see if I did have someone following me, but no one was there.

I arrived back at the Viceroy shortly thereafter and took the elevator up to our suite. All the while I kept wondering if my imagination was playing tricks on me, and if not, then why would anyone be want to be following me. I didn't like not knowing the answer.

Weed looked like he was ready to go out on the town. His nap reenergized his battery, and he was dressed like the dapper blues man that he is.

"Did you get a chance to call Maggie?" Weed asked.

"Sure did," I said. "It was great hearing her voice. She's busy but doing fine."

"And, how was your walk, Clay?"

"My walk was very good. Saw some incredible historic homes. Nothing that I'd trade our brewery complex for, though. I did have something happen that was a bit unusual."

"Oh?!" Weed asked inquisitively. "Good unusual or bad unusual?"

"Honestly, I'm not sure, but I felt like I was being followed. I saw the same person twice, and he was staring at me. I know it's probably nothing, but it got my attention."

"I can tell," Weed said. "Did you happen to bring any 'devices' along with you?"

By "devices", I knew that Weed meant any of the antique detective cameras that he and Mace had weaponized for me.

"Yeah, I always carry the Demon camera with me in my camera bag."

The Demon Detective Camera is a hand-sized metal camera that was originally built by the American Camera Company around 1890. Weed and Mace had taken some extra parts I had stored in the camera museum and converted them so the Demon could release an angry zap of electricity. When discharged at night, the camera casts a beautiful blue bolt. Alas, for the recipient, it's lethal as hell.

"Bring it along!" Weed suggested. "Just in case."

Chapter 6

Weed and I arrived at Snow Auctioneers a little after six o'clock to preview the items that would be auctioned tomorrow beginning at noon. The legendary auction company is housed in a stately old limestone townhouse whose first-floor interior walls had been artfully rearranged to provide a larger seating capacity. The building's hardwood floors and millwork, stained glass windows, and crystal chandeliers displayed its history of opulence. Beyond question, Snow Auctioneers is the most prominent auction company in Chicagoland, so it only made sense that the paintings from the Land Foundation would be sold here.

The owner, Gordon Snow, greeted us amicably and pointed out the various salon rooms where the art and artifacts were on display.

"Ah, you're Clay Arnold, aren't you?" Gordon Snow said. "I know you've participated in some of our auctions in the past by telephone, and it's a pleasure to finally meet you, sir. I assume you're here to view the Morse daguerreotype camera."

"Yes, Mr. Snow, I'm Clay, and this is my associate, Weed Rawlins. It's a pleasure to meet you, too. I'm sure the paintings you'll auction tomorrow are all wonderful, but yes, I'm mainly here to view the Morse camera. I imagine there's been quite a bit of interest in it."

"Yes, indeed," Gordon Snow proudly confirmed. "As you might expect, we've had inquiries from collectors all over the world."

We chatted a few more moments and then Gordon Snow directed us to a small salon room to see the camera I had only read about in books. There were several people already in the room when we arrived, and it took every ounce of patience that I could muster to wait my turn. I saw a couple of collectors that I recognized from previous camera shows or from articles written about their photography collections. Judging from those present, I knew that the final hammer price for the Morse camera would be astronomical.

Finally, the small crowd dissipated a bit, and Weed and I were able to get an up close and personal view of the holy grail of photographic history.

"It's bigger than I thought it would be," Weed said.

I didn't respond immediately. I was that caught up in the moment. To think that this camera before us was built in 1839 by Daguerre's brother-in-law, Alphonse Giroux, as the world's first practical camera, and then was gifted by Daguerre to Samuel F. B. Morse, was difficult for me to fully comprehend. I just knew I had to have it!

"What's with the other wooden boxes with it?" Weed inquired.

"They're the original fuming boxes," I replied. "Through a lot of trial and error, Daguerre learned that by exposing a silver plate to iodine vapors, it created the light-sensitive properties of silver-iodide that created a photographic image. Then, this fuming box contained mercury that enhanced the image before it was permanently fixed in a bath of hyposulfite. The fact that these other pieces of ephemera are still with the camera makes this collection even rarer. And, look, there's a box with an early Morse telegraph key and some coiled copper wire."

I inspected the camera as well as I could from its perch on its original studio stand two feet away. Giroux's original maker's label on the side of the

wooden sliding box camera confirmed everything I needed to see.

"There's only one other camera like this in the world, Weed, and it's in the permanent collection of the Eastman Kodak museum in Rochester. This one, though, is even rarer because of its provenance as a gift from Daguerre to Samuel Morse. It's essentially the first camera ever used in America."

Weed whistled and nodded his appreciation of its significance.

A few more people entered the small salon to view the camera, and I recognized a fellow who I knew I'd likely be bidding against.

"Good evening, Clay," said Roland Ross. "I had a feeling that you wouldn't be able to resist this auction. I recall that you outbid me at the last auction for the Mathew Brady camera, and I hope to give you a pricier run for your money for this gem."

"Hi, Roland, it's good to see you again." Although it really wasn't. "Quite a special piece, wouldn't you say?"

We made idle chitchat for a few moments longer, and then Weed and I exited the room to look at the paintings from the Land Collection that would be auctioned as well.

"Friend of yours?" Weed asked sarcastically.

"Not really. Roland has been collecting vintage cameras for quite a long time, and he's put together an impressive collection. We've competed against each other on more than one occasion. Some I've gotten, and some he has."

"Apparently, he carries a grudge against you for losing the Brady camera," Weed said.

"Yeah, well, imagine how pissed off he'll be when I outbid him on the Morse daguerreotype," I said. "Frankly, there's no way that I'm losing that camera to a stuffy old coot like him!"

"Oh boy!" Weed laughed. "Tomorrow's auction ought to be quite a spectacle!"

Weed and I wandered around the Snow auction house looking at art for a little while longer, and then I registered for the auction and got my bidder's number. We said goodnight to Gordon Snow who was still stationed by the front door, and we stepped outside. We were preparing to walk to a trendy restaurant for dinner a few blocks away when I felt a little tug on my coat sleeve. I turned to look and saw a woman in her midthirties who I didn't recognize.

"Pardon the intrusion, Mr. Arnold, but I want to introduce myself. I'm Lucretia Land, and this is my friend, Drew Thomas. We've actually met before, but it was only briefly and a number of years ago at that."

"Well, hello, Lucretia, it's nice to remeet you then. This is my buddy, Weed Rawlins." I replied. "Are you here for the auction preview as well?"

And then I recognized my mental lapse and said, "Land. Of course, I remember now. Your father's Ralston Land, right? And, that means that a lot of the important art that will be auctioned tomorrow is from your family's collection."

"Was," she said. "My father passed away last week."

"Oh, I'm very sorry, Lucretia. I didn't know. Your father was the consummate art collector, and I felt very honored when he purchased one of my photographs for your family's collection a few years ago."

She managed a bit of a wistful smile and asked if the two of us could speak privately for a moment. We left Drew and Weed at the building's entrance and walked several feet away.

"As you may know, the Morse camera is from our collection, too," she shared. "It was a bit outside of the genre of artwork that my parents normally collected, but father always knew rarity when he saw it, and he snatched it up from a descendant of Samuel Morse's family when it became available some twenty-five years ago."

"I see," I replied. "Honestly, Lucretia, I'm surprised that it's even available for sale, and I hope to be the winning bidder tomorrow."

"To be frank, Clay, none of these paintings or the camera would be up for sale if it were up to me.

My brother, Malcolm, seized control of the family foundation when father died, and he has organized this sale through Gordon Snow to generate cash that he apparently needs."

I wasn't quite sure how to respond. Then, I heard a loud crack and felt the sonic disturbance of a bullet as it crossed in between Lucretia and me. I immediately grabbed her, and both of us dropped to the pavement. Instinctually, I climbed halfway on top of her to protect her and hollered over to Weed to call the cops. We heard the wheels of a car screech and rapidly drive away.

"Are you all right, Lucretia?" I asked.

"Yes, Clay, I believe I'm okay, but I might be able to breathe a little better if you got off of me."

I moved off and helped Lucretia to her feet. Both Drew and Weed joined us a second later, and security personnel from the auction company arrived shortly thereafter.

"What the hell was that all about?" I wondered out loud.

Gordon Snow approached us a moment later and turned pale with fear when he learned that Lucretia Land and Clay Arnold had just been shot at in front of his establishment.

Uncle Drew immediately attended to Lucretia who seemed to be all right with the exception of some abrasions to her knees and elbow. Weed saw that I was okay, and quietly asked me, "So, who was that bullet meant for … you or her?"

"Damned if I know," I confessed, "but I have to wonder if the guy who tailed me on my walk earlier and the shooter are the same person." We walked back over to Lucretia and Drew.

"Are you okay?" I asked Lucretia again. She said she was, but the look on Drew's face told me that he was seriously concerned.

"As I was about to share with you, Clay, before we were so rudely interrupted, there has been a lot of family turmoil swirling around ever since father's death, including the death of our longtime attorney just two days ago. I'm afraid that it's too late to stop the auction at this point, and I just wanted to say that if anyone else is to own the Morse camera, I certainly hope it's you."

I was stunned by the family drama that Lucretia was describing and asked if she was planning on coming to the auction tomorrow, or if it would be too emotional an experience.

"I haven't decided yet, but our getting shot at hasn't scared me off. If anything, it's strengthened my resolve. We both have to be wondering, though, who that bullet was actually meant for."

Both Weed and I nodded our agreement.

"However, like I said a little bit ago, if the Morse camera is, indeed, to be sold, I hope it finds its way into your museum, Clay."

"Thank you, Lucretia, I appreciate that very much. If I am the winning bidder, I assure you that it will be displayed with the highest honor."

Snow approached us to say that the police were on their way, and Weed and I took that as our cue to slip away and try to regain our equilibrium over drinks, dinner, and soulful blues.

We said goodbye to Lucretia and Drew, and halfway down the block I turned to Weed and said, "Please, not one word about this to Maggie, okay?!"

He nodded his understanding.

Chapter 7

MALCOLM LAND WAS GIDDY with excitement. Alas, his poor father, Ralston, had finally departed the living, and now everything that his parents had owned, with the exception of that monstrosity of an old house, was his and his alone. Cash, stocks, real estate, and, of course, art! He grinned when he thought of the shock his dear sister, Lucretia, must've felt when that old cuss of an attorney, Benton Pettengill, informed her of daddy's new will. Cut Out!

Currently, Malcolm was in his newly rented condo overlooking the Chicago River. Given all of the hullabaloo he expected his sister would create

over the estate and auction, he thought it was a good time to choose a new domicile so no one knew his exact whereabouts … at least until the dust settled a bit. Besides, he liked the view.

His doorbell chimed, and he showed his attorney, Ernst Kline, into the living room. In the early days of his career, Ernst actually was a rising star. He was both an attorney and a certified public accountant, and was in demand by both legal and financial firms.

Ernst particularly enjoyed solving vexing tax problems, and that drew the attention of some very wealthy clients who also made tons of money in various nefarious ways. Before too long, Ernst had fixed a few problems rather unscrupulously, and his shady clients had him under their control. He now was a very well educated patsy and served at the will of others. Along the way, Malcolm Land met Ernst through some mutual contacts, and thus began a personal business relationship.

"Good job on the will, Ernst, I think you got all the important points very well covered. I doubt that dear Lucretia will go quietly about this though."

"I concur," Ernst replied.

"And, I think we have everything ready to go for the auction tomorrow. The Land family has purchased and sold a great many pieces of art through Snow Auctioneers over the years, resulting in some substantial premiums being paid to the firm. I reminded Gordon Snow of that fact, and I made it abundantly clear to him that he should endeavor to keep me as a good reference, too."

"So, he understands where his loyalties should lie?" Ernst asked.

"I think he understands that he can either cooperate with me and be well compensated, or go against me at his peril."

The two men sat quietly for a few minutes, and Ernst finally said, "I don't feel comfortable having been a party to your father's death." He let those words hang in the air like a frozen rope.

"Oh, well my friend, you were definitely a party to Ralston Land's death. In fact your suggesting that we very slowly poison him to death using diluted arsenic was a stroke of genius. A bit Victorian in its vintage but effective nonetheless."

"I don't feel good about it," Ernst said again.

"Well, I suppose it doesn't make you feel any better that you also poisoned good ol' Benton Pettengill the other night, too, eh? Why don't you just accept that you're very good at killing people?"

Ernst looked at him with steely eyes.

"And remember, Ernst, that I have video recordings of your repeatedly administering low doses of arsenic to Ralston's food and beverages over a couple of weeks. Fear not though, Ernst, I have them very safely tucked away. Alas, I don't have anything directly incriminating you with murdering poor Benton, but I don't think the authorities would have to delve too far before they'd realize the same poison was used in both deaths. Fortunately, for you, I am magnanimous of spirit, and as long as you do exactly as I say, you will be wealthy and safe. Or, if you prefer the contrary, then *que será, será*." Malcolm just let those sobering words hang in the air.

"Now then, Ernst, tell me about your visit tonight to Snow Auctioneers. Did you see Lucretia, and did you send her, uh, a message?"

"Yes, I saw Ms. Land outside the entrance to Snow Auctioneers. She and Drew Thomas were talking with two men. I recognized one as Clay Arnold, the famous photographer, and another guy. Lucretia and Clay walked away from the other two and stood talking privately. That's when I fired a shot close to them. I left immediately thereafter."

Malcolm nodded at the news. "Perhaps now Lucretia will take the hint that I'm not fooling around. As for you, Ernst, I need you to remain available to me. I believe I'll have other potentially vexing problems for you to solve, and we both know how much you enjoy solving problems."

Ernst Kline nodded his understanding and submissively exited Malcolm's new abode.

"Now then where was I?" Malcolm murmured aloud to himself. "Ah yes, all of those valuable paintings …"

Chapter 8

"HOLY CRAP!" I EXCLAIMED as I rolled over in bed and looked at my watch. "It's nine o'clock, and the auction starts in three hours!" I went over and knocked on Weed's bedroom door and heard what sounded like a man who was sorry he drank too much the night before. But, that's only because we both did.

After Lucretia and I literally dodged a bullet last night, Weed and I found the Blue Wisp supper club and treated ourselves to some good Chicago steaks, some great blues tunes, and entirely way too much booze. But I have to say that we had a great time, highlighted by Weed leaping on stage with the other

musicians and crooning away until we eventually closed the bar. Weed was a hoot! He knew one of the other musicians from a previous blues gig and recognized a few others by reputation. By the time the evening was over, the blues band leader invited him to join their troupe at an upcoming engagement in Indianapolis. This morning, however, Weed was having a little trouble locating his business card. Like I said, we both drank way too much.

I heard Weed stagger off to the bathroom, accompanied by sounds of the toilet flushing, water running, and a congested nose being blown.

"You okay in there?" I called out to Weed.

"Coffee! I need coffee!" came Weed's pitiful reply.

Fortunately, for both of us, I had our coffeemaker brewing, and I handed a steaming cup to Weed when he exited the bathroom.

"Thanks!" was about all he could manage to say. We both sat around in our underwear alternately laughing about how much fun we had at the club and nursing some serious head-clanging hangovers.

I left Weed to fend for himself and went back in my room to call Maggie. "Good morning, darling," I managed to say with as bright and chipper a voice I could muster.

"Good morning to you, too," she replied, "and how was your evening last night?"

Inasmuch as I really want to be honest and transparent in all things with Maggie, I saw absolutely nothing to be gained by telling her that I had been shot at the night before and then proceeded to get rip-roaring wasted watching Weed commandeer a night club act.

"Oh, pretty tame," I fibbed. "We went to the auction preview event last night and then over to the Blue Wisp for dinner and music. A nice quiet evening, and how about you? Are you making progress with work stuff and getting your home under control again?"

"Yeah, I think I'm in pretty good shape which makes me feel a lot better about leaving town again to join Rita's family for Thanksgiving."

"Please send everyone my love," I said. "Weed and I are just having coffee and enjoying the view from our great suite. We're going to head for some breakfast in a little bit and then go back to Snow Auctioneers and wait for the auction to begin."

"So how was the camera that you're interested in, Clay? Did it meet your expectations?"

"Boy, did it ever!" I exclaimed. "And there are some other photographic items that go with it, so I'm more excited than ever about trying to get it. Plus, there's even a very early version of Morse's telegraph key with some copper wire. I saw a couple of other camera collectors at the preview, and I know there's going to be a lot of very active bidding."

"Well, I hope it goes exactly the way you want," Maggie said.

I wasn't sure if she really meant that considering I had told her previously about how much the Morse camera might cost, but she was being a very good sport. I decided to change the subject.

"I miss you so much, Maggie! Weed and I are having a great time, but I miss reaching over at night and having you there."

"Me, too, Clay, but soon we'll be back together, and we can get ready for the holiday season and make plans for baby Arnold. You know we still need to pick out a name for our little bundle."

"Yeah, I've been giving that some very serious thought," I joked. "Do you think naming him/her Louis Jacques Mande Daguerre, after the inventor of photography, would be too much?"

Maggie chose not to dignify my silliness with a response. We talked a few minutes longer and then said our mushy goodbyes.

I showered, then finished getting cleaned up, and put on a fresh suit so I looked sharp for the auction. "Hey, Weed, are you about ready? We should get a move on!"

Weed came out of his bedroom to join me. He didn't look very chipper.

"Coffee! I need coffee!" he declared again.

We went downstairs to the Viceroy's dining room and proceeded to refuel our vitamin-depleted bodies. "You were something last night, Mr. Rawlins!" I said to Weed.

"Yeah, well, I may be getting a little old for that kind of carousing," he admitted.

We finished our breakfast, came back up to our suite to make a final pit stop in the bathroom, and then walked the few blocks to Snow Auctioneers. The crisp Chicago air helped bring our brains back to full functionality.

Gordon Snow greeted us once again at the entrance to his auction house. "Good morning, gentlemen, I trust you've recovered fully from the, uh, excitement with the gunshot last night. The police arrived shortly after you left. I believe Lucretia Land gave them all of the details that they needed, and they've pretty much written it off as a random drive-by street shooting. This is Chicago, after all."

"Yeah, we're fine," I said. "Do you know if Ms. Land and Drew Thomas will be attending the auction? I asked her last night, but she wasn't sure."

"I'm not sure, either," Gordon admitted. "Auctioning off the Morse camera is one thing, but I'm sure it will be extremely difficult for her to witness their paintings being sold. I know she's especially fond of the Georgia O'Keeffe painting which her father bought for her mother. She says it's one of two paintings by O'Keeffe that her father purchased, but she and Drew can't seem to locate the other one. Apparently, it was her mother's favorite."

Weed and I left Snow to greet his other guests, and we entered the main salon where the auction would be held. It was scheduled to start in a few minutes, and we were lucky to find some reserved seats near the front. I glanced around the room and recognized a few fellow camera collectors, including my bidding nemesis, Roland Ross. We exchanged frosty smiles. A few moments later Snow approached the podium to deliver his welcome, and to go over the rules for bidding. At three minutes before noon Lucretia Land and Drew Thomas slid into the seats next to Weed and me. They had chosen to come, after all. Lucretia offered us a brief smile, but otherwise her demeanor was stoic.

"Good afternoon, ladies and gentlemen, and welcome to Snow Auctioneers. I'm Gordon Snow, and I'm delighted that you've chosen to attend what promises to be one of the most exciting auctions that our firm has hosted in quite some time. We have a number of excellent offerings today, but I am especially pleased to present a few very special paintings from the Ralston and Miriam Land Collection.

In addition to them, we have an extremely rare daguerreotype camera that was originally owned by Monsieur Daguerre himself, and the father of American photography, Samuel F.B. Morse. Please be advised that we are accepting bids from registered individuals present here today, as well as by telephone and via the Internet. So, without further ado, let the bidding begin!"

The bidding that followed for one important painting after another was brisk. There were some occasional lapses in the auction's momentum as the telephone and Internet bids took a little longer to be received. However, by one o'clock a string of paintings by Andrew Wyeth, Mary Cassatt, Grant Wood, Jackson Pollock, and other luminaries became the property of the highest bidders.

I looked over at Lucretia to gauge her reaction to the sales. Largely, she remained stoic, but she offered Weed and me another brief smile like someone who could use a lifeline but is too proud to ask.

Gordon Snow adjusted his reading glasses, took a sip of water, and began, "Next up, ladies and gentlemen, are three paintings from the Ralston and Miriam Land Collection that are described in great detail in your auction catalogue: A stunning western landscape by Albert Bierstadt, an engaging scene of boys in a pasture by Winslow Homer, and an iconic floral by Georgia O'Keeffe."

It came as no surprise to anyone in the room that the Bierstadt and the Homer fetched multimillion dollar prices. Lucretia was spared the pain of having to see bidders in the room get the paintings as the winning bids were submitted over the phone.

Snow took another sip of water and continued, "The third painting from the Land Collection is a work by Georgia O'Keeffe entitled "Moonflowers."

He removed the cloth drape from the painting, and a murmur of excitement rose within the salon. I looked over at Lucretia again and noticed that her eyes were closed. Her stoicism had given way to sadness. Minutes later, after a bidding bloodbath between two stubborn and very wealthy bidders, Gordon's hammer announced a $32 million sale. I saw Lucretia slump against Uncle Drew's shoulder and small tears fall from her heartbroken eyes. Her mother's O'Keeffe was gone.

At that point Snow suggested that we take a twenty-minute break and return for the final auction of the day: The Morse daguerreotype camera.

"Welcome back, everyone," Gordon Snow began, "and now for you photography aficionados, we have a most unique offering, also from the Ralston and Miriam Land Collection. Up for auction is the 1839 daguerreotype camera that Alphonse Giroux constructed for his brother-in-law, Louis Jacques Mande Daguerre. Historically, it is regarded as the world's first successful camera. This camera is also significant because Monsieur Daguerre gave it to Samuel Morse as a gift when Morse visited him in Paris to learn the daguerreotype process. It was with this particular camera that Samuel Morse introduced photography to America."

Snow continued, "I understand that this camera was passed down through successive members of the Morse family until some twenty-five years ago when Ralston Land had the foresight and resources to purchase it. It may well be the most valuable camera in the world, and this is the first time it's ever come to auction."

Again, a murmur of admiration rose in the audience. I have to admit that I was among that chorus.

"So, let's open the bidding at five hundred thousand dollars," Snow announced. Immediately, a hand was raised in the audience and the bidding was underway. I chose to hold back my bids at first to see what the action was like; plus I saw no sense in entering into the bidding at this early stage and driving the price up.

"We now have five hundred and fifty thousand," Snow declared. "Can I have six hundred thousand?" A staffer handling the phone lines raised his hand to acknowledge that six hundred thousand had been bid. Over the next few minutes there was a lot of back and forth among bids from the floor, the phone and the Internet. When the bid finally crossed the million dollar mark, I sat up a little straighter in my chair and prepared to join the action.

"One million one hundred thousand is now the bid," Snow announced. I noticed that it came from Roland Ross. A couple more bids came in from the phone lines, and before too long the camera's price was approaching a million and a half. Ross was staying silent at this point, but I had a feeling that he wasn't finished.

I finally declared a bid of one million seven hundred thousand just so folks knew that I was in the hunt. Snow then announced, "We now have a bid of one million eight hundred and fifty thousand!" I gulped a bit and raised my paddle at $1.95 million. The room fell silent. I glanced over at Roland Ross to see if he was done or not, but Snow quickly announced a phone bid at $2.1 million. I looked over at Weed with my eyebrows arched, and he calmly said, "Go for it, Clay!" And that's what I did.

Roland made a final attempt to own this historic camera with a final bid of $2.2 million. Ten seconds later his dreams were dashed when an Internet bid came in at $2.35 million. That was it for Roland. He was done.

Now it was between me and some unknown bidder out there. Gordon Snow took another sip of water and began anew. "We are at two million three hundred and fifty thousand. Can I have two million four hundred and fifty thousand?" There was dead quiet for a few moments, and then Snow said, "Final calls everyone. Are there any other bids?"

At last a staffer working the phones urgently raised his hand to indicate he had a bid of $2.45 million. The murmurs in the room grew louder in anticipation.

"Final bids everyone … two million four hundred and fifty thousand dollars is the bid … last chance, going once, going twice …" And then I stood and declared my final bid of $2.85 million. The audience gasped, and Weed damn near micturated himself. The seconds of silence that followed seemed interminably long. "Going once, going twice!" Snow announced, and before I knew it, Snow rapped his gavel, and the Morse daguerreotype camera was coming home to our museum in Indiana.

Weed clapped me on the shoulder, grinning like a Cheshire cat. Drew Thomas shook my hand eagerly, and Lucretia gave me a warm smile and a nod of sincere approval.

Gordon Snow rapped his gavel again to get everyone's attention. "That concludes our auction today. Will the winning bidders please come to the office to discuss payment and to provide us with shipping instructions? And I hope you'll consider using Snow Auctioneers in the future. Thank you very much!" He rapped his gavel a final time.

At that point a small crowd was gathering around us; people probably wanting to see the lunatic who just spent almost three million on an old wooden camera. Anyway, everyone was polite and gracious including Roland Ross who stopped by to congratulate me.

"Well, you did it again, Clay Arnold!" Roland said with a smile on his face. "You got another great camera. The greatest! And you won it fair and square. I prefer to think that you just saved me over two million dollars by your buying it instead of me."

"Thanks, Roland, You've always been a tough competitor. Anytime you're around Indy, give me a buzz. You're always welcome to visit the Morse daguerreotype at our museum."

The crowd thinned out, and Weed and I walked back to the office to settle payment. "Sorry, guys, I didn't bring that much cash with me," I said in jest. They didn't seem to find my quip very amusing. We exchanged account details for a wire transfer and confirmed contact information.

"And where would you like the camera, studio stand, and the other boxes to be shipped, Mr. Arnold?" the clerk asked.

"My buddy and I are taking them with us. If you have someone who can lend us a hand, we should be able to do this very quickly." Fortunately the camera and equipment came with sturdy shipping crates, so everything was protected and also out of sight. Ten minutes later we had the Tacoma loaded up.

Weed and I saw Lucretia and Drew standing outside, and we walked over to say goodbye.

"It's certainly been a pleasure meeting you both," I said. Weed concurred, and we all said that we'd like to keep in touch.

"Are you guys heading back home tonight or do you plan to celebrate another night in Chicago?" Lucretia asked.

"I'm not sure we can handle another night of partying in Chicago like last night," Weed confessed.

"Besides," I added. "I think I prefer to get our new three million camera into the secure surroundings of our museum rather than keeping it locked in the truck in a garage overnight."

"You showed a lot of moxie during the bidding, Clay," Lucretia said. "I respect that. Plus, you probably saved us from being shot last night. If we can ever be helpful to you and Weed down the road, just give us a call. Despite my being cut out of our Land family's holdings, I still wield some influence in the art world. My offer is sincere."

We said our final goodbyes, and Weed and I climbed aboard the Tacoma. The drive home was relatively peaceful especially in comparison to the two days we'd just spent in Chicago.

I turned to Weed and said, "You know, buddy, it's not every weekend I get shot at, then get rip-roaring drunk, and spend three million dollars. Surely, life couldn't get more exciting than that!"

Weed laughed out loud and said, "Oh, I don't know, Clay, I have total faith in your ability to turn tranquility into turmoil … but that's just one of your many endearing qualities that we all love!"

"Swell," I replied. "By the way, Weed, I want you to have the early telegraph key and copper wire. You've definitely earned it."

"Wow, Clay, that's very generous," Weed said. "It definitely looks like a rare Morse prototype. I'll keep it in my backpack in case we ever want to send a message to old Sammy boy," he joked.

"Why don't you call Mace, Rennie, and Tori and let them know we're about ninety minutes from home? I'm really excited for us to take a close look at the Morse camera and get everything set up in the museum. This acquisition takes our collection to a whole new level."

"What're you going to tell Maggie about the price?" Weed asked.

"The truth … well, sorta … kinda … maybe …" I replied. "Come to think of it, she didn't throw me away when I told her I'd been an avenging vigilante. Maybe she'll go easy on me with a three million dollar purchase. What do you think, Weed?"

His reply was direct. "I think you're screwed, and the cost of her wedding ring just went way up!"

Chapter 9

WHEN WE PULLED INTO the courtyard at home, everyone was there to greet us, including Lex and Satchmo. Mace had a huge grin on his face as if it were Christmas morning, and he just found a great gift under the tree.

"Well, let's do this," I asserted. "Let's bring the camera and the rest of the gear up into my living quarters, and Weed can tell you all about our adventure, well, most of it, anyway."

I picked up the Morse camera while Weed and Mace lofted the studio stand, and Rennie and Tori carried the fuming boxes. Satchmo led the way and Lex kept trying to sniff the new acquisitions.

Once we got settled inside, Tori said, "I'm a little confused. I thought Samuel Morse invented the telegraph and the code named after him, but you said he introduced photography to America, too."

"That's right," I said, "Before we went to Chicago for the auction, I began reading a little about Morse. First and foremost he trained as a painter, and during his earlier years he was regarded as a premier portrait painter in America. His artwork also included large, heroic scenes. After Morse returned home from studying painting for three years in London and Paris, he was eager to teach us backwoods Americans about European art, so he founded the Academy of Arts in New York. Alas, the popular appeal of Morse's paintings was far less than what he'd hoped for, and he turned his interest to other things like photography and trying to figure out a way to use electricity for communication. It's very ironic that today Samuel F.B. Morse is virtually only remembered for his contributions to the telegraph and the Morse code, and his great love of painting and photography have become mere footnotes in history."

After Weed regaled everyone with descriptions of our suite at the Viceroy Hotel and the paintings auctioned at Snow Auctioneers, Tori and Rennie took off to complete a project that they'd been working on together, and Mace and Weed and I hung back to inspect the rarest camera in the world, and to discuss how it should be displayed in our museum.

"This camera is just amazing!" Mace praised. "I mean, the wooden construction, this great brass Chevalier lens, and the rest of the equipment are all in immaculate condition. Really unbelievable, Clay!"

"I know, Mace. I'm still pinching myself. Weed and I thought you'd be excited about teaching museum visitors about this special piece, and I've got some good literature for you to look at to help get you up the learning curve about Daguerre, Morse, and the daguerreotype process."

"Can't wait!" he said.

The three of us spent more time examining the camera and the fuming boxes closely. We also told Mace about meeting Lucretia Land and Drew Thomas, and the turmoil with the Land family assets, and also about us getting stinking drunk at the Blue Wisp.

"Good lord!" Mace exclaimed. "You guys are really a couple of juvenile delinquents!"

"Oh, and we haven't even told you yet about Clay getting shot at," Weed added.

Mace just shook his head in disbelief, and I simply shrugged.

"Hey guys, let's open up the back of the camera and look inside," I suggested. I carefully lifted the plate holder and the ground-glass viewing screen from the back of the camera, and we shined a light inside the dark box. I couldn't help but think that both Louis Daguerre and Samuel Morse had done just as we did although many decades apart.

"Looks pretty clean," Weed said. "I can see some old discoloration on the wood from photo chemical spills, but aside from that, it looks totally original and in great shape."

I ran my fingers inside the chamber of the camera and felt around for any separation of the wooden joints after years of storage. The sides and corners were solid, and the brass Chevalier lens was a little dirty, but intact. I shined the light inside again and noticed what appeared to be a small paper label tucked in a recess near the back of the lens. Neither Weed nor I had noticed it before, but there was definitely something there.

"Hmm, hey guys, what's this?" I said, and I gave the label a gentle pull. It didn't want to come free, and so I asked Mace to go to my medicine cabinet in the bathroom and bring back a tweezer. He did.

With Weed shining the light inside the camera, I tried to grab the corner of the label with the tweezer. It didn't want to come free at first, and so I very gently jostled the paper back and forth until I felt it give. A moment later I had a very old folded piece of paper in my hand, and I carefully unfolded it.

There was a message written on it, but I didn't have a clue what it meant. It looked like this:

.. ..-. .... -.-- --- ..- ....- .-. . ... -. . .- -.. .. -. -.
.... - .... --.-- ....- -- ....-.. .. -.-. . .-.. -.-
.... -. . --- ....-.. --- -. -.. . .-. ....- -- --- -. -.. .... - ....
. ...-.. .. ..- .. -. -.. --.-- ....- -. .-. .... -.-- --- ..- ....
.... .- ...- . ...-. . --- ... ... --- -. .... --- ..-. .... -
....- -- --- -. .-. -. --- .- ... . -.- .- -- . .-. .- .... --
--- -. ... .- .-. .... -.. .- --. .. .. --. .. ..-. - .
-.. .... -- . ... -. ....- --- --.. ..- --- . .- .- ....
-.-- --- ..- ....- .-. .. ... --- .... --- .- .-. -.. .... - .... .
.... -.- .- .-- .... - .-- ....-. .. -. -.. .. -. -. ....- -. ....
.- -- .- --.. .. -. --. .... - .-. .- .. ... .- .-. . .- .-.- ....-..-
.- -- .. -. -. . ... - .... --- -. .-. --- ....- .. .. - ....
- .... --. .- -. -.. .- .- .-- .... --- ..-. .... - ....
.-.. --- ..- ..- .-. . ... - --- .... -.- --- -- -- . -. -.-. . ...
-.-- --- ..- .-. ....- -.. ..- . - .-. .- .-. .-.- ....--
.- -- .. -. -.. . ... - .... -.- .-. --- ... . . .-. -.-- .... -. ....
.. - ... . -. - .. -. . .- -.-- --.- .... -.-- --- ..- .-.
....-. .-. --- -. . .- ... . -- .. .-. .-. .... -... . ...-.
. .-- .- .-. -.. . . .-.. ....- -. .-.. ... --- -- . .-. -.-- --.- ....
.... -... --- -. .... -.-. .... .- -. -.-. . ...- -- ..- . .-..
....-. .-.-. .... -... .-.-. .... -- --- .-. ... .

"What the ...." I began. "Why would anyone put this jibberish inside the Morse camera?" I asked aloud to no one in particular. It made no sense to me. I showed it to Mace and Weed, and Mace shook his head quizzically, too.

"Clay, let me take a look at that," Weed said. "I have an idea what this might be."

I handed the paper to Weed, and he looked at it for a long time. "It looks like Morse code to me," he declared. "We had to study it in my freshman year at MIT. I never thought I'd ever actually use it, though. Here, let me take a picture of it with my phone, and I'll see if I can come up with an app that'll allow us to convert it to English text."

"So, who do you think put it in there?" I asked my friends. "Daguerre? Morse? Someone else?"

"Let me have a few minutes to try and translate the message, and that may shed some light on who placed it inside there," Weed said.

Mace and I sat patiently while Weed pulled up an app on his iPhone. He scanned the coded message and inserted it into the app's conversion window. Within seconds the translation was revealed, and all three of us were thunderstruck by what we read:

"If you are reading this, I am likely no longer among the living, and you have possession of the wondrous camera Monsieur Daguerre gifted me in 1839. You also hold the key to finding an amazing treasure trove. You need only visit the Gallery of the Louvre to commence

your adventure. Examine it closely … in its entirety.
Your efforts will be handsomely rewarded. Bon chance!
Samuel F. B. Morse."

"Is this for real?" Mace asked. "I mean seriously … is this for real?!"

The three of us looked at each other incredulously and read the message over and over again.

"So, let me get this straight," Weed deadpanned. "Samuel Morse is speaking to us from the grave, and he's prodding us to embark on a treasure hunt. Is that right?!"

"Seems like," I said. "And the Louvre is in Paris, and he says we should go there."

"And what would we do when we got there?" Weed asked. "Besides, the Louvre is huge. It has scores of galleries, and good old Samuel didn't say which one."

I couldn't argue with his reasoning. At this point the hour was growing later, and I was starting to feel pretty weary after experiencing the emotion of the auction, the drive home from Chicago, and the startling revelations that we discovered inside the Morse camera.

"This is a lot to digest, guys," I said. "Why don't we call it a night, and talk about it more in the morning. I sure don't relish the thought of flying to

Paris on a wild goose chase, especially if Maggie needs me. On the other hand, the idea that Samuel Morse, who died in 1872, could lead us to 'an amazing treasure trove' nearly one hundred and fifty years later is the stuff that dreams are made of."

Chapter 10

DESPITE FEELING WIPED out from our trip to Chicago, I had difficulty falling asleep. When I finally did, I had strange dreams. I dreamed about an old bearded man who was waving for me to follow him into a dimly lit vault. There were classical paintings on the walls and old photographs mounted in antique gutta percha frames, and around the doorframe I saw what looked like surreal charges of static electricity. I somehow knew I was dreaming about Samuel Morse, but I couldn't quite divine its meaning.

I awoke sometime around 2:00 a.m. and was tempted to call Maggie, but I knew if I woke her up

and started talking about a treasure hunt because of a note I found inside an old camera, she'd likely divorce me before we even got married. Several minutes later, I got up and went into the living room to look at the Morse camera again. It sat quietly on its studio stand, and yet in the silence of the room, it felt like it was almost shouting at me to seek what the coded message had prompted us to do. At this hour of the morning, it was hard for me to determine which was stranger, my dreams or reality.

I eventually managed to fall back to sleep, and when I woke up around eight, the dream was still fresh in my mind, and I was eager to talk about Morse's message more with my two friends.

I texted Weed and Mace to see if they wanted to go to Stella's Diner for breakfast and to continue last night's discussion. I didn't have to text them twice. Twenty minutes later we climbed into my Tacoma and rooster-tailed a little gravel as we exited the courtyard.

Truth is, the three of us love going to Stella's Diner because we crave diner food, but also because we enjoy Stella so much. We've known her a long time now, and we appreciate her business acumen as well as her fame as a local celebrity. Heck, what's not to like about a smart businesswoman who chooses

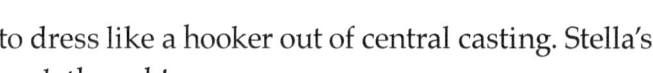

to dress like a hooker out of central casting. Stella's cool, though!

We pulled into the parking lot at the diner and exited the truck. Stella herself greeted us at the entrance. "Howdy boys, where y'all been lately?" she sang out. "C'mon over here and give old Stella a big hug!"

"Mace, you look handsome as ever. You, too, Weed!"

"Hey, what about me?" I complained.

"Yeah, well, you're already taken, sir, and these studs aren't!" Stella lobbed back at me.

Mace was delighted that at age seventy-two, a good-looking woman would still call him a stud.

"C'mon fellas, I've got you a clean table over here in the corner and fresh, hot coffee on the way. I'll get your orders in a minute, okay?"

We sat down and waited for a family, who had been seated at a table next to us, to finish their breakfast and leave before we starting talking about the coded message.

"How'd you sleep last night, Clay?" Weed asked me.

"About as restlessly as you might expect," I admitted. "Between thinking about the camera and this really weird dream I had, sleeping was an elusive state of mind last night."

"I suspected so," Mace consoled.

Stella came by and took our orders and then promptly left to seat some new guests who had just arrived.

"What do you think about all of this, guys?" I asked earnestly. "You know, the whole hidden coded message thing about visiting the Gallery of the Louvre. I'm a bit bewildered."

"Yeah, it's a mystery," Weed confirmed. "And I've gotta say that I stayed awake thinking about it last night, too. Here, I wrote down the translated message Let's take a look at it again."

Weed unfolded the paper he had in his pocket, and the three of us looked at it very closely. *"You need only visit the Gallery of the Louvre to commence your adventure. Examine it closely … in its entirety."*

Stella returned and brought our breakfast platters with another round of coffee.

"The Gallery of the Louvre," I said aloud. "But which one?"

We ate our breakfasts deep in thought. *"Examine it closely … in its entirety,"* Weed followed. He shook his head in frustration, too. "I wish I knew the Louvre Museum well enough to figure out what Samuel Morse had in mind. The museum is enormous, though, and I imagine they change the exhibits around, so how do we even know where to begin?"

"We don't," I acknowledged. "Perhaps we should just celebrate the fact that we have the world's rarest camera in our collection and leave it at that," I suggested. Although, I immediately looked into Mace and Weed's eyes and knew that none of us really believed in giving up so easily.

"Your efforts will be handsomely rewarded," Mace quoted from Samuel Morse's message. "Sounds pretty darn intriguing to me, guys!"

We enjoyed a hearty breakfast together, and Weed told Mace more about our meeting Lucretia Land and Drew Thomas, and about Lucretia and me getting shot at.

"Man, there's never a dull moment with you is there, Clay?" Mace chided playfully.

"Tell me about it, Mace! All I wanted to do was go to Chicago and buy a camera, and someone takes a shot at us. Believe me, I'm ready for a few dull moments!"

We finished our meals, waved our goodbyes to Stella, and climbed back into my truck. When we got home, Mace asked me how I felt about his rearranging a couple of display cases in the camera museum to better accommodate the Morse daguerreotype.

"Sounds like a very good idea," I encouraged. "You may need to redirect the lighting a little, too."

Fact is, I'm tickled that Mace has taken such an active interest in the museum. He's learned the story behind most of the cameras we have on display and knows the history of predigital photography as well as anyone.

After Mace left us to work in the museum, Weed and I sat in my living room listening to music and reflecting on the last seventy-two hours. I noticed him sitting there staring at the piece of paper with the translated message, and he finally looked up at me.

"You know, Clay, if we're serious about seeking Samuel Morse's treasure trove, we're going to need some help."

"Well, I'm definitely interested in taking this adventure to the next level, and I also agree that we definitely need help, but who?" I asked. "We sure don't want to trust just anyone."

Weed began, "We need someone who is intimately familiar with the art world, someone who is knowledgeable about the Louvre Museum in particular, and someone who is more familiar with Samuel Morse's art and history than we are ... plus someone with integrity who we can trust."

"Yeah?!" I said expectantly. "That's a pretty tall order, Weed. Who do you have in mind?"

"One ... no actually two people!" he declared. Lucretia Land and Drew Thomas!"

We just stared at each other, and I thought very carefully about Weed's suggestion. "Lucretia and Drew!" I said. "Hmm!" We began weighing any pros and cons we could think of, but within a few moments, we agreed that contacting Lucretia was a sound idea.

"Good thinking, Weed! I've got her business card here on my desk. Let's give our friend, Ms. Land, a call. Maybe she'll know which gallery of the Louvre Museum we should begin our search."

Lucretia Land picked up the phone on the third ring and was surprised to hear my voice on the line. "Good morning, Clay, and to what do I owe the honor of this call?"

"Good morning, Lucretia, I hope I'm not taking you away from anything important. Weed and I have come across something rather intriguing, and we think you might be able to shed some light on a little mystery we're facing. Weed's with me now, and I have the phone on speaker."

"Good morning, Weed," she said. "A mystery, huh, and how can I be helpful to you guys?"

Lucretia listened attentively over the next few minutes as I described our finding the coded message that Samuel Morse had ostensibly hidden inside the daguerreotype camera.

"Wow, you're kidding!" Lucretia exclaimed. "It's hard to imagine that someone hadn't found it before you."

"I agree. Weed and I are honestly stymied by what the message means, and we don't have a clue where to begin at the Louvre Museum."

"Well, I'm certainly not an expert on Samuel Morse's artwork," Lucretia admitted, "but my parents collected some of his paintings a long time ago, and between Drew and me, we might be able to help. Tell me again what the message said."

I read the message slowly to her over the phone, and at the end she paused and said, "I think I may know what you're looking for, and the good news is that you don't have to go to Paris."

"I'm confused," I admitted. "I thought that the Louvre Museum is in Paris?"

"Of course it is," Lucretia replied. "However, I believe that Samuel Morse was referring to his large painting, entitled the *Gallery of the Louvre* that he completed around 1833. I don't think he was referring to a physical location within the actual museum."

"Seriously?!" was about all my challenged brain could manage to utter. Weed and I looked at each other with a look of amused befuddlement on our faces.

"Well, I'm certainly glad I called you, Lucretia. We were ready to fly to Paris and search every inch of that museum if we had to!" I exaggerated. "What can you tell us about the painting, and do you have any idea where it is now?"

"Considering that my parents bought the painting in 1992, and that it's part of the Land family collection, Drew and I can probably shed some light on your, uh, mystery."

"Seriously?!" I repeated. "Please go on!"

"The *Gallery of the Louvre*," Lucretia began, "is a monumental six foot by nine foot painting that Samuel Morse painted as a way to educate Americans about Italian and French Renaissance art. It depicts thirty-eight masterpieces from that period in a single gallery view. Morse copied paintings by masters such as DaVinci, Titian, Caravaggio, Raphael, and others. Since America at the time had no museums to display European masterpieces, Morse's plan was to bring his large painting back to the United States and to charge admission to the viewing public."

Weed and I were mesmerized by what Lucretia was sharing with us.

"Since the Land Foundation owns the painting, do you have any idea where it is now?" I asked hopefully.

"The Foundation loans quite a few of our paintings to other museums. I'm not sure where it is currently, but after we hang up, I'll e-mail Drew at his office and ask him to look into it."

"That sounds perfect!" I said, "And I'm thrilled that we don't have to fly to Paris on what would've been a huge wild goose chase. Weed and I certainly appreciate all of the guidance you and Drew can provide us."

"Happy to help, Clay. You two have been there for me, and I want to return the favor," she shared. "Why don't I get back to you in a little while after Drew has had a chance to check the Foundation's loan records?"

We hung up a few moments later, and I patted Weed on the shoulder for coming up with the great idea to contact Lucretia.

"You're a genius, my friend!"

"Aw shucks!" he replied with feigned modesty. "Alas, Paris is so lovely this time of year."

Chapter 11

WHILE I WAITED FOR Lucretia to get back to us, Weed went to the farmhouse to check on Tori and Rennie, and I contacted my agent, Lily Deupree, to see if I had any photographic assignments coming up. I had previously told her about Maggie's pregnancy and my not wanting to schedule any projects outside of the country. Now, with the prospect of going on a treasure hunt of sorts, I asked her not to schedule any work until after the first of the year. She said that she'd just booked a project for me at Balboa Park in San Diego in early December, but that she didn't see a problem rescheduling.

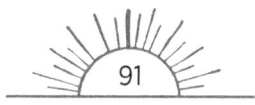

I then called Maggie to share the latest news with her.

"You what?!" she said laughing when I told her about finding the coded message from Samuel Morse inside the camera I just bought. "And you think you're going to find a valuable treasure if you go see an old painting by some bearded geezer who's been dead for a hundred and fifty years?"

Stated in that context, I could easily understand her skepticism, but I assured her, that with Lucretia Land's help, Weed and I both thought this was something worth pursuing.

"I swear, Clay Arnold, you do enjoy the little adventures you get involved in, but frankly, darling, I do think it sounds mighty intriguing. I hope you know I support whatever you want to do. Any idea what Morse's treasure trove might have?"

"I'm not sure, of course, but given his love of art, it might be a rare painting," I conjectured.

"Very cool!" Maggie replied. "Maybe it's a painting of Elvis on black velvet," she teased.

"You never know!" I teased back. "Old Sammy boy was a man way ahead of his time!"

We talked a little bit longer; mostly mushy stuff, and then Maggie remembered to ask me how much I paid for the Morse camera.

"Well, it cost a little more than I thought it would," I said evasively.

"Oh, how much more?" she asked pointedly.

"Actually quite a bit more, but it was definitely worth it," I countered pseudo-bravely.

"How much?" she persisted.

And then I did what any spineless guy would do when caught in an untenable situation with the woman he loves: I lied! I told her we had a bad phone connection, and I was having trouble making out what she was saying.

Naturally, she didn't accept my condemnation of AT&T and told me we could discuss it later.

Feeling like I'd just gotten a reprieve from a life sentence, I resorted to flattery and told her she's the prettiest girl on the planet. That helped a little, maybe, and I got off the phone to await Lucretia's return call.

About ninety minutes later I heard back from Lucretia, and I quickly texted Weed to join me again.

"Hi guys," Lucretia began. "I e-mailed Drew about Samuel Morse's painting, *Gallery of the Louvre,* and he looked into its current location. Apparently, it's on loan for the next six months to the Rothman Collection in Cincinnati, Ohio. As you may know, the Rothman Collection refers to both the museum that houses the private art collection of the founders, Elias and Winifred Rothman, and the collection itself. They have approximately twenty-five hundred paintings, prints, photographs, autographs, rare books, and diverse ephemera. In that regard, it's similar to the Land collection, but on a smaller scale."

"Well, Cincinnati is a lot closer than Paris!" Weed offered.

"Any chance we could get in to see the painting privately?" I asked Lucretia.

"I don't see why not," she acknowledged. "Joseph Daniels is the director of the collection, and I've known J.D. for a very long time. Actually he was an attorney with a venerable law firm in Cincinnati for many years until he was wooed away from the practice of law to oversee the renowned Rothman Collection. In fact, as I think about it, I recall that J.D. and Benton Pettengill worked together on some legal issues for my parents several years ago."

"Would you feel comfortable calling J.D. to see if Weed and I can drop by for a visit?" I asked hopefully.

"Sure, I can do that. I'll be happy to make the introduction for you, and you can take care of scheduling a time after that. How's that sound?!"

"Perfect!" I said. "We sure appreciate your help, Lucretia."

"Well, I'm certainly curious to see what, if anything, you learn after viewing the *Gallery of the Louvre*."

"We'll definitely be in touch afterward. Please just text or call me once you and Joseph Daniels connect." We hung up shortly thereafter.

"So, what do you think?" I asked Weed.

"I think we're going to Cincinnati … and I think it's darn helpful to have a friend like Lucretia Land."

Meanwhile, from his condo high above the Chicago River, Malcolm Land looked out across the gray expanse of Lake Michigan. He had just been informed by the Land Foundation's security chief, George Titus, that Drew Thomas had been communicating via e-mail with his estranged sister, Lucretia.

Malcolm's initial reaction was to use this as the excuse to go ahead and fire Drew. He'd been planning on it anyway ever since he seized the Land Foundation's reins after his father's death. Instead, he thought it might be wise to let them continue to communicate without their knowing he was privy to all they said.

Malcolm looked again at the message that the security chief had forwarded to him. "Hmm," he wondered out loud. "The *Gallery of the Louvre,* Samuel Morse, and the Rothman Collection.

I wonder what this Clay Arnold fellow is up to, and why my sister is interested. I'll just have to stay tuned."

He texted his compromised attorney, Ernst Kline, and wrote, "I believe I have another assignment for you. Drop by later this evening."

Chapter 12

TRUE TO HER WORD, Lucretia made contact with Joseph Daniels at the Rothman Collection a few hours later, and Weed and I followed-up with him by phone. We scheduled a visit in Cincinnati the following afternoon.

The three-hour drive to Cincinnati was visually appealing to me. Once Weed and I got south of Indianapolis, we took the ramp for I-74 east, and within a very few miles we were seeing an attractive combination of rolling farmland, stands of mature trees, and the occasional cluster of modest-looking homes. As a photographer I learned a long time ago that if I try to compare the grandeur of the American

west with the subtle beauty of the midwest, I'll be disappointed. Regardless of its subtleness, however, the midwest is an inextricable part of my DNA, and seeing the scenes flow past my window made me proud of our region as a heartland.

"I don't know about you, Clay," Weed said, "but I haven't spent that much time in Cincinnati. Generally, I've headed to Chicago or to St. Louis mainly for their music scenes, but not so much to Cincinnati."

"I think I've had a similar experience, too, Weed. It's a great city with decent-enough sports teams and enough places to go for entertainment, but I guess as a photographer, I never really felt like there were any galleries that took photography seriously. So, I went to cities where they did instead. In any event, I'm open to giving the city a fresh new look, and from the way Lucretia described the Rothman Collection, we'll be in for a treat."

We arrived in Cincinnati around three fifteen and were early for our four o'clock appointment with J.D., so we decided to drive around town a little. Traffic was congested in the downtown area, so we used our GPS to direct us to some of the older neighborhoods. We went through North Avondale, Clifton, Mount Auburn, and Hyde Park. The neighborhoods were as visually appealing as any I could recall in a major midwestern city.

"I need to come back here with my camera," I said aloud to myself as much as to Weed. I made a mental note to do it. Next we drove over to Eden Park where the Rothman Collection is located. From a quarter mile away, I could see that it was an artfully designed, contemporary edifice, certainly fitting for a progressive museum. The structure was largely constructed of steel and glass, and it commanded an impressive view of the Ohio River as it wended its way to the heart of downtown.

About four o'clock Weed and I exited my Tacoma and entered the naturally-lit expanse of the Rothman Collection's lobby. A fresh-looking ingenue at the information desk named Lainy greeted us warmly. We introduced ourselves, and I said that we had an appointment with Joseph Daniels.

"Of course, Mr. Daniels is expecting you," she said. "Please follow me."

Now I don't mean to be crude here, but I know my friend, Weed, and even though he's always a gentleman with the ladies, I knew his eyes were glued to the young woman's rear end. I looked over at him, and sure enough, I was right. He saw me looking and offered me a guilty grin. Busted!

Lainy rapped lightly on Joseph Daniels's office door and led us inside. He immediately stood up from his desk and walked around it to welcome us. He thanked Lainy, and I know Weed cast one more admiring glance at her delightful figure before she left the room.

"Welcome, welcome!" Daniels said effusively. "Any friends of Lucretia Land's are certainly friends of ours here at the Rothman Collection."

"Thank you, Mr. Daniels, Weed and I sincerely appreciate your seeing us on such short notice. We promise not to take too much of your time."

"Please call me J.D. At Lucretia's request, I've cleared most of my calendar although I have a previously scheduled conference call in a few minutes with two of our trustees."

"We'll try not to unnecessarily detain you," Weed said.

It was hard not to be impressed by J.D. He was tall in stature with a full head of wavy dark hair and black eyeglasses that gave him a rather professorial look. His office was diversely decorated and equally impressive. His teak desk and office furniture had the sleek design of Danish modern that went very well with the overall contemporary architecture of the building, but that's where the modernity stopped. A stunning Tiffany dragonfly lamp illuminated his desk, and a massive Miro painting dominated the wall behind his chair. The other walls were adorned with important paintings representing several centuries, and sculptures by Auguste Rodin and Henry Moore occupied pedestals in the room's niches. J.D.'s bearing and his office accoutrement were the definition of refinement.

"So, gentlemen, Lucretia mentioned that you are especially interested in viewing the *Gallery of the Louvre* by Samuel Morse," J.D. intoned.

"Yes, that's correct," Weed said.

"Anything in particular you care to know about the painting? Lucretia simply said you're on a personal assignment about the painter, but she didn't go into any specific details."

Weed and I were both relieved that Lucretia hadn't mentioned anything to J.D. about the coded message we'd found inside the camera and Morse's instructions to seek the painting. Despite his honorable appearance, the mere mention of the word "treasure" can weaken a person's ethics, and we saw no point in risking J.D.'s sense of moral resolve.

"No, nothing in particular," I fibbed. "Lucretia may have told you that I purchased a daguerreotype camera from the Land Foundation last week that Morse once owned. Since then I've learned that Morse was an acclaimed painter prior to his commitment to photography and the invention of the telegraph. We're basically interested in viewing his paintings to get a fuller sense of the life and artwork of Samuel Morse."

"I see," said J.D. "Well, Samuel Morse was a fascinating individual. In many ways he was like a latter-day Da Vinci given his skill as an artist and his understanding of mechanical invention. Let's walk down to the main salon where we have his work on view."

The museum closed at four thirty, so there were no visitors present when J.D. led us into the main salon and the lights flicked on. There, on the opposite wall, was a massive six foot by nine foot painting, depicting a Louvre gallery of European masterpieces. Morse had reproduced some thirty-eight paintings into one scene.

"Essentially," J.D. began, "Samuel Morse was interested in showing his prowess as a painter, and he also wanted his masterpiece to showcase great renaissance art for American audiences who couldn't travel to Paris to see the originals. He brought his painting home to New York, where his plan was to charge twenty-five cents for admission by the viewing public. Unfortunately, the public wasn't very intrigued by Morse's mega opus, and he felt crushed by the lack of popular appeal, and that disappointment was a watershed in his painting career. He lost the desire to paint, and as history points out, he went on to other endeavors."

The large painting on the wall before them was indeed impressive in both its subject matter and its dimension.

"Look here!" J.D. pointed. "This figure in the painting is the author, James Fenimore Cooper, who Morse met while studying art in Paris. As the story goes, Morse included Cooper in the scene with the hope that the author would buy the painting. These figures in the front and center are actually Samuel Morse himself teaching his daughter, Susan Walker Morse."

Weed and I sat on the padded bench opposite the painting and hoped for divine intervention to solve Morse's mysterious message: *"Visit the Gallery of the Louvre. Examine it closely … in its entirety."*

The three of us looked carefully at every painting represented on the massive canvas. J.D. was kind to spend thirty minutes with us waxing on professorially about each painting and artist depicted, but despite his giving us great information, Weed and I were at a loss to understand what Morse's message was prodding us on to see.

At that point Lainy reentered the salon, and informed J.D. that the trustees were on the line for their conference call.

"Please excuse me, gentlemen, but duty calls. Feel free to stay as long as you like. This call is likely to last a while, and Lainy will be happy to show you out whenever you're finished. Naturally, if I may answer any further questions that you have, I'll be happy to do so. As I mentioned earlier, any friends of Lucretia Land's are friends of the Rothman Collection."

We thanked J.D. and told Lainy we'd find her when we're ready to leave. After they exited the room, Weed and I continued to examine virtually every inch of the *Gallery of the Louvre*. We looked closely at each painting, every figure, even the background of the massive work, but nothing of note revealed itself. Nothing.

"Well, I'm beginning to feel like a real doofus looking at this old painting waiting for inspiration to lead us to a treasure trove," Weed lamented.

"Yeah, I know what you mean," I concurred. "Recite the message again, Weed. We've got to be missing something."

"Visit the Gallery of the Louvre. Examine it closely … in its entirety," Weed replied. "Well, we're here with your painting, Sammy boy, talk to us!" Weed exclaimed theatrically.

Again, we began examining every inch of the canvas, but we still came up with nothing … no words, no symbols, no pictures of treasure, nothing but a nice painting showing a bunch of other really nice paintings.

"Examine it closely … in its entirety," Weed repeated out loud. He thought for a moment and then said, "You know, Clay, we may be going about this search all wrong."

"How so?" I said looking for any ray of inspiration. "We're visiting the *Gallery of the Louvre* like Morse instructed, and we've both examined the painting very closely."

"But not in entirety," Weed declared.

"What do you mean?" I said with frustration growing in my voice. "We've been over every single inch of this thing … repeatedly!"

Weed shook his head no. "We haven't looked at the back of the painting. Morse said to examine it closely which we've done, but not in its entirety … yet."

I learned a long time ago that Weed Rawlins is one smart fella, and I've trusted his judgment for years, but his suggestion to look at the back of the painting surprised me.

"Seriously?!" I said.

"Yeah," Weed declared. "C'mon, we have to heave this puppy off the wall and turn it around."

"Holy shit, what if we get caught?" I said.

Weed laughed at me. "You're ordinarily the person leading the charge on wacko stuff, so just get down there at the end of the painting, and we'll just lift it off its hanger."

"With its frame this thing's gotta weigh nearly two hundred pounds. Just be careful!" I replied, speaking the obvious.

Each of us went to opposite ends of this nine-foot wide American masterpiece and gripped the frame as securely as we could. I looked Weed in the eyes, and he nodded. We struggled a bit to lift the heavy painting, but managed to get it off its wall cleat and rested it carefully on the floor. We both took a second to catch our breath and then lifted it again and turned the painting around so it was facing the wall. We leaned it against the wall, and now the rear side was exposed to us.

What stuck me first when I looked at the back of the *Gallery of the Louvre* was its originality. The canvas itself showed very little deterioration, and the original wooden stretchers showed minimal wear. No doubt, Samuel Morse went to great lengths to make certain his masterpiece was properly prepared for framing.

Weed and I took our time examining the rear of the canvas to see if there was anything noteworthy there. Morse's words, *"Examine it closely … in its entirety"* kept coming back to me.

Weed and I both were about ready to concede defeat when I spotted what appeared to be worm or beetle marks in the wooden stretcher near the bottom of the canvas. I thought it wouldn't be the first time insects had taken up residence in old, dry wood. But these marks looked different, and

I kneeled on the floor to take a closer look. I was stunned by what I saw.

"Hey Weed, come here and tell me what you think of this," I urged.

Weed kneeled down next to me, looked to where I was pointing, and then he glanced at me with the same look of intrigue. There in the wooden stretcher someone had carved or stamped a definite series of dots and dashes into the wood.

... . . -.- .... -- -.-- .... -- ..- ... .

"Looks like Morse code to me," he said

I nodded my head in agreement. "Listen ,Weed, we need to quickly see if there are any other similar marks in the wood and get this painting rehung before anyone comes back. Can you write down exactly what you see and take a picture with your cell phone so we can convert the code into English text after we're gone. I prefer that we have the painting back in position before J.D. or Lainy returns."

Weed carefully transcribed the marks in the wood onto a pad of paper and took a close-up picture as well. Next we carefully turned the large painting around and lofted it onto its wall cleat. I had a little difficulty on my end, but Weed patiently held his end of the frame in place until I finally managed to secure my end to the wall. We backed away to see how we'd done, and it looked like it had before.

"Good thing you reminded us to view the painting in its entirety or we never would've found these marks," I complimented Weed.

Both of us were shaking a little, partially because of the physical exertion of lofting the heavy painting, but mainly because we were both excited by what we found, and what it might mean. We were stoked!

We walked back to the lobby, and Lainy was still stationed at the front desk with the same friendly smile on her face. We wanted to be polite to her, but we sure didn't want to dawdle with drawn-out pleasantries. We couldn't wait to see what the coded message said.

"Well, did you learn what you came for?" she asked us enthusiastically.

"I believe we may have," I said noncommittally. "It's a magnificent painting! Would you please thank Mr. Daniels for us again? You've both been very gracious, and I'd love to come again to see more highlights from the Rothman Collection." We then promptly said goodbye.

Weed and I exited the museum and walked with purpose to my Tacoma. He was already entering the code into his phone's conversion app as he climbed inside. I drove us a short distance to the lovely Eden Park overlook and we parked the truck.

"I almost have the coded message entered into the app," he declared. "Just a few more key strokes ... and voila!"

We both stared at the text: *"Seek my muse."*

"Seek my muse?!" I said quizzically. "Oh swell! Another vague clue. Here we go again!"

Chapter 13

THE SUN WAS SETTING over Lake Michigan as Ernst Kline approached the door to Malcolm Land's condominium. He hesitated outside the door before ringing the bell. He didn't like Malcolm Land one bit, but he disliked himself even more for what he had become … a stooge for bad people and a killer of good people. He cringed and rang the doorbell.

"Ah, Ernst!" Malcolm said convivially, "How good of you to visit me."

"As if I had a choice," Ernst murmured under his breath.

"Please come inside and have a seat. I have some things I wish to discuss with you," Malcolm said imperiously.

Ernst entered the lavish condo but chose to remain standing. "Yes?" he said. "What is it you wish to discuss, Mr. Land?"

"As I informed you earlier, Ernst, it has come to my attention that my sister, Lucretia, and Drew Thomas have been e-mailing each other about Land Foundation artwork. Apparently, they gathered some information about Samuel Morse's painting, *Gallery of the Louvre,* and shared it with this Clay Arnold fellow and a friend of his. You'll recall that Arnold is the famous photographer who just paid three million dollars for a stupid camera last week."

Malcolm continued, "First of all, I don't like her nosing around our Land Foundation business because it no longer concerns her, and, secondly, I want to find out what they're after."

"And what do you want me to do about it?" Ernst asked reluctantly.

"I want you to remain available to me by phone twenty four seven. My security chief will let me know about any further messages sent between Lucretia and Drew, and I want you to follow Clay Arnold and his pal. I suspect that he and Lucretia are up to something, and I want to know what it is."

"Why don't you just ask Drew. He still works for the Land Foundation, doesn't he?" Ernst queried.

"Yes, for now, but I see no point in letting them know that I'm watching them." Malcolm confirmed.

"I'll do what you want for now, Mr. Land, but may I suggest we find an end point to this hostile family business takeover and get on with life?" Ernst tried.

"Look here, Mr. Kline!" Malcolm said with all of the polish removed from his prep-school training. "I have all of the incriminating evidence against you that I need for murdering both Ralston Land and Benton Pettengill. You watch your mouth with me, sir, and do as I instruct you. Is that understood?"

"Yes, Mr. Land. It is clearly understood." Ernst replied. "Is there anything else you require?

"Just remain available and your payments will keep coming," Malcolm concluded.

Ernst Kline closed Malcolm Land's condo door and walked down the hallway toward the elevator. He shook his head in thoughtful disgust. "God, I hate that son of a bitch!"

Weed and I were perplexed. The drive back home to the brewery complex from Cincinnati was pleasant enough, but we couldn't get the message we found on the canvas stretcher of the *Gallery of the Louvre* out of our minds … *"Seek my muse."*

"It could be anyone," I said. "Morse's muse could be his wife, his sister, a friend, a lover. Where do we go with this new clue?"

"You're right," Weed acknowledged. "It could be anyone, and again we need some help solving this piece of the puzzle. You know, Clay, we wouldn't have gotten this far if it hadn't been for the help Drew and Lucretia provided us. Besides, we promised we'd get back to her to share what we learned at the Rothman Collection. I suggest that we call Lucretia and see if she and Drew can work their magic again for us."

"Yeah, I agree," I said. "I have a feeling good old Sammy boy is going to have us chasing our tails in search of his treasure trove. I only hope there's something worthwhile at the end of the rainbow. Why don't you call Lucretia and bring her up to date with where we stand?"

Weed placed the call and was greeted by Lucretia's voice on the third ring.

"Good evening, Clay," she said. "How was J.D. and the Rothman Collection?"

"Hi Lucretia, it's me, Weed. Clay's driving, and I'm using his phone. I have it on speaker so the three of us can communicate."

"Evening, Lucretia," I said. "Our trip to Cincinnati was very helpful thanks to you and Drew. J.D. was very gracious in allowing us time to examine Morse's painting. Honestly though, we would've come away clueless if Weed here hadn't reminded us to view the *Gallery of the Louvre* in its entirety. Please don't tell J.D., but when he left the salon to handle a conference call, Weed and I lofted that heavy picture off the wall and examined its back side."

"Oh my!" Lucretia gasped. "I doubt that J.D. would've approved of that without his staff's help. In any event what did you find?"

"Well, fortunately, we got the painting securely rehung after we examined it closely. J.D. shouldn't be any wiser of our manhandling the artwork. One thing's for sure, Samuel Morse was one clever dude. Weed and I found more Morse code stamped into the wooden canvas stretcher."

"Any idea what it said?" she inquired.

"Yeah, we do," Weed replied. "I used a code conversion app on my phone, and it said, 'Seek my muse.' Any idea who Morse could be referring to?"

"No, I'm not sure, but I'll e-mail Drew when we hang up and see if he can do a little research for us. You two certainly have an interesting adventure going on, don't you? Wouldn't it be incredible if Samuel Morse really did have a treasure trove hidden away somewhere?"

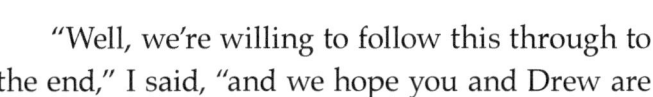

"Well, we're willing to follow this through to the end," I said, "and we hope you and Drew are amenable to helping us with the clues."

"With the exception of trying to figure out a way to legally reclaim my inheritance, I don't have a lot more going on. Besides, you've gotten me excited about this search, too. It's intriguing to say the least. I'll e-mail Drew, and we'll see where Morse's muse leads us."

"Sounds like a plan," Weed said, and we disconnected the call.

"So, now we try to practice some patience and wait to hear back from them," I said stating the obvious. We arrived home about two hours later, and Weed and I were still practicing patience.

Mace greeted us in the courtyard as we pulled into the brewery complex. "Hey guys, after you get settled let's meet in the museum. I just finished re-arranging some of the displays, and I want you to see the place of prominence I've given the Morse camera."

"Cool! What say we meet in the museum in thirty minutes? That'll give me time to put stuff away and try to reach Maggie."

"Thirty works!" Weed said, and we temporarily went our separate ways.

Satchmo joined me, and we raced each other up the steps to my bedroom. He won. "So, what do you think, Satchmo? Am I nuts to be pulling Weed and Lucretia and Drew into this crazy adventure? "

Satchmo uttered a low "meow," and I took that to mean that he absolutely thought I was nuts.

"Hey Sir Cat! That was meant as a rhetorical question!" I said with feigned indignation. "But why would Samuel Morse go to all of this trouble with his coded messages hidden in obscure locations in his paintings if there weren't a real treasure?"

At that point Satchmo found more satisfaction in molesting a ladybug than in being an audience for my monologue about hidden treasure. Frankly, I wasn't entirely sure I could blame him.

I called Maggie's cell phone, and her voice mail kicked in. "Hi Honey, sorry I missed you. Weed and I got back from Cincinnati a little while ago. We had a very revealing visit to the Rothman Collection, and I wanted to let you know about another clue we discovered. Looks like we may be going on another trip somewhere. Lucretia Land and Drew Thomas are helping us out with a little research about our new clue, and we'll know more when they get back to us. So, stay tuned! Love you!"

Chapter 14

EVERY TIME I ENTER my antique camera museum, I'm reminded about how much I've enjoyed the hunt for each item. As a professional photographer, I'm not satisfied with just being very good at my art. I feel compelled to also understand the evolution of the equipment and processes that began with Daguerre's monumental achievement in 1839. That's why owning the daguerreotype camera that Daguerre gifted to Samuel Morse is so important to me. I love the hunt for landmark pieces and sharing photohistory with others.

Weed and Mace joined me a few minutes later, and we admired the place of honor that Mace provided the Morse camera.

"Great job, Mace!" I said. "I love the way you situated the camera on the studio stand and positioned the fuming boxes nearby. It looks like an original photography salon. I imagine that both Daguerre and Morse would be shocked to know that their camera had taken up residence in a museum in central Indiana."

"Thanks, Clay, I think it works pretty well there, too," Mace replied. "So, what did you guys find out at the Rothman Collection?"

"Well, thanks to our clever friend, Weed, we found another clue on the back of the *Gallery of the Louvre,* and we're waiting to hear back from Lucretia and Drew to see if they can shed some light on its meaning."

"So, what did the clue say?" Mace asked.

"Seek my muse. Whatever that means," I said.

Shortly thereafter my phone rang, and I saw that it was Lucretia calling Weed and me back. I put the phone on speaker and answered. "Hi there," I said. "What's the good word?"

"Sorry it took me a while to get back to you, Clay, but Drew wanted to thoroughly research whatever he could find out about Samuel Morse's muse."

"And?" I asked expectantly.

"And, it turns out that his muse was none other than his eldest daughter, Susan Walker Morse. Samuel painted the portrait sometime around 1836, and it was first exhibited at the National Academy of Design in 1837. It depicts his daughter at about seventeen years of age, holding a sketchbook with her eyes raised in contemplation."

"Interesting," I replied. "Any idea where the painting is now?"

"I do," Lucretia said. "It's in the permanent collection of the Metropolitan Museum in New York."

Weed and I glanced at each other and nodded. We knew we'd be heading to New York very soon.

"Well, let me ask you, Lucretia, do your contacts in the art world extend to the Metropolitan Museum? Any chance you could facilitate a visit for us to examine *The Muse?*"

"Of course!" she replied without hesitation. "Since the Land Foundation collected mostly American art, we know many of the curators at major museums who specialize in that area. If I'm not mistaken, Clifton Maguire is still the curator for the American art department at the Metropolitan. I'll e-mail Drew to confirm that and let you know, okay?"

"Sounds great, Lucretia," I said. "We can't thank you enough."

I hung up with Lucretia and looked at Weed. "Keep your backpack handy, my friend, it looks like we'll be taking our show on the road again. Mace, do you mind holding down the fort here while we're gone?"

"Not at all, Clay, especially since I've got the rarest camera in the world to keep me company!" he beamed.

After the three of us tinkered around in the camera museum for a while longer, Mace said, "I've got something else I want to show you down in the subbasement."

The subbasement is a testing laboratory of sorts that is two floors below where we're standing. Back in the days when the brewery complex actually brewed beer, the Block brothers used the subbasement as a place to store kegs of beer. The last couple of years, Mace, Weed, and I have used it as a subterranean testing lab for the weapons I've taken with me during my time as an avenging vigilante. Those violent days are pretty much over since Maggie and I got together, but honestly, in these crazy times, I feel more secure carrying a concealed weapon. Plus, getting shot at in Chicago didn't exactly turn me into a pacifist. Maggie's not thrilled that I do it, but she understands my attitude, especially after we had to rescue her niece, Laura, from that wacko Dr. Mortimer Chestnut a few months ago.

We took the elevator from the museum down to the subbasement and Mace led us over to the main workbench.

"Now, Clay, I know you prefer to use the Demon detective camera for your forays into evening the score with bad guys, so I rooted around the camera parts bin and found enough pieces to redesign the Demon into a smaller, yet more powerful device."

"Mace, I swear you are incredible … and incorrigible!" Weed laughed. "You should be teaching at MIT or working for the CIA."

"Yeah, well," Mace said. "I learned most of what I know from you, Weed!" he countered.

"Take the Demon, Clay, and stand about twenty feet away from that paper target on the wall," Mace instructed.

"That's probably ten feet further than its previous range," I said.

"My point exactly!" Mace said. "Now get in position and press the shutter button."

I did, and an angry blue charge of electricity shot out from the Demon and engulfed the paper target. It was fried in a matter of seconds. Weed whistled his show of appreciation.

"How many zaps do you think I can get out of this before the charge is totally depleted," I asked.

"About three, I reckon," came Mace's reply.

"I think we have a winner!" I said about the new, improved Demon camera. "Thanks, Mace, I'll swap this one out for the one I've been carrying."

Between driving to Cincinnati, finding the clue on the back of the *Gallery of the Louvre,* driving home, and hanging out with Weed and Mace, it had been a long day. I was tuckered.

"I think I'm going to call it a night, guys," I said to my two friends. "I'll be sure to let you know when I hear from Lucretia, okay?"

We parted company, and I took the stairs up to my living room. Halfway up the steps I was passed by a large fluffy gray streak, and Satchmo stood at the top of the stairs waiting for me.

"Okay, you win," I said. "But you're younger, sneakier, and you have two more legs than I do! C'mon, let's grab a bite to eat and get some shut-eye."

Satchmo replied by rubbing his furry flank against my lower leg. Definitely a cat of few words.

After dinner I was feeling physically sated and mentally exhausted. I wanted to call Maggie again, but I was honestly too bushed to be much of a communicator. Besides, I knew she was at her sister's house now, and that they'd be having a good time. I texted her to say that I was heading to bed and that I love her. I knew we'd talk tomorrow.

"Seek my muse," Morse's message had read. I lay in bed and stared at the ceiling and thought about everything that had occurred since I bought the Morse camera. "Wouldn't it be incredible if there really is a treasure trove," I murmured to myself. A few moments later I drifted off to sleep.

Malcolm Land hung up the telephone after a late night call from his security chief, George Titus, at the Land Foundation. At Malcolm's instructions Titus had been secretly monitoring Drew Thomas's e-mails with Lucretia.

"Hmm," Malcolm said aloud to himself, "What's the big deal with them looking into Samuel Morse's paintings. First, the trip by Clay Arnold and his buddy to the Rothman Collection, and now their looking into some obscure painting by Morse at the Metropolitan Museum. Huh, that rumpled old cuss of a curator, Clifton Maguire, apparently still works there. Perhaps it's time that I had Ernst Kline pay Dr. Clifton a little visit. Ernst has such a special knack for gleaning information from folks, and, if necessary, taking care of, uh, loose ends."

Malcolm placed his call to Ernst and then settled in to watch the boats cruise along the Chicago River into Lake Michigan.

"Oh, Lucretia, I daresay our mother and father wouldn't be very happy with me, would they? Oh well, I can live with that."

Chapter 15

"GOOD MORNING, Lucretia!" Clifton Maguire gushed from his finely appointed office within the Metropolitan Museum. "And to what do I owe the pleasure of your call?"

"Good morning to you as well, Clifton, I wasn't sure if you'd remember me," Lucretia said.

"Of course I remember you. I was very sorry to learn of your father's recent death. Very few art collectors ever acquired the the scope of American paintings that your parents did. I wish we owned several of those paintings, but alas, the power of the Metropolitan's purse only goes so far. Please accept my sincere condolences on their passing."

"Thank you, Clifton, I appreciate your kind words."

"Now then, how may I help you, Lucretia?"

"I'm calling about Samuel Morse's painting, *The Muse,* which I understand the Metropolitan owns."

"Yes, indeed," Clifton confirmed. "It's a lovely painting. If I'm not mistaken it is currently undergoing a little restoration and is presently off display."

"I have two friends who recently purchased a daguerrotype camera from the Land Foundation that Samuel Morse once owned. Subsequently, my friends have kindled an interest in Morse's art as well, and they are traveling to various museums to view his artwork close up. They just returned from visiting the *Gallery of the Louvre* that our Foundation has loaned to Joseph Daniels and the Rothman Collection. They're hoping to see *The Muse,* and I offered to call you on their behalf to see if you'd be willing to allow them to do so. I'd be most appreciative."

"Well, ordinarily our restoration staff prefer no visitors in their clean lab, but I think we could probably make an exception for you. What are your friends' names and when do you think they'll be in New York?"

"I imagine you know the name, Clay Arnold, the famous photographer. It's Clay and his friend, Weed Rawlins," Lucretia stated.

"Ah, who hasn't heard of Clay Arnold?" Clifton asked rhetorically. "Please just ask them to give me a call, and it would be an honor to share *The Muse* with them. I'll alert our restoration staff as well. I imagine they would very much enjoy meeting Mr. Arnold, too."

"Thank you very much, Clifton, I will let Clay and Weed know you're awaiting their call."

Clifton Maguire and Lucretia ended their conversation, and she promptly called me.

"Good morning, Clay," Lucretia said. "I just got off the phone with Clifton Maguire at the Metropolitan, and he's happy to meet with you and Weed. He said The Muse is currently undergoing some minor cleaning and restoration, but that he'd arrange a special, behind-the-scenes viewing for the two of you."

"He doesn't know the real reason why we want to see the painting, does he?" I asked.

"No, of course not. I told him that you and Weed have developed a keen interest in the artwork of Samuel Morse ever since you purchased the daguerreotype camera he once owned."

"Thanks, Lucretia, and please thank Drew for us as well. I'll give Dr. Maguire a call and see about arranging our visit. I'll definitely keep you informed. Plus, I have a nagging feeling that good old Samuel Morse isn't finished leaving us a string of clues to follow."

After we concluded our call, I texted Weed to let them know that Lucretia had paved the way for our visit to the Metropolitan.

"I'll e-mail my agent, Lily, and ask her to book a flight for us and maybe she can get us a suite at the Plaza Hotel. How's that sound?!"

"Sounds like a plan, my man, I think I need to travel with you more often!" Weed declared. "How's Maggie gonna feel about you going to New York without her?"

"Oh, it'll probably mean one more thing I need to make up to her," I acknowledged. "Although I think with her pregnancy she'll be more comfortable hanging out at her sister's home through Thanksgiving. I'll let you know what travel and hotel arrangements Lily comes up with for us, okay?"

Lily did her scheduling magic for us, and some twenty-four hours later Weed and I boarded our flight from Indianapolis to LaGuardia. I had called Clifton Maguire earlier in the day to let him know we are on our way, and we agreed we'd meet at the museum around five o'clock. Our flight went fairly smoothly, and Weed and I checked into our spacious suite at the Plaza around three o'clock.

"Holy crap!" Weed said when we opened the door to our large hotel suite with a great view of the city. Do you always travel like this, Clay?"

"Never!" I said. "But, I figured you're going out of your way to make this treasure hunt a success, so I thought I'd splurge for us a bit. Besides, it's only for a night or two."

"You know, Clay, I've never asked you how much dough you really have, mainly because it's not important to me. And, you've always been so generous with all of us in your own quiet way. Then even more recently you gave me the early Morse telegraph key which on the open market has to be pretty pricey in its own right. I just want you to know we all appreciate your generosity very much."

"You're right, Weed, it's not something I talk much about. When my parents died in that car accident when I was in college, I received a rather tidy inheritance, mainly from my mother's side of the family. Fortunately, I've also enjoyed a successful career in photography. I've been very lucky, with the exception of losing my parents, of course, and I don't take my assets for granted. What I do believe in is sharing what I have with people that are important to me. Life's not a dress rehearsal, after all."

"I get it, buddy," Weed acknowledged. "Does Maggie know you're well off?"

"Yeah, she has a pretty good idea, especially when I told her how much the Morse camera could be. I never did summon the courage to tell her I spent around three million dollars for the camera. I did tell her, however, that I'd share my financial status before we got married."

"Like I said, Clay, you're being wealthy isn't important to me, or to Tori, Mace, or Rennie, either. On the other hand, it's damn sweet to benefit from your largesse. So, you can book the Plaza for us anytime you want, my friend!"

I called Clifton Maguire's office again to confirm that we're still meeting at five o'clock. His assistant, Olivia Hudson, acknowledged that we are, and that I should ask the information desk to ring her when we arrive. And two hours later that's what we did.

"Ah, Mr. Arnold and Mr. Rawlins, it's so lovely to meet you both," a lithesome Ms. Hudson chirped. Dr. Maguire is finishing up a few details and asked me to bring you to the restoration lab. He'll join you there momentarily."

Ms. Hudson led the way down a corridor lined with musical instruments from around the world. I looked over at Weed to see if he was eyeing Ms. Hudson's derriere like he did with the sweet ingenue at the Rothman Collection. Sure enough, he was.

"What?!" he said when he looked back at me and saw me smiling. "I was admiring the instruments!"

"Yeah, and I'm Ansel Adams," I replied sarcastically.

Ms. Hudson approached a locked door and entered a numerical code into the touch pad. The pad flashed green, and she opened the door to the restoration room. Inside, an art restorer was seated at a well-lit bench assiduously examining a darkened Rembrandt painting.

"This is Grace Sawyer," Olivia announced. She's working on a new acquisition which was recently bequeathed to the museum.

Weed and I introduced ourselves and listened as she explained the arduous process she was undertaking to remove the painting's old varnish.

"Once I dissolve the old varnish, clean the painting a bit, and revarnish it, we'll see detail that has been obscured for centuries," she said. "We don't want it to look like a new painting, but just fresh enough to reveal the additional details."

I was about to ask Grace a question about the cleaning process when the lab door swung open and a gentleman in his mid-fifties wearing a conservative-looking suit and a flamboyant tie strode into the room with a broad smile on his face. It was Clifton Maguire, curator of American art for the Metropolitan museum.

"My sincere apologies, gentlemen, for my tardiness. I'm Clifton and it is, indeed, a pleasure to meet both of you, and I must say, Clay, I have been an admirer of your photography for quite a long time."

"Thank you," I said, "and this is my good friend, Weed Rawlins. We certainly appreciate your allowing us to view *The Muse.* We promise not to take too much of your time. I know that with the holidays upon us, it must be a very busy time at the museum."

Weed and Clifton exchanged pleasantries, and then Clifton asked Grace where Morse's *The Muse* was located. She pointed to another workbench across the room, and we strode over to see it.

Clifton continued, "*The Muse* is a full-length portrait measuring roughly five feet by six feet. It is a portrait of Morse's eldest daughter, Susan Walker Morse, although some art historians say that it is also a personification of the art of drawing and design. It's historically significant because Samuel Morse painted it around 1837, a crucial period in his development of the telegraph. Apparently, Morse had grown depressed that his artistic career wasn't met with more popular appeal, and after completing *The Muse,* he turned his attention away from painting and to science and invention instead."

"Fascinating!" Weed said. "I see that you have removed it from its frame."

"Yes," Grace said. "We always do that when we restore and clean a painting. The canvas itself is in very good condition, but the wooden stretcher that the painting was attached to had experienced some dry rot, and we had to replace it."

I'm sure that Weed and I shared the same sinking feeling that we were totally screwed if we couldn't examine the original wooden canvas stretcher. I glanced over at him briefly, and he was looking at the floor in disappointment.

"You wouldn't still happen to have the original stretchers, would you?" Weed inquired evenly. "Clay is the art aficionado, and I really appreciate seeing how the great artists also physically prepared their masterpieces for framing."

"Good for you, Mr. Rawlins!" Grace evoked. "It's not everyone who appreciates all that goes into preparing a fine work of art for presentation. I'm impressed. Now, as to where the old stretchers are, we ordinarily toss them in the trash bin. Hmm, ah yes, let's look over here. Fortunately, our housekeeping staff have not collected this bin yet."

While Clifton and I discussed art and photography, Weed and Grace walked over to the trash bin. "You're welcome to look in here if you wish, Mr. Rawlins. I believe it should still be relatively intact."

Grace went over to speak with Clifton Maguire a moment, and Weed did a refined version of dumpster diving. He pulled out old rotten canvases, broken pieces of frames, and at last saw what appeared to be an old wooden canvas stretcher. He gently lifted it from the trash bin and laid it on a work table. It was, indeed, intact, and Weed quickly examined it for signs of Morse code. Sure enough near the bottom of the wooden stretcher, Weed saw the characteristic marks of dots and dashes.

- .-. .- ...- . .-.. .... - --- .... - .... --- ..- ... .

He pulled his phone from his pocket and took pictures of the code. He carefully examined the rest of the wood and saw nothing further. Presently, Grace returned, and Weed was already replacing the stretcher into the trash bin.

"Find anything interesting?" Grace asked.

"Oh, nothing earthshaking, really," Weed replied. "But I appreciate your letting me root around in your garbage," he joked.

Weed gave me a brief nod affirming that he had what we came for, and after we asked polite questions for about another three minutes, we thanked them both, and Clifton escorted us back to the main entrance.

"Please do give Lucretia Land my best regards the next time you speak," Clifton said. "Her family certainly has an eye, and a wallet, for great art."

We parted company, and it wasn't until Weed and I were totally outside of the Metropolitan that either of us began breathing normally again.

It was getting dark outside, but we walked into Central Park and plopped down onto a park bench. Weed was already entering the Morse-coded message into the conversion app on his phone. A minute or so later, he read the text message out loud, *"Travel to the house."*

Weed and I looked at each other quizzically. "I think we need some dinner and a couple of stiff drinks to figure this one out," Weed said.

"Yeah," I agreed. "Looks like we'll be calling Lucretia again in the morning, huh?!"

Weed concurred, and we hailed a cab back to the Plaza Hotel.

At seven thirty in the evening Clifton Maguire was still in his office completing some last minute details before leaving for the day. His assistant had already gone home as had most of the museum's staff. At this hour the only staff that remained were typically from security and housekeeping.

Clifton was deep in thought. He was excited about the opening of the museum's upcoming exhibition of artwork from the American West and hadn't heard his office door open and close. A few

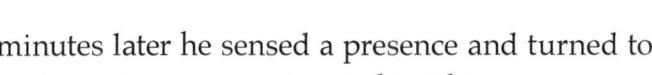

minutes later he sensed a presence and turned to notice a stranger standing behind him.

"Oh my!" he declared. "Who are you and how did you get in here? The museum is closed for the day."

"I am well aware that the museum is closed, Dr. Maguire, and who I am is of little consequence. Suffice it to say that I am here on behalf of my bene-factor, and I have have a few questions for you."

Clifton Maguire reached for his phone to sum-mon security and was rewarded with an angry rap on his hand from the stranger's ebony walking stick.

"Yeoww!" he bellowed in pain. "Who are you and what do you want?" he cried out with fright.

"Like I said, who I am is of little importance. Tell me about the visitors you had late this afternoon," Ernst Kline demanded.

"Who, what, which visitors?! We have thousands of visitors at the Metropolitan every day."

"That photographer, Clay Arnold, and his asso-ciate, Weed Rawlins," the stranger's voice com-manded. "What did they want, and what did you tell them?"

Clifton was confused and frightened. "They wanted to see a painting by Samuel Morse. Now I really must insist that you leave at once," Clifton voiced with false bravado, and he reached for his phone again.

Ernst sharply rapped the curator once again on his hand with his ebony cane. "What about the painting? What is its significance? What did you tell them?"

"I, uh, told them the history of the painting and showed them the restoration work we were doing on the canvas down in the lab," Clifton managed.

"What else?!" Malcolm Land's attorney asked as he raised his walking stick for another savage strike.

"That's all," Clifton cried out. "Well, Mr. Arnold's friend was also interested in seeing the painting's original wooden canvas stretcher."

"Why?!" the stranger hissed at the hapless curator.

"I don't know why," Clifton replied meekly. "He said he likes to see how the paintings are assembled prior to framing."

None of that made any sense to Ernst Kline, but he let the curator's comment slide because he figured at this point he would say anything to extricate himself from this terrifying situation.

"What else?" Ernst Kline demanded again. "Did they say where they're staying in New York?"

"Clay said that they were staying at the Plaza Hotel, but please, sir, I can't think of anything else to tell you about their visit. They were only here briefly and then they left."

Ernst considered the curator's words carefully and decided he didn't want to risk being seen dragging Clifton down to the lab to look at *The Muse* and the stretchers. But, he also didn't want to risk Clifton Maguire calling for help as soon as he departed his office.

"Well, this has been rather fruitless!" Ernst said to Clifton as he turned to leave. Then, with lightning speed he wheeled around and delivered a bone crunching smash to the curator's forehead with his walking stick. Clifton slumped face forward on to his desk, and Ernst savagely brought his cane down on the back of his head to conclude their "fruitless" conversation. He was quite dead. Ernst turned off the office lights, locked the door behind him, and managed to exit the Metropolitan as surreptitiously as he'd entered.

Chapter 16

THE NEXT MORNING brought sunlight streaming through the windows of our suite at the Plaza Hotel. I woke up in a bit of a fog and tried to go back to sleep. Then, I remembered the new Morse-coded message that Weed had converted to English text: *Travel to the house.* I bolted upright in bed trying to understand some meaning from yet another bewildering clue.

Weed shuffled out of his bedroom in his underwear and headed for the coffeemaker. He saw me sitting on the side of my bed and grunted, "G'morning." Neither of us were really morning people, but Weed especially wasn't. His career as a

blues musician had seen him close many a nightclub, and it wasn't unusual for him to sleep till after ten in the morning. It was only eight o'clock now.

Five minutes later the coffee was ready, and we each grabbed a cup and walked over to the window to admire our view of the city. After a couple of sips, the caffeine jump-started my brain, and I looked over at Weed.

"So, what do you think?" I asked him.

"What do I think about what?" he replied. "Are you asking me about last night's coded message? Or, where we're going next? Or, are we out of our minds to be doing this treasure hunt? Or, perhaps you're asking me about that young woman's rear end who escorted us to the restoration lab?"

"Yeah, pretty much all of that with the exception of the young woman's rear end," I said. "I already know what you think about that."

"Which house?!" Weed queried out loud. "Which house was Morse referring to? I imagine he lived in a number of cities during his life: Charlestown, New Haven, New York, London, Paris. It could be in any of those cities, or someplace that we're not even aware of."

"You're right," I acknowledged.

"Now, as to whether or not we're out of our minds for going on this merry chase," Weed continued. "Yeah, I think we're both a little nutty, but

I sure don't see us stopping the search at this point. Do you?"

"No, I sure don't!" I asserted. "I've got to hand it to Samuel Morse. He knew he'd get someone's undivided attention if his coded message was ever found inside Daguerre's camera. Hard to pass up a chance to find treasure. So, shall we give Lucretia a call and see if she and Drew can help us solve a riddle … again?!"

"They've sure been helpful up to now," Weed said. "We'd be virtually nowhere without their guidance, and I think at this point they're probably starting to get a little excited, too. Yeah, Clay, let's give her a call. Breakfast and showering can wait." And that's what we did.

"Good morning, Lucretia," I said when she answered the phone on the third ring. "I hope I'm not calling you too early."

"Good morning to you, too, Clay, and I presume Weed is there with you."

"I am!" Weed called out from across the room. "G'morning, Lucretia!"

"And no, you're not calling too early, Clay. In fact I presumed that I'd hear from you bright and early, especially if you and Weed have some good news to report."

"We do!" I replied earnestly. "First of all, thanks again for introducing us to Clifton Maguire. He and his staff were very generous with their time. And, of course, while I chatted with Clifton, Weed managed to find the old canvas stretchers for *The Muse* that the art restorer had tossed in the trash. He found and converted another Morse-coded clue which we can't figure out, so once again we could sure use some help from you and Drew about the meaning."

"So what did you guys come up with?" Lucretia asked.

"*Travel to the house*," Weed said. "That's it. *Travel to the house.*"

"Hmm," Lucretia exhaled. "I see why you're stymied. Considering that Morse lived to be about eighty, that could refer to a lot of different places where he'd resided. I'll send an e-mail to Drew at work and see if he can shed some light on this. I need to also send a quick message to Clifton Maguire thanking him for his time."

"Thanks, Lucretia," Weed and I said in unison. "We knew we could count on you guys. We'll stay in New York until we hear back from you."

We ended our call, and then Weed and I had another cup of coffee and enjoyed a continental breakfast that we had room service send up.

"Well, there's no telling when Drew and Lucretia will get back to us, and this is New York City after all, anywhere in particular you want to visit today?" Weed asked.

"You know, I was just thinking," I said. "The Hayden Planetarium is just on the other side of Central Park. "Their director, Alex Konstantin, contacted me a couple of months ago about possibly exhibiting some of my photographs of the Milky Way. We might swing by there and see if he's free to chat for a couple of minutes, and if not, we can always see their latest star show while we wait to hear back from our friends in Chicago. How's that sound?"

"I'm game," Weed said. "I actually know Alex, too, from our days together at MIT. It would be good to see him again."

I told Weed I needed some time to get cleaned up, and that I wanted to try to reach Maggie again at her sister's house. "Besides, I doubt that the Hayden is open before ten o'clock."

I went into my room and called Maggie.

"Hello," came her drowsy voice.

"Good morning, Maggie. Sounds like I just woke you. Sorry," I said.

"Hi sweetheart," she replied. "You did, but that's okay. I was hoping I'd hear from you this morning."

"Do you want to go back to sleep and call me back later?" I asked.

"No, that's fine. I'm awake now. So, tell me about what kind of mischief you and Weed have been up to."

I told Maggie about our successful visit to the Metropolitan museum yesterday afternoon and Weed's finding another clue for us.

"*Travel to the house*?" Maggie said out loud. "Which house?" she asked.

"That's what we're trying to figure out," I replied. We called Lucretia Land this morning, and she's going to e-mail her friend, Drew Thomas, at the Land Foundation to see if he can do some research for us."

"Any idea when they'll get back to you?" she asked.

"Not really. Probably later today. Weed and I are going to visit the Hayden Planetarium to see if their director is available to chat about a possible photography exhibition with my work and to kill some time."

We chatted for a few minutes longer mostly about how she's feeling with her pregnancy, and what she and her sister and her niece have been doing. Then we engaged in a little naughty phone sex. After giggling way too much for grown adults, we hung up and I got ready to meet Weed and head over to the planetarium.

We took the elevator down to the Plaza Hotel's opulent lobby, and I stopped briefly at the front desk to confirm that Weed and I would be staying an additional night.

"We're delighted that you'll be with us a little longer," Marlita said from the desk. "Do you and Mr. Rawlins have special plans today?"

I told her that we were going to the Hayden Planetarium, and she voiced her approval of our choice of venues.

Weed and I walked along West 59th Street and turned on to Central Park West. It was a lovely November day, and we enjoyed seeing the activity in Central Park. Despite the invigorating walk, I had a nagging feeling that we were being followed, but each time I turned to look around, I didn't see anything or anyone unusual.

"What's up?" Weed inquired. "Do you think we're being followed?"

"I don't know," I admitted. "Just a weird feeling, I guess. It's at times like these that I'm glad I have the Demon camera though."

Earlier that morning Ernst Kline had called his malefactor and chief tormentor, Malcolm Land, to report his recent activities.

"You killed Clifton Maguire in his office?!" Malcolm exclaimed with surprise and a mild twinge of amusement.

"I did," Ernst replied evenly. "He didn't have anything useful he could share about Clay Arnold and his buddy's visit, so I decided it was best to not leave any witnesses about our, uh, activities."

"Jesus! You do enjoy your little executions, don't you?" Malcolm noted without any ethical concerns.

"Not really," Ernst replied. "But dead men tell no tales, and I prefer not to spend the rest of my life behind bars."

"Good!" Malcolm replied. "It's important that you remember that, and it's good that I have all the incriminating evidence I need to keep you in line. Eh, Ernst? All in a safe place. Heaven forbid, you'd ever decide to turn on me!" he said with malice in his voice. "So, what's your plan for today?"

"Well, thanks to that curator at the museum, I learned that Arnold and Rawlins are staying at the Plaza Hotel. I waited outside for them to leave the hotel, and I'm tailing them now. I'll get back to you when I learn more."

"Be sure that you do," Malcolm said. "My security chief just intercepted an e-mail that my dear sister, Lucretia, sent to her beloved Uncle Drew. Apparently, she wants him to figure out the location of a house that Samuel Morse referenced. I'm not sure what they'll find there, but I want you to keep tailing Clay Arnold and his buddy. Understand?!"

"Perfectly," Ernst responded. They hung up, and the blackmailed attorney stared at his phone and said, "I hate that bastard."

Weed and I entered the Hayden Planetarium and paid for our admission. I introduced us to the desk clerk and asked if she'd please call Alex Konstantin's office and see if he has time to say hello. She called his office and said that his assistant, Rosemary, would be down to speak with us shortly.

A few minutes later a portly woman in her midforties joined Weed and me. "Ah, Mr. Arnold and Mr. Rawlins, Dr. Konstantin is in Chile visiting the Atacama observatories. He'll be so sorry that he missed you."

"That's too bad," I said. "Actually we weren't even sure we'd be coming here today, so we just took our chances. Would you please tell him that we dropped by, and that I would enjoy speaking with him further about a possible exhibition of my photography?"

"I sure will," Rosemary said. "I recall your communications about this several weeks ago, and I know Dr. Konstantin will be very pleased that you're interested."

Rosemary offered to have a member of their staff give us a personal tour of the planetarium which we politely declined since we didn't know when Lucretia would call us back, plus we were happy just to wander around on our own. Weed and I spent the next hour or so going from one exhibit hall to the next and also watched a video about the development of the James Webb Space Telescope which is scheduled to replace the Hubble telescope when it's launched in 2020.

When we finally exited the Hayden around noon, we were approached by a serious-looking man in a dark overcoat.

"Are you Clay Arnold and Maurice Rawlins?" the man said as he flashed his NYPD credentials.

"Uh yeah," I said nervously. "What's this about?"

"I'm Detective Nelson Tweedie from the homicide division. Would you please come with me? I have a few questions I'd like to ask you."

From a safe distance, Ernst Kline watched the man approach Weed and me and slinked further back in the shadows when he saw the officer show us his police badge.

"Uh yeah," I said again. "What's this about?"

The homicide detective led us to an unmarked car, and we were instructed to get inside the back seat.

"What's going on, Detective Tweedie? I don't understand how we can help," I tried.

"Do you know a Dr. Clifton Maguire from the Metropolitan Museum?"

"Yes," I responded. "We were at the museum yesterday afternoon visiting with him. Is there a problem?"

"Quite so!" Detective Tweedie replied. "He was found beaten to death in his office early this morning." He closely watched our reactions.

Both Weed and I were stunned by this revelation. "Holy shit!" Weed exclaimed. "You don't think we had anything to do with it, do you?"

"Not at this point," Detective Tweedie replied. "We've watched the surveillance videos and saw the two of you exit the museum without incident. However, I'm curious if you saw anyone or anything suspicious."

We told him we hadn't. The truth was that when Weed and I left the Metropolitan after visiting with Clifton Maguire and Grace in the restoration lab, we were so intent on trying to decipher the new clue Weed had found that a brass band could've marched down the street, and we wouldn't have noticed it.

"I can't believe he's dead," I said sadly. "Do you have any suspects aside from us, of course?"

"Not at this time," the detective said. "That's why I wanted to speak with you."

"How did you even know we were here today?" Weed asked.

"Well, given your good reputations, we thought you might be staying at one of the better hotels in the area, so after phoning around to a few notable places, we spoke with the desk clerk at the Plaza

Hotel, and she informed us that you said you were going to the Hayden this morning."

Both Weed and I were impressed by the detective's effective police work.

"Honestly, Detective," I said, "Dr. Maguire's death is shocking news to us. I'm not sure what else we can offer in the way of help."

Detective Tweedie detained us for about five minutes longer, and when he realized that we had nothing substantive to offer and that we appeared to be forthright with our responses, he let us go.

We exchanged our contact information, and he told us to contact him immediately if anything else came to mind. Then, as quietly as he had first approached us, he melted away into the crowd and was gone.

"That was weirder than shit!" Weed exclaimed. "We haven't done anything wrong, and I still feel nervous."

"Yeah, homicide cops can do that to you. I'm just glad he didn't search us. No telling the questions he would've had about the Demon camera in my pocket."

Weed and I walked down Central Park West trying to understand why anyone would want to murder a museum curator, but we were both bewildered. We stopped at a delicatessen to grab some lunch and ponder this tragic information, and my phone rang. It was Lucretia calling us back.

"Hi guys!" came Lucretia's friendly greeting. "How's your day going so far?"

I shared the news about Detective Tweedie's detaining us and his questioning us about Clifton Maguire's murder.

"Oh no!" she cried out. "That's horrible! Why would anyone want to do that to that kind man?"

"We don't know, but I have a sinking feeling it may be related to our following Samuel Morse's clues from the paintings," I admitted.

"But how would anyone else know what you're doing?" she asked.

"We don't know," Weed said, "but Clay thinks someone may be following us."

"Did you share that with the detective?" Lucretia proposed.

"I thought about it," I said, "but saying something to the detective seemed pointless since it's pure speculation on my part."

"I wonder if this has anything to do with that person taking at a shot at us in Chicago, Clay." Lucretia proposed.

"I've thought about that, too," I said. "No way to know for sure, but it's definitely a possibility. Weed and I are sure going to keep our eyes peeled for anything suspicious."

"So, Lucretia," Weed asked. "Were you and Drew able to come up with any ideas about the meaning of Morse's last clue, *Travel to the house*?"

"Yes, we think so," Lucretia said. "I'm just heartbroken about Clifton, though."

"I know. What did Drew's research find?" I tried to ask her patiently.

"Drew doesn't believe that Morse's message refers to a specific house that he ever lived in," Lucretia said.

"Well, what else could it mean if not that?" I asked.

"According to Drew, Samuel Morse wanted to secure his reputation as a great artist by painting a grand work of historical significance entitled *The House of Representative'*. He completed the painting in 1823 and toured it nationally. Unfortunately, the lack of sensational subject matter failed to attract popular appeal and ultimately proved to be a financial disaster. That's the house you're looking for. Morse's painting, *The House of Representatives*."

"Fascinating!" Weed said. "So, that apparently rules out our having to find a house that he resided in. Any idea where that painting is now?"

"Indeed, we do!" Lucretia replied. "It was acquired from the Corcoran Gallery by the National Gallery of Art in Washington in 2014."

I looked at Weed, and we both knew that we'd be hopping a train to Washington soon.

"No sense in spending another night in New York," I said. "We might as well check out of the Plaza and take a cab to Penn Station."

"Lucretia, do you have any contacts at the National Gallery?" Weed asked. "You're batting a thousand for us so far."

"I imagine we do," Lucretia replied. "I asked Drew the same question, and he said he'd make a couple of phone calls for us. I'll call you later today with a name, okay?"

"Sounds good, Lucretia. We'll look forward to hearing back from you," I said.

We chatted a few minutes longer, and Lucretia ended the call with a bit of sage advice for Weed and me. "Watch your backs!"

Chapter 17

W EED AND I CHECKED out of the Plaza Hotel and made a beeline for Penn Station. Given the number of trains that run daily between New York and Washington, we didn't have to wait any longer than forty-five minutes before we departed.

As for many people, being on a train evokes fond memories from youth. It was definitely the case for me. I remember taking the train with my parents to Cincinnati and St. Louis, and the fun times I'd have riding the train to summer camp in Northern Wisconsin. I closed my eyes and listened to the rhythmic clatter of the train's wheels on the

tracks. It was a mesmerizing sound that drew me into a welcome sleep.

Before long I was dreaming again about an old bearded man who was beckoning me to follow him. No words were spoken. The spectral figure waved for me to follow him, and I felt no fear in doing so. The old man waited for me by the entrance to a crypt-like structure that appeared to be glowing with some sort of static electricity. And then, I felt Weed touching my shoulder and drawing me back to wakefulness.

"We're here," he said. "We're just pulling in to Union Station."

I managed to shed the cobwebs from my brain, but the memory of the old bearded man stayed with me. I knew it had to be a dream about Samuel Morse.

Weed and I collected our belongings and exited the train. The station was bustling with hundreds of travelers, and instinctively I looked around to see if we were being followed. Nothing seemed unusual to me. I texted my agent, Lily, and apologized for being lazy, but asked if she'd be kind enough to book us a hotel suite somewhere near the National Mall. She replied promptly and told me she was on it and would get back to me soon.

Weed and I decided to take a taxi from the station to the National Mall. We cruised down Louisiana Avenue, then Constitution Avenue, and we were standing near the steps of the National Gallery in a few minutes. Since we hadn't heard back yet from Lucretia with the name of a contact within the museum, and since Lily hadn't had time to book a room for us, Weed and I did the only sensible thing. We found an appealing-looking restaurant and had a very late lunch.

Sometime between my French onion soup and my Cobb salad my phone rang, and it was Lucretia getting back to us.

"Hey guys, sorry it took so long, but we've been a little distracted here," Lucretia related.

"Oh, what's going on, Lucretia?" Weed asked.

"I had another visit from Detective Cioffi with the Chicago Police. He left a few minutes ago. Apparently, my attorney, Benton Pettengill, did not die from a heart attack. He was poisoned. The toxicology reports came back, and the killer used arsenic."

"On no!" Weed and I said almost in unison.

"Wait," Lucretia said, "there's more. On a hunch, Detective Cioffi wanted to compare the blood work between Benton and my father, and it turns out that both had lethal amounts of arsenic in their systems. That naturally leads him to believe that they were murdered by the same person.

"I explained the turmoil that I've been experiencing with being cut out of our parents' estate and getting fired from the Land Foundation's board of trustees," Lucretia shared. "Detective Cioffi told me that my brother, Malcolm, is pretty much missing in action. They have an all points bulletin to bring him in for questioning if they spot him, but so far he's managed to stay below the radar."

"Whew!" I exhaled. "This news certainly raises the bar on the danger we're facing. Three murders now with Clifton Maguire, plus you and I got shot at in Chicago. Your brother, or someone, is certainly willing to do whatever it takes to stop us from achieving our objective."

"I feel so badly for father and for poor Benton. Malcolm has so much money. I just don't understand his greed," Lucretia said tearfully.

"Drew and I have attempted to reach Malcolm both at his Land Foundation office and at home, but it appears that he has moved to another location. Now I understand why."

"I think it's time that we all watch our backs a little more closely," I said.

"Detective Cioffi agrees with you, and he's posted plainclothes officers to watch my home around the clock."

"Speaking of Drew, Lucretia, have the two of you communicated more about a contact for Weed and me at the National Gallery?" I asked.

She composed herself more and said, "Yes, we have. Drew has spoken with Dr. Kenneth Schubert, who is the senior curator for the National Gallery. He is well aware of your reputation, Clay, and said he could make some time available for you and Weed this afternoon. Here's his direct line."

We spoke for a little while longer, and Lucretia repeated the sage advice she'd given us earlier, "Watch your backs!"

"You, too!" I returned. "We'll let you know if we learn anything from *The House of Representatives*, and please thank Drew for us."

Ernst Kline called Malcolm to let him know that he had managed to tail his two targets well enough to catch the same train they'd taken from New York to Washington.

"Where are they now?" Malcolm asked.

"They're having lunch in a bistro right around the corner from the National Gallery," Ernst replied.

"You should know, Ernst, that my security chief has read Lucretia's e-mails to Drew Thomas. The Chicago police are aware that both my father and Benton Pettengill were murdered with arsenic. Obviously, I'm the likely culprit since I'm the one who materially benefits the most from my father's demise, so I will continue to stay out of sight. Just thought you'd like to know that we are both at significant risk, and if push comes to shove, given the video evidence I have, you're the one who will be implicated. Not me!"

"You've made that abundantly clear, Malcolm. Perhaps it's time we cut bait. You obviously have a lot of money squirreled away in offshore accounts, and I have a little. What difference does it make that Clay Arnold and his pal may be on to something big? Let's just call it done and go our separate ways?

"Not yet!" Malcolm declared. "And, don't you go getting cold feet on me. If Lucretia and Drew and these two yahoos from Indiana are searching for something, I want to know what it is!"

"Jesus, Malcolm, how much money do you need?" Ernst implored.

"As much as I can get my hands on. That's how much, and don't go getting all sniveling on me. I told you before to do exactly as I say. I'll let you know if and when it's time to cut bait. Understand!? You just keep following these two guys, and well, if you need to get a little ugly with them, just don't get caught!" Malcolm disconnected the call.

Ernst stared at his phone, shook his head in disgust, and said, "I swear … one of these days …"

As Weed and I finished our lunch, I received a text from Lily confirming that she had booked a suite for Weed and me at the Congress Inn. Now that we had spoken with Lucretia, filled our bellies, and gotten the night's accommodations squared away, I placed a phone call to Dr. Kenneth Schubert's personal line at the National Gallery of Art.

"Yes, hello, this is Kenneth Schubert," the voice said upon the second ring.

"Dr. Schubert, good afternoon, this is Clay Arnold calling you. I believe my friend, Drew Thomas, spoke with you earlier."

"Oh yes," Schubert said, "Mr. Thomas told me that you are interested in a private viewing of Morse's *The House of Representatives.* Is that correct?"

"Yes, if possible that would be great. My friend, Mr. Rawlins, and I are on a personal quest to view as many of Morse's paintings as we can," I fibbed.

"Well, you've chosen an interesting artist to follow," Schubert said.

"Certainly not the greatest painter that our country ever produced, but in his day, Morse commanded much respect in the American art world, especially as a portraitist. Then, of course, when Morse shifted his energies to science and changed the world with his telegraph, his success spurred many art historians to also reconsider his talent as a painter."

"Weed and I know you are a very busy man, and we promise not to take up too much of your time. We've already viewed *Gallery of the Louvre* at the Rothman Collection and *The Muse* at the Metropolitan, and we're excited to see the *House of Representatives*."

"So sad about my colleague, Clifton Maguire at the Metropolitan," Kenneth Schubert exclaimed. "I just learned of his death. Shocking!"

"Yes, we agree," I replied. "I believe Weed and I were among the last people to see him alive."

"Well, I certainly hope it's not catching!" Schubert quipped darkly.

"Why don't you come over in an hour. I should be free by then. I'll meet you in my office. The front desk staff can show you here."

We had an hour to kill which isn't an unpleasant task along the National Mall. We walked to the Smithsonian Castle and admired its beautiful red sandstone construction. Across the mall I saw the National Museum of American History which is my second favorite museum in the world after the George Eastman House.

"Hey Weed, what say we visit the American History Museum when we're finished at the National

Gallery? They've also got a terrific antique camera collection."

"Sounds fine to me," Weed said. "But, let's see how we do with *The House of Representatives* first. I have a feeling that may dominate our plans."

"You're right, of course. First things first. Besides, I'd probably want to back a truck up to their collection and start hauling stuff out," I laughed.

An hour passed, and Weed and I walked up the wide limestone steps leading to the entrance to the National Gallery and entered its realm. Unbeknown to us, a solitary figure traced our footsteps from several yards away.

"Good afternoon," I said to one of the women staffing the main desk. "I'm Clay Arnold and this is Mr. Rawlins. We have an appointment with Dr. Schubert."

"Oh yes, gentlemen, I'm Kelli. Dr. Schubert's office phoned us a bit ago and told us to expect you. Would you please walk this way?"

In anticipation of what was going to occur next, I leaned over to Weed and said, "Please do try to keep your eyes on the artwork and not the young lady's derriere this time!"

Weed grinned at me and said, "But it's such a nice derriere!"

"I heard that!" Kelli replied with a barely perceptible smile.

I rolled my eyes in embarrassment.

We arrived at Dr. Schubert's office, and I straightened my jacket while Weed watched Kelli's backside glide rhythmically down the hall. I gave him a friendly elbow to the ribs and said, "Try to remember why we're here, stud!"

Dr. Kenneth Schubert was a patrician-looking man of about seventy years of age. Silver was the dominant color of his wavy hair, and it gave him a regal bearing. His suit was off-the-rack, but his tie looked like a fine Countess Mara design. When he stood to greet Weed and me, he towered over us.

"Hello, gentlemen, I'm Kenneth Schubert. Welcome to our humble abode," he said in amusement given the large size of the museum. "As you know I spoke with Drew Thomas from the Land Foundation about your interest in the Morse painting. Drew was very keen on your being able to view it privately, and so I've asked two of our art handlers to bring it here in my office."

"That's very gracious of you, Dr. Schubert," I said.

"Only partially true, Clay. I leaned a little on Drew about loaning a Winslow Homer and an Edward Hopper to the National Gallery in exchange for my, uh, graciousness."

"Ah yes, no good deed goes unpunished," I quoted.

While we were waiting for the painting to be delivered, Kenneth Schubert asked more about our interest in the art of Samuel Morse.

I dodged his question somewhat and only explained that my interest in Morse had newly risen as a result of my buying the camera Daguerre gave him.

"Morse was a fascinating figure in American history, almost Da Vinci-like in some ways. Yet, his reputation today is a mere footnote, and his artwork is all but forgotten. You've chosen a peculiar individual to study."

"We agree. But that's what you get when a blues musician and a photographer hook up in their spare time!" I joked. I don't think Dr. Schubert caught the humor, but that's okay.

There was a knock of his office door, and his assistant opened it to permit two men with a large painting on a cart to be delivered. It was *The House of Representatives.* Dr. Schubert instructed the two handlers to leave it on the cart which still provided viewing of all sides. Once they left, Dr. Schubert and Weed and I approached the monumental work with assiduous inspection.

"Wow!" I exaggerated. "Very nice painting." In truth, I did find it to be a nice painting, but it was really rather subdued in terms of dramatic subject matter. I understood why paying audiences were underwhelmed when Morse exhibited it nationally, but I wasn't about to say anything derogatory.

While Dr. Schubert gave me a brief overview of Samuel Morse's life and times, Weed did what he'd done in the Metropolitan's restoration lab and casually inspected the rear of the canvas. Despite Dr. Schubert's presence, Weed immediately looked to where he'd seen the previous coded marks in the bottom of their canvas stretchers. The stamped marks on both the *Gallery of the Louvre* and *The Muse* were in the same place. Here, he saw nothing.

"Dr. Schubert, I'm curious," Weed said. "Has the canvas ever been removed from its stretchers for cleaning and restoration?"

Dr. Schubert thought for a bit and then he moved over to his desktop computer and typed in something. "According to our records, it was restored back in 1994, when it was still owned by the Corcoran Gallery. So yes, I would assume that it was removed for restoration and then reattached to the original stretcher upon completion."

"Thank you," Weed said, and he returned to the rear of the canvas while Kenneth Schubert told me about Samuel Morse's virulent anti-Catholic and anti-immigrant views for America. He was a genius, but definitely not a tolerant fellow.

Weed had a flash of an idea that the painting may have been reattached improperly when it was restored, and he gazed up to the top of the stretchers. He wondered if it was now upside down. He noticed that the canvas was loosely covering the stretcher, and he casually peeled it away. Dots and dashes were stamped into the wood, and it was all that Weed could do to conceal his excitement. He and I made eye contact, and I instantly knew he'd found what we were looking for.

"Dr. Schubert, would you mind if Weed took some pictures of you and me standing by the painting? It's part of our Morse art archive."

"Of course, that would be fine," he beamed.

Weed took several pictures of us with the painting and then surreptitiously snapped a few pics of the rear, including close-ups of the Morse code imprints. He nodded at me when he was done.

We spent several more minutes with Kenneth, and we both genuinely enjoyed his company. I actually felt a little guilty about our clandestine visit to his inner sanctum, but he had wangled the loan of an Edward Hopper and a Winslow Homer from Drew Thomas, so I didn't feel too terribly.

When we exited the National Gallery, the sun was close to setting, and Washington was aglow with the reflections of thousands of lights. We walked down the museum's steps to the street and crossed into the mall. There were still quite a few tourists and residents milling about, but Weed and I managed to find a bench away from the throng.

"Here's the picture of the coded message I found," Weed said.

-.-- --- ..- .-. .... - .- ... -.- ....-. -.-. ..- .-.. . .- -.

At this point neither of us was surprised that we didn't know what it meant. Weed took his time entering the coded message into his phone app, and a moment later the converted text was revealed: *Your task is Herculean.*

"Wow!" I exclaimed. "So, Sammy boy, tell us something we don't already know?" I voiced sarcastically.

Just then something happened that I'll remember with sadness all of the days of my life. I heard gunshot pierce the silence of the night, and I screamed at Weed to duck. We both hit the dirt in front of the bench, and the sound of screams rose up all around us. Then the sirens started to blare. I started to get up and motioned for Weed to do the same, but he didn't move.

"C'mon pal," I said. "Let's get out of here and give Lucretia a call."

When he didn't move, I dropped down in the grass next to him and saw that he was bleeding profusely from a bullet wound to his neck. I wrapped my jacket sleeve around his neck to try to stem the flow of blood and screamed for help. Somehow I managed to call 911, but amid all of the confusion, it took several minutes for the paramedics to arrive. When they finally did, it was too late, and my lifelong friend, Maurice "Weed" Rawlins, had already died in my arms. His hand still held his phone with the converted message still on the screen, but the light was gone from his eyes.

I sat with him in total shock and didn't want to release Weed from my arms even when the paramedics began to lift his lifeless body onto a gurney for transport. I placed Weed's phone in my pocket and took his knapsack which held his personal belongings. I insisted on riding with him to wherever they were taking him. I finally looked at myself and saw that I was covered in my friend's blood. I sobbed for a loss I knew I'd never, ever fully recover from. Weed was gone, and I was alone.

Chapter 18

SINCE THERE WAS NO need for speed at this point, the ambulance driver had turned off its emergency lights and pulled quietly into an underground garage beneath a major hospital. It was near the entrance to the morgue. I got out and was met by a police officer and two nurses. I didn't want to leave Weed, but they insisted that I needed to be checked out as well, and, of course, the police wanted to ask me about what happened.

I was led into a private examination room, and the shock I had been feeling morphed into absolute mind-wrecking grief when I thought, "Oh my god, what will I say to Tori?!"

The following hour saw a blur of personnel in blue scrub suits and police officers entering and exiting my room. Physically I was fine, but mentally I was a mess. "I need to make some phone calls," I said to no one in particular.

A kindly nurse brought me an extra change of clothes since mine were soaked in Weed's blood and virtually unsalvageable. She threw them away which was fine because I knew I'd never wear them again, anyway. A police detective entered my room and asked me what I recalled seeing. I told him the truth. Weed and I hadn't seen anything. We heard a gunshot split the night, and the next thing I knew my friend and I were on the ground, and he was dead. I thought about telling the police about being shot at in Chicago and the turmoil our friend, Lucretia, was living through, but I couldn't think of anything substantive that would help them in this investigation. I remained quiet about those things.

Ninety minutes later, the police dropped me off at the Congress Inn where Lily had reserved a suite for Weed and me. Once inside my room, I fell on a bed and sobbed like I hadn't done in years. After a while, I regained some composure and picked up the phone. Even though I really wanted and needed to hear Maggie's voice, I knew Mace was the first person I needed to connect with. Mace was as close with Weed as anyone, and I needed his strength to help bolster Tori from what was soon to be a life-altering shock.

Mace answered the phone on the first ring and said, "There you are, Clay. What's the good word?"

From the quietness of my voice, Mace immediately knew something was wrong, and he braced himself for what was to follow.

"Mace, Weed's dead. He was shot as we were leaving the National Gallery. He's gone, Mace. Our friend is gone."

"Oh no, please tell me this is a bad joke," Mace moaned, but he knew I'd never joke about something like this.

"Where are you now?" he asked.

"I'm in a suite at the Congress Inn in Washington. I'm going to talk with the authorities again in the morning and see what arrangements I can make to have his body flown back to Indy. We need to talk with Tori and Rennie. I just can't do it by myself, Mace. Will you please go over to the farmhouse so she's not alone when I call?"

"Of course," he said solemnly. "I'll go over now. Give me two minutes. Rennie's already spending the night there."

A couple of minutes later I made the call to Tori that I was dreading. I tried to be as sensitive and gentle with her as possible, but there's no good way to tell a loving sister, and a blind one at that, that her wonderful, doting brother had been murdered. She sobbed as if someone had ripped her heart from her chest, and there was nothing that any of us could do to ease her anguish. In truth, we all cried together. Weed was gone.

Mace told me that he and Rennie would spend the night in the farmhouse with Tori. I told him I'd call them in the morning once I knew when Weed's body would be released for transport back to Indy. This was a conversation none of us believed would ever be possible, but it was.

Next, I debated whether to call and share the tragic news with Maggie. Thanksgiving was coming the day after tomorrow, and I didn't want to spoil a holiday she'd been looking forward to sharing with her sister's family. Regardless, I knew I had to make the call. I knew she'd want me to.

"Hey there, Maggie," I said when she answered the phone.

"Hey there yourself, handsome, I was wondering when I'd hear from you. Have you and Weed been up to more mischief?"

"Weed's dead, Maggie. He was shot a few hours ago after we left the National Gallery."

"What?!!" was the only word she could immediately summon.

"Clay, please tell me this isn't so," she cried.

"I wish I could. He was shot in the neck by some unseen assailant, and he died in my arms. He's gone."

"Oh no, Clay, I am so very sorry," Maggie lamented. "I'll fly right back to Indy. Does everyone know back home?"

"Yes, they do. I called Mace and asked him to go over to the farmhouse so he and Rennie could be there when I called Tori. I still need to speak with the police tomorrow about when Weed's body can be released to us. I'll let you know as soon as I know, but it would be very helpful if you could return home to Indiana and help look after my friends. I'm so sorry about interrupting your Thanksgiving with your sister's family. I know how much this visit means to you."

"I'll make travel plans as soon as we hang up. How are you doing, Clay?"

"Not very well," I admitted. "I never should've dragged Weed on this stupid adventure we were on."

"Please don't be too hard on yourself, Clay. I know this is horrible, but Weed wouldn't want you to feel this way."

While I knew that Maggie's words were true, I nonetheless couldn't accept Weed's death without feeling some responsibility.

"I know he wouldn't," I agreed. "But, I …" words failed me.

"Please come home as soon as you can," Maggie said. "We'll all be waiting for you whenever you get there."

We hung up a minute later, and I was alone again in a strange room, in a strange city holding Weed's backpack as if my clutching his personal belongings could bring him back to life.

I wandered around my hotel room and stared vacantly out my window. None of what had occurred made sense to me. I sat on my bed and held Weed's backpack. I looked inside and managed a wistful, sad smile when I saw his harmonica. I knew I'd never be able to hear harmonica music again without thinking of my friend. I saw Weed's change of clothes and his toilet kit, and I held the old Morse telegraph key and coil of copper wire that I'd given him when I won the camera auction. I'd give the Morse camera and everything back if I could only have my buddy here with us again. I eventually got myself cleaned up and put on a fresh change of clothes. My phone rang, and it was someone from the hospital saying that the police had authorized Mr. Rawlins's release. I never did catch the person's name, and I doubt that I would've remembered it anyway given the grief I was feeling. They told me that the hospital would make the necessary travel plans including transport of his body to a funeral home of my choice. It was way too much reality for me, but at least it got me thinking about things other than the painful loss of my lifelong friend. I called Lucretia next.

"Good morning, Clay, how're you and Weed doing today? I assume you have more news to report from your visit at the National Gallery," Lucretia said warmly.

"I wish I did, Lucretia," I said softly.

"Oh, what's up?" Lucretia asked cautiously.

"Weed's dead, Lucretia. He was shot after we left Kenneth Schubert at the museum yesterday evening."

"Oh my goodness, no!" she said. "I am so sorry, Clay."

"Me, too," I said sadly.

I told Lucretia about what had happened, and that I'd be returning home to the brewery complex later in the day.

Before we hung up, I told Lucretia that my plans to follow-up on Samuel Morse's clues were definitely on hold and that I might chuck the entire search. She understood my grief.

"Well, it would sure seem that Morse's last message from *The House of Representatives* painting was somewhat prophetic," I finally said.

"What was the message?" Lucretia asked supportively.

"Your task is Herculean," I replied. "That's pretty much how my life feels right now," I said somberly. "Maybe we can talk again in a few days," I offered, and then we hung up.

Chapter 19

"**Y**OU DID WHAT?!" Malcolm Land verbally hurled at Ernst Kline when he told him about shooting Clay Arnold's buddy. "Sweet Jesus, you sure do like your executions, Kline."

"Not really," he replied evenly. "I just wanted to scare them off. Guess it was just a lucky shot."

"Not lucky for Rawlins, was it?" Malcolm chirped.

"Do you still want me to tail Clay Arnold, or should we give it a rest for a little while?" Ernst asked. "I imagine Arnold won't be chasing around looking at Samuel Morse's paintings for a few days anyway," Ernst stated matter of factly.

"Yeah, let's give them time to bury their dead," Malcolm said charitably. "My security chief, George Titus, can keep me posted about any further e-mails between Drew Thomas and Lucretia. We'll see what the future holds. Just lay low for now, and I'll let you know if and when I need you further."

They ended their call.

I arrived back home at the brewery complex as the sun was beginning its descent toward the horizon. It felt like it had been a lost day. I remembered very little about where I'd been and who I'd seen. I felt like I had simply gone through the motions. Going from point A to point B until I pulled my Tacoma into our courtyard and stared sadly at the farmhouse where Tori and Weed lived.

Tori heard my truck enter the courtyard and came outside to the front porch. She waited for me. Then, Maggie came running out of our home in the old brewhouse, followed shortly thereafter by Mace from the power-plant. Rennie walked very slowly out of the farmhouse and stood by Tori's side. And then, of course, Lex and Satchmo joined us.

We all moved to the front porch, and the sadness that welled up in each of us was overwhelming. A piece of us had died yesterday, and the only solace from that wreckage was that we were together.

We each took a seat on the porch despite the November chill and watched the sun's bright light succumb to darkness. The day was done, and the nighttime suited our mood.

"I'm so sorry," I said with tears streaming down my cheek. Maggie took my hand and leaned against me. "I am so very sorry."

Tori also sat next to me, and she took my other hand. She held it up to her cheek, and I could feel the wetness from her tears. Tori began softly humming a tune that sounded like an old Negro spiritual. She gently rubbed my hand and hummed.

Several moments of quiet reflection passed, and Mace asked, "Where is he now, Clay?"

"He's at the Weil-Gordon funeral home in Indy," I said. "I hope it's okay with all of you that I've scheduled the funeral for the day after Thanksgiving."

Then Tori broke into tears and the rest of us were swept away with their flow.

A few more moments passed and Tori softly said, " You know, I sit here on this porch, and what I think of most is his sitting in that chair with his feet propped up on the handrail playing a tune on his harmonica."

We all nodded and murmured our agreement. Rennie had been uncharacteristically quiet up to that point, and he finally said, "We were friends.

Weed and me were good friends. I don't want him to be gone."

"None of us do, Rennie," Mace offered. "He loved you."

The sun had totally set now, and I told everyone I'd like to spend some time with Maggie. We hadn't seen each other in nearly a week, and especially since Weed's murder, I'd been missing her even more than usual. They understood.

Maggie and I walked arm in arm across the courtyard, and I kissed the top of her hair. Satchmo fell in stride with us, and the three of us climbed the stairs to our bedroom.

"I've missed you so much, Maggie. Thank you for being here."

"Here is where I belong, Clay. I'm so very sorry about Weed, too. He was wonderful, and you guys were like brothers."

We held each other for a long time, and Satchmo rubbed against our lower legs. We stayed like this for a little while longer, and then I said, "Can we just get into bed and hold each other?"

She whispered, "Of course." And that's what we did.

Before too long I fell into a deep sleep comforted by the security of Maggie's arms. My sleep was like the mythological river Lethe whose waters supposedly gave a sense of forgetfulness to those who drank it. I drifted even deeper into sleep, and before long, I became aware of an apparition. The old bearded man had again invaded my dreams, and all sense of forgetfulness was gone. As in the previous dreams, the old man beckoned me to follow him, and again I saw him leading me toward a crypt whose entrance was alive with blue electricity. I tried to resist the old man's urgings to follow, but my feet moved steadily in his direction. Then, thankfully, I finally woke up and peered into the magic of Maggie's emerald eyes.

"Hey there," she said softly. "You were dreaming."

"Yes, I was. It was similar to dreams I've been having recently."

"You seemed agitated. Was it frightening?"

"No, not really," I replied. "This old bearded man, who I presume to be Samuel Morse, was beckoning me to follow him. It's weird.

"What time is it anyway?" I asked.

"About four a.m." Maggie yawned. "Do you need anything?"

"No, I'm all right," I returned. Then I pulled her close to me. "I'm sorry, Maggie. It sure seems that I drag you into some damn frightening messes."

"It's okay, Clay," Maggie said calmly. "None of it has been your doing, including Weed. Please don't be too hard on yourself. None of us want that for you. You and Weed were like brothers. Now, let's try to fall back to sleep, okay? We both need the rest, and I promise you we can talk about Weed and any of this as much or as little as you want tomorrow."

I laid my head on Maggie's chest, and listened to her beating heart. Its rhythm lured me back to the waters of forgetfulness.

———

Two days later it was Thanksgiving. Tori, Rennie, and Maggie worked together to create a festive fall look to the farmhouse and the dinner table. Despite all of their best efforts, however, none of us felt particularly thankful. I thought about how Thanksgiving was always my favorite holiday, but now it had lost its appeal.

Three years ago our Thanksgiving had been spoiled when the Hacker men attacked us at home, and now with Weed gone, well, I'm not sure that the specialness of Thanksgiving can ever be revived. Tori asked Rennie if he wanted to offer thanks when we sat down at the table, but he politely declined.

Tori then had us all take hands, and she offered her personal thanks for friends and family. She had almost gotten through her blessing when her words failed her. We all bowed our heads somberly. I looked at the empty chair where Weed always sat and thought about our treasured friend and the impermanence of life. Tori had placed a harmonica by his place, but it was only our memories that played a soulful tune.

The next day was Weed's funeral at the Weil-Gordon funeral home. None of us wanted to be there, but our spirits were buoyed by the outpouring of love and respect that the large group brought to us and the memory of Maurice "Weed" Rawlins. In addition to Weed's many admirers in the music business, Stella was there from the diner and our close buddy, Trent Reynolds, was seated in the second row.

It was a very large crowd, and I was particularly surprised and grateful that our new friends, Lucretia Land and Drew Thomas, had made the drive to Indy to pay their respects. I actually smiled to myself when I thought how much Weed would've enjoyed the attention.

When the funeral was over and Weed's body had been interred, a small group returned to the brewery complex with us for a little celebration of Weed's life. Trent came, as did Lucretia and Drew.

Trent Reynolds is the assistant superintendent of the Indiana State Police, but his real importance to us is because he grew up with Tori, Weed, and me. He's a special friend, and we've all shared some heartwarming and tragic times together.

"Any word from the DC police about finding Weed's killer?" Trent asked.

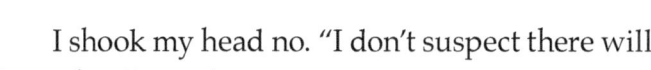

I shook my head no. "I don't suspect there will be, either," I said.

"I'll place a call up there to see what I can find out," Trent said. "Maybe being a squeaky wheel can help motivate them."

I nodded my understanding but didn't really hold out much hope to find the killer. One thing I knew for certain, I wasn't going anywhere in the future without carrying the Demon camera with me.

"Thanks, Trent, we appreciate whatever you can do. And, thanks for being here today. I know Weed would be pleased."

Trent left to resume his official duties, and I went over to talk with Drew and Lucretia who were speaking with Maggie and Mace.

"You've got a terrific place here, Clay," Drew exclaimed. "It's wonderful that you all live on this property together."

"Yeah, it's a great home," I replied, and Maggie leaned affectionately against me.

"Would you like to see our little camera museum and the place where we positioned the Morse camera?" I asked.

They said they did, and Satchmo took up the lead position and led us across the courtyard to the museum entrance.

"This is wonderful!" Lucretia said as we entered the realm of cameras from bygone eras. "I love the way you have each camera displayed with spot lighting."

"Look over here, Lucretia," I directed. "Here's the Morse daguerreotype camera with the fuming boxes.

"Oh nice! Great display!" she gushed.

"Thanks. Mace deserves the display credit, plus he's our senior curator for tours. I provide the vision and the cameras, but Mace is the heart of our museum."

Mace smiled and nodded his appreciation to me.

"I must say that if the camera had to be any place other than at the Land Foundation, I'm pleased it's here with you guys," Lucretia said.

After touring the museum a bit, Maggie said, "I think I better get back and help Tori and Rennie with things. I'll catch up with you before you head back to Chicago."

Mace said he needed to tend to some things also, and that left Drew, Lucretia, and me with the chance to catch up. We rode the elevator up to my living room, and after getting some beverages for us, we sat down.

"How are you holding up, Clay?" Lucretia asked.

"Oh, about as you might expect." I replied. "You know the pain of losing loved ones, Lucretia. Right now I just feel very sad, and I believe the sadness will be with me for a very long time. But, I'm also feeling another emotion, and that's anger, and I don't like myself very much when I feel angry."

Drew and Lucretia looked at me sympathetically.

"I understand," Lucretia said, "and I don't blame you one bit for feeling angry. I'm angry, too. My brother is a murdering liar, and I want him to pay for his transgressions."

Drew sat by quietly, but it was clear that he totally agreed with Lucretia.

"Let's do this," I said. "I need a couple of days to get myself recentered emotionally, and Maggie's presence here will help me a ton. Is it okay if I call you in a few days, and we can discuss where we are in this search? I have a feeling Weed would want us to continue, but I still need a little time."

"Absolutely, Clay," Lucretia replied. "You can count on Drew's and my help whenever you're ready.

Chapter 20

THE NEXT FEW DAYS passed in a bit of a blur. No matter how much I tried to focus on the mundanities of life to find some normalcy, I couldn't elude the sadness and the anger I felt about Weed's murder. Maggie, of course, was very loving and helpful to me, but she knew that only time could heal the huge gaping hole I felt without Weed's friendship.

"Your task is Herculean." These words, which Weed had converted from the Morse-coded message stamped into the wooden stretcher of the *House of Representatives,* haunted me. The phrase was always just below the surface of my thinking. *"Your task is Herculean,"* Samuel Morse had written.

Maggie and I were sitting outside on our roof-top balcony just off our bedroom. She saw me staring into the distance and gently touched my hand.

"Oooh, I just felt a kick," she said. "Seems like little Sputnik is trying to let us know he wants to get out and join the world!"

We're both thrilled that our baby will be born in a few more months, but we still hadn't settled on a name. For now, calling the little one, Sputnik, was good enough.

Out of the blue I said, "I think I'm ready to call Lucretia and Drew."

"Oh!" Maggie replied.

"I can't get Morse's last message out of my mind, and I feel like I have unfinished business."

"I think you do, too," Maggie added. "Seems like finishing the search that you and Weed began will bring you closer to healing. At the very least you can do something that is proactive rather than waiting for the grief to end."

"So, you won't mind if I go off for a few more days?" I asked seeking her permission.

"No, I don't mind. I'm feeling fine still with my pregnancy, and I think this is something you need to do. Do you want me to come with you?" she asked.

"No," I said quickly. "There's been enough violence, and I don't want to put you and our baby in danger. I've been thinking about asking Mace if he'd consider coming with me, though."

"You know, Clay, Mace isn't getting any younger," she added. "Do you think he'd be willing to join you?"

"Only one way to find out, I guess. I'll ask him in a few minutes. Then, I want to call Lucretia."

With the late November chill in the air, we didn't linger long outside. From the balcony I looked across the courtyard to the farmhouse, and I felt very sad. Then, my blood begin to boil as the anger within me thirsted for justice for my friend's murder. Maggie and I went inside, and I texted Mace asking him to join me in the camera museum.

Several minutes later Mace and I stood face to face, and I posed the question to him, "Any chance you'd care to join me on finishing the search that Weed and I began?"

"Did you really think that there's any chance that I wouldn't?" my older friend queried. "We stick together, remember?!"

"By my count, four people have been killed, Mace," I stated. "It'll be dangerous."

"Yeah, and one of them was a best friend to both of us," he said with conviction. "I don't want that son of a bitch to get away with murder. Besides, Weed wouldn't want us to quit, would he?"

I smiled wistfully and said, "Not likely."

"So, let's give Lucretia and Drew a call, and see what Herculean task Morse was referring to, okay?"

I nodded my agreement and dialed Lucretia's number.

"Hi Clay, how're you doing today?" Lucretia asked.

"I'm okay, I guess. Mace and I are together in the camera museum talking about continuing the search."

"Hi there, Mace," Lucretia voiced. "It was a pleasure meeting and talking with you despite the sadness of the occasion. I hope you're holding up okay."

"Yeah, I think we're all starting to slowly come around, but well, you know it'll take time, and I think Clay and I both believe that getting on with the search is the right thing to do."

"Lucretia, did Drew get a chance to do any research about the Herculean task?" I asked.

"He did," Lucretia responded. "I didn't want to interrupt your privacy, so I decided to wait until you were ready to talk about it."

"We're ready now," I declared, "and Mace wants to join me. So, what did Drew find out?"

"Drew and I have been e-mailing each other, and he believes that the reference to Hercules's task probably relates to Morse's painting entitled *Dying Hercules*. It's a large painting that Morse completed in 1812. After years of studying and drawing human anatomy, he finally produced his first notable painting. It was his masterpiece."

"So, where is it now?" I asked.

"In 1866 Morse donated it to his alma mater, Yale University. It's been in Yale's art gallery ever since," she said.

Mace and I looked at each other, and he nodded his understanding that we would be leaving soon for New Haven, Connecticut.

"Thanks, Lucretia, I don't suppose that you and Drew have a contact at their gallery, do you?" I inquired.

"We knew you'd ask that question if you were still interested in the search," she admitted. "The director of the museum is a chap named Gilbert Throckmorton."

"Seriously?!" I said. "His last name is really Throckmorton?"

"Apparently," Lucretia said, "but it's no weirder than my parents naming me Lucretia," she added. "If you and Mace think you'll be leaving in a day or so, I'll be happy to call Gilbert to see if he's available to meet with you. The Land Foundation name still carries some weight even at Yale. I'll let you know after I speak with him, okay?"

"Yeah, that would be great, Lucretia! We'll await your call. Please thank Drew for us again."

We hung up, and I asked Mace, "Are you up for this?"

"I wouldn't miss this for anything," Mace replied. "I know Weed would want me to go, too. Besides, I've never met anyone named Throckmorton before."

I told Mace I'd let him know as soon as I heard back from Lucretia, and I returned upstairs to talk with Maggie.

"Are you sure you're okay with Mace and me going away for a couple of days?" I asked her again.

"Where do you want to go?" she asked apprehensively.

"The Yale University art gallery," I said. "Samuel Morse has a painting there that might contain another clue."

"I'd be less than honest if I didn't tell you that I'm concerned," Maggie confessed. "I'll worry the whole time you're gone, Clay. With Weed being murdered how can I not?!"

"It'll only be a few days, I promise, and if we come up with a blank from this trip, I'll seriously consider giving the whole thing up."

We held each other, and I promised her I'd be very careful. I didn't tell her that I'd be carrying the Demon camera with me, and that Mace would probably be armed as well. She'd only worry more.

Malcolm Land sat at his dining table considering his future. He knew that the police would eventually find him if he stayed here, but he hoped to be long gone to the south of France with a huge cache of cash. He read a new message from his security chief, George Titus, who was growing increasingly nervous by the police contacting him about communications with Malcolm.

They're looking for you, Mr. Land, and I don't feel comfortable lying to the police, Titus e-mailed.

Malcolm called Titus directly. "Now, now, Mr. Titus, no cold feet! You and I have already agreed to a generous financial incentive for you to communicate certain things to me and to be, uh, vague with the police. Now, haven't we?!"

"Yes, Mr. Land, we have, and you're being very generous. It's just that I could go to jail for lying and obstructing justice. I'm not very comfortable with this."

"Of course, you're not, Mr. Titus. You are a man of high morals and principles. I, on the other hand, don't much care that you're uncomfortable and could give a whit about your principles. Beyond that, let me simply add that if you flip on me, if you go to the authorities, you may not live to enjoy all of that money I've paid you. How's that sound?!" Malcolm said like the imperious prick that he is.

George Titus gulped. He knew that his boss had him right where he wanted him. "Yes, sir, Mr. Land, I hear you loud and clear."

"Good! Now then what do you have to report?" Malcolm asked calmly as if he hadn't threatened the man's life a moment ago.

"Drew Thomas recently received an e-mail from your sister asking him for information about a message that Clay Arnold and his friend gave her."

"What did the message say?" Malcolm inquired.

"*Your task is Herculean* was the message," Titus replied.

"Hmm, I wonder what that means," Malcolm posed to himself.

Titus continued, "Drew wrote Lucretia back an hour after he received her request and told her he thought the message referred to a painting entitled *Dying Hercules* by Samuel Morse."

"Hmm," Malcolm voiced. "Did Drew mention where that painting currently is?"

"Yes, he did. It is in the permanent collection of the Yale University art gallery. A person named Gilbert Throckmorton is the director."

"Oh yes, I remember good old Throckmorton. We met a few times over the years at art conferences and exhibitions. Did you find a telephone number for Gilbert? I believe I'll give him a call."

George Titus gave Malcolm the number, and the two of them ended their call.

Malcolm sat in a comfortable chair that gave him an unimpeded view of Lake Michigan. It reminded him of the view from the garden of his parents' home that his sister now owned. He entered a telephone number into his cell phone, and waited for an answer.

"Yale University Art Gallery, this is Diana speaking, how may I direct your call?"

"Good day, Diana, this is Malcolm Land calling. Would you kindly direct my call to Gilbert Throckmorton's office?"

"Certainly, Mr. Land. One moment please, sir."

Ten seconds later an officious-sounding woman named Constance answered the phone. "Yes, this is Dr. Throckmorton's office. How might I help you?"

"Constance, this is Malcolm Land calling from the Land Foundation in Chicago. Is Dr. Throckmorton available that I might speak with him? I have an exciting proposition for Yale's art gallery."

"Please hold, Mr. Land, while I see if he's available. It'll just be a moment."

Twenty seconds later Malcolm Land was greeted by the mellifluous voice of Gilbert Throckmorton. "Why Malcolm, what a lovely surprise. To what do I owe the honor of your call?"

"Hello Gilbert, it's been too long. What is it? Four or five years ago that we were in Cincinnati together at the Rothman Collection exhibition?"

"Too long, Malcolm, entirely too long! And, I haven't forgotten that incredible painting by Albert Bierstadt that you managed to outbid us on as well."

"Yes, that's one of my favorites, too!" Malcolm fibbed.

"So, how may I help you today?" Dr. Throckmorton inquired.

"This may sound rather juvenile," Malcolm began, "but you're going to be receiving a phone call very soon from a friend of mine named Clay Arnold. Perhaps you know his reputation as a photographer. In any event, Clay and I go way back, and I was hoping you'd be willing to help me play an innocent trick on him."

"Oh, do say! I spoke with your sister, Lucretia, and subsequently with Mr. Arnold not two hours ago. We've scheduled an appointment the day after tomorrow for him and an associate to see a painting by Samuel Morse. I've had the painting delivered to my office for a private viewing."

"Excellent!" Malcolm lied. "When they arrive would you be willing to fib by telling them that you were mistaken when they called you, and that the Yale art gallery no longer has the *Dying Hercules* painting?"

"Now, that doesn't seem like a very nice joke to play on them," Gilbert exclaimed.

"I know, I know," Malcolm replied. "Clay and I have been pulling these silly pranks on each other for a while now, though," he lied.

"Malcolm, with all due respect, I have too much on my plate to be involved in your, uh, silly prank," Dr. Throckmorton admonished.

"What if I were to sweeten the pot for you to make it worthwhile?" Malcolm responded.

"Oh, what did you have in mind?" he asked curiously.

"Well, you mentioned the Albert Bierstadt painting a minute ago. How would the Yale art gallery like to have it on a long-term loan?" Malcolm prodded.

That certainly got Throckmorton's attention. "What do you mean by 'long-term loan'?" he queried.

"Actually, why don't we consider it more of a gift from the Land Foundation rather than a loan if you help me with this little ruse," Malcolm replied.

"Oh my!" Throckmorton chirped with delight. "That certainly changes the situation, doesn't it?! What would you like me to do?"

The two men spent the next few minutes discussing Malcolm's proposed prank.

"Well, as long as this really is just a silly ruse, I think I can go along with it," Throckmorton exclaimed. "When can Yale expect to receive the Bierstadt painting?" he inquired.

"Would next week be soon enough?" Malcolm offered.

"That would be lovely!" Throckmorton gushed.

"Now remember," Malcolm cautioned, "not one word to Clay or anyone about this. I want him and his friend to come there and leave without having seen *Dying Hercules*. I'll spring the joke on him after their unsuccessful trip here. Do we have a deal?"

"Yes, we do," the director confirmed. "Not one word!"

They ended their call, and Malcolm stared out his window at the steel-gray expanse of Lake Michigan. "For being so well-educated, museum directors are such dumb asses!" he chortled out loud.

Next, he called Ernst Kline. "I have new instructions for you, Ernst. Pack your bag and catch a flight to New Haven, Connecticut. I want you to keep an eye on Clay Arnold and another friend at the Yale University art gallery. Here's when they're likely to be there …"

Chapter 21

TWO DAYS LATER Mace Davis and I chartered a plane from Indianapolis to the Tweed New Haven Regional Airport. We arrived shortly before noon, rented a car, and did an early check-in at the Ivy League Inn. Mace and I were traveling light. We each carried an overnight bag, and Mace brought along Weed's knapsack which, among other things, contained Weed's phone with the Morse code conversion app.

After getting settled in our room, we still had a couple of hours before meeting with Gilbert Throckmorton so we decided to take a driving tour of the Yale campus and New Haven. I was curious

to watch Mace's reactions. Mace Davis is one of the most resourceful men I've ever known, but growing up as a poor kid in the Bahamas, he never had the benefit of a great formal education or the lessons learned from world travel.

"Wow, Yale University!" he exclaimed. "Never thought I'd ever be at a place like this."

"Yeah, a lot of famous people got their degrees here," I acknowledged, "but don't let that buffalo you, Mace. There are plenty of folks who attended college here that were mediocre in their careers."

I shared with Mace a story I read in my own freshman English class entitled "Young Man Axelbrod." It was a story about a man who never went to college and felt inferior to other people as a result of his lesser education. When he retired he made the decision to finally go to college, but when he did, he realized that college ranks are filled with plenty of students who really didn't appreciate the opportunity.

"I'd rather have you watching my back than anyone, Mace. I'd put your education from the school of hard knocks above a lot of folks with Ivy League educations."

"I appreciate that, Clay, but still …" Mace said.

We enjoyed seeing the great architecture on Yale's campus, and the bustle of students who had recently returned from their Thanksgiving holiday.

At five o'clock we pulled into the parking lot for Yale's art gallery and admired the contemporary steel and glass structure that housed a painting hopefully containing a clue that would propel us on our search. We approached the main information desk, and yet another lovely young ingenue welcomed us. I immediately felt a pang of sadness when I thought about how much fun Weed had had enjoying the callipygian shapes of various women who'd greeted us.

"Hello, I'm Clay Arnold and this is my colleague, Mace Davis. We have an appointment with Gilbert Throckmorton."

"Just one moment, gentlemen, I don't seem to have you down on our visitors' list. Please have a seat while I make a quick phone call," she said.

A few minutes later a sturdy-looking middle-aged woman named Constance came to the lobby to greet us. "I'm sorry, gentlemen, I thought Dr. Throckmorton had been in touch with you. There's been a little glitch."

"Oh!" I said with surprise rising in my voice.

"Dr. Throckmorton is still in his office and said he'd be happy to meet with you nonetheless," Constance said. She led us down a long hallway to the director's office. "One moment, please."

A few moments later she led us into his spacious office, and a studious-looking man in his fifties

came around his desk to greet us. He had a look of embarrassment on his face.

"Ah, Mr. Arnold and Mr. Davis, it is a pleasure to meet you." Dr. Throckmorton said. "I tried to reach you earlier at this phone number but without success. He showed me the phone number but two of the numbers had been accidentally transposed.

"Oh?!" I said again. "Is there a problem?"

"Alas, quite so!" said Throckmorton. "We can't seem to find the Morse painting anywhere in the gallery."

"You're kidding!" I said, and Mace and I looked at each other with surprise and annoyance.

"You realize, Dr. Throckmorton, that Mr. Davis and I have gone to considerable effort and expense to meet you today. It was our understanding from Lucretia Land that everything was in order for our visit."

"I know, I know, and I certainly can appreciate your disappointment," the director replied. "I tried to reach you by phone, but I apparently had the wrong phone number. Mea culpa!"

A minute later Throckmorton's phone rang, and he said, "Excuse me just a moment, please. I've been awaiting this call from one of our curators."

"Do you need us to step out of your office while you take the call?" I asked.

"No, it's okay. Please look around while I speak with her," he said without showing much concern for the disappointment Mace and I were feeling about a wasted trip to New Haven.

Mace and I took our time looking at signed letters and photographs from former American presidents and dignitaries from across the globe. When Throckmorton ended his call, I spoke with him some more while Mace continued to admire the historic art and letters adorning the walls.

I noticed a particularly interesting photograph by Mathew Brady and asked Dr. Throckmorton about it. While I did, Mace walked over and stood near a large painting that was propped against a wall in the corner of the office. It was draped with a white muslin cloth. Out of curiosity, Mace casually lifted the cloth and saw an ornate, gold-leafed frame with a brass nameplate centered at the bottom. It read, "Morse". Mace noticed that Throckmorton and I still had our attention turned to the Brady photograph, and he surreptitiously lifted the drape for a better look. There was an image of a muscular man who looked to be in the throes of dying. Mace thought to say something to us, but chose to remain silent instead since Dr. Throckmorton had been so adamant in saying that they couldn't find the painting anywhere.

"I'm so sorry, gentlemen, that this has been a wasted trip for you. If only I had recorded your phone number properly, I could've saved you the effort … alas!"

Mace gave me a curious look and motioned to me that it was time to leave. I took his cue, and after gushing his apologies for the umpteenth time, Gilbert Throckmorton asked Constance to show us out to the main lobby.

"Well, that was total bullshit!" I said to Mace after Constance left. "They've got some of the smartest people in the world on this campus, and these numbskulls can't locate a valuable painting in their own collection!" I was royally pissed, and I knew that Lucretia would be, too.

Mace glanced at me with a knowing smile on his face and said to me, "*Dying Hercules* is in his office. I spotted it under a drape while the two of you were looking at the Brady photograph."

I was stunned by Mace's revelation. "Why the hell would he do that?! Why would he allow us to visit the art gallery and lie about the location of the painting? It makes no sense," I declared.

"I don't know," Mace said. "Perhaps someone got to him and convinced him not to show it to us."

"Well, considering that Weed was murdered and that Lucretia and I got shot at, that does make some sense. I can't prove it yet, but it wouldn't surprise me if Malcolm Land has something to do with this. The question now is what do we do about it. We sure didn't come this far only to be turned away by some pedantic jerk!"

"Break in!" Mace said evenly.

"Beg pardon!" I replied.

"If Throckmorton is so willing to obstruct our seeing the Morse painting, I feel even more determined to do it. Let's break into his office and find another clue."

I looked at Mace and nodded my agreement. "Screw 'em!" I said. "Let's do it for Weed!"

The late November sun had already set by the time we exited the gallery. We noticed a sign indicating that the art gallery would close at eight o'clock, so we decided to reenter the gallery and hide out in their library until closing time. From our perch behind the stacks, we saw Constance leave at about seven forty-five, and Throckmorton exited the building a few minutes later. All other students and visitors departed by eight o'clock, and Mace and I managed to stay hidden from view until then.

"You realize, of course, that if we get caught, we're totally screwed," I said to Mace.

He smiled at me and calmly said, "Yeah, so let's not get caught."

We stayed hidden in the library well past eight o'clock. The art gallery's hall lights automatically turned very low to conserve energy, and from time to time we noticed the sweep of a flashlight beam as a security guard made his appointed rounds. We waited until we saw the guard disappear down a long corridor, and Mace and I made our move toward Throckmorton's office. Mace looked inside Weed's knapsack that he carried and saw a headlamp along with Weed's phone and the old Morse telegraph key I had given him. Mace placed the headlamp on his forehead and switched on the red light to provide some additional visibility. We listened intently for the guard and watched for signs of his flashlight. So far, so good. Mace and I scurried down the hallway like the nighttime skulkers that we are and thirty seconds later we stood in an alcove outside of the entrance to the director's office. Mace turned off his red headlamp, and we listened in the dark.

At first I thought it was an errant headlight from a car outside, but the security guard had returned and was coming our way. Mace and I squeezed down behind a life-size statue of James Fenimore Cooper and held our breath. We prayed he didn't point his flashlight our way. Forty feet, twenty-five feet, fifteen feet. The guard stopped. He looked our way but didn't direct his beam toward us. He held his watch up and shined his light on it. He pulled a hankie out of his jacket pocket, blew his nose liberally, broke wind, and sauntered off down the hall. Mace and I finally exhaled.

"That was close," I said. We waited for a few moments longer to see if the security guard would make a surprise return, then turned our attention to Dr. Throckmorton's locked office door.

Mace pulled out the handy Leatherman multi-tool kit he wore on his belt. In the dim light he selected the stout screwdriver and began working on the wooden frame near the lock. Bits of shredded wood fell away as he gouged as quietly as he could. When the door bolt was finally exposed, he chipped away at the door frame some more until, with one swift motion, he managed to jimmy the lock open.

"Cool!" I exclaimed. "How'd you know how to do that, Mace?"

"Years of futzing around the brewery complex. Can't beat a Leatherman tool kit for breaking and entering!" he joked.

We entered Gilbert Throckmorton's office and quietly closed the door behind us. The red beam from Mace's headlamp cast an eerie hue throughout the room. We walked past the wall with the Mathew Brady photograph, and for a brief moment I thought about swiping it to go with the antique camera in my bedroom that Brady once owned. Fortunately, I realized that I would be Dr. Throckmorton's first suspect since we had just spent time discussing it earlier that afternoon. I left it alone.

"Over here!" Mace whispered to me, and I followed him to the opposite wall where the shrouded painting leaned. "Let's turn it around so the rear is facing us.

It was not a light painting, but we managed to lift and turn it so it faced the wall. Mace tilted his head in slightly different directions so the red beam scanned the rear of the canvas and the wooden canvas stretchers.

"There!" he said as he pointed to the bottom left area of the wooden stretcher. Sure enough, stamped into the wood was the unmistakable impression of dots and dashes. Morse code.

Mace pulled out a pen and pad of paper and began exactly transcribing the marks Samuel Morse had made over one hundred and fifty years earlier. "I'll take a picture, too," Mace said, and he attempted to cover the flash from the camera as best he could.

I walked over to the door to listen for the guard and stopped to briefly admire the Brady photograph again. Man, I wanted that image. It would serve Gilbert Throckmorton right for steering us in the wrong direction. Again, I came to my senses and left it alone.

"Hurry up!" I whispered hoarsely to Mace. "We've got what we came for, now let's get out before the guard returns."

"Almost done," Mace said as he returned the iPhone and his pad of paper to Weed's knapsack.

Just then, the office door swung open, and I was confronted by the security guard with his revolver drawn. I'd been caught red-handed, but Mace managed to duck down behind a sofa near the *Dying Hercules*.

"Gotcha!" the guard voiced with satisfaction. "Next time you might try hiding the wood chips from where you forced the lock," he said arrogantly. "Now, get face down on the floor while I call for back up."

I began to do as he said, when all of a sudden a blue charge of electricity emanated from Mace's location and engulfed the hapless security guard. He twitched and slobbered and fell to the floor in a heap.

"Holy fuck!" I said out loud to Mace. "Is he dead?"

"Naw!" Mace declared. "He's just a little incapacitated."

"I have the Demon camera with me," I said. "What did you zap him with?"

"Well, when Weed and I gave you the updated version of the Demon last week, I took your original one and modified its power level so it had a stun setting in addition to full-blown electrocution. The guard should be okay in a few minutes, but we'd better scoot on out of here!" And that's what we did.

We moved the security guard behind Throckmorton's desk and returned Morse's *Dying Hercules* to its original position against the wall. We quietly exited the office, and I scattered the incriminating wood chips with my shoe. Thirty seconds later we bolted out the front door of Yale's art gallery and ran like the wind to our car as the emergency alarms started to wail.

Mace fell in to the passenger seat, and I did my best to drive as casually as possible from the art gallery's lot. Between being out of breath from our sprint to the car and laughing our asses off at what we'd just done, I was amazed that I didn't run off the road. Thank goodness there was a fair amount of traffic at this hour so we blended in well as police cruisers came screaming toward the museum.

"Oh, so this is the kind of mischief you get into when you leave the brewery complex, huh?" Mace teased me. "Damn, if I knew you were having this much fun breaking into places and zapping folks, I would've signed up a lot sooner! Holy, holy shit, did we really just do that, Clay?"

"Uh yeah!" I managed to say. "And, I just have one major favor to ask you: that you never mention any of this to Maggie!"

Mace stopped laughing and said to me supportively, "All right, your secret's safe, my friend, not one word. But, I gotta say I haven't had so much fun since the pigs ate my brother." Mace pretty much grinned all the way to the Ivy League Inn.

From his hidden position near the parking lot, Ernst Kline watched Clay Arnold and his friend run out of the art gallery and leap into their car. Ernst had done as Malcolm Land instructed and flown to New Haven to watch them. He managed to follow their car to the Ivy League Inn and saw them enter the motel. He parked and phoned Malcolm Land to report in. "Just keep tailing them," Malcolm commanded him.

Chapter 22

WHEN WE GOT TO our room, we sat down at a table and peered at Mace's handwritten transcription of the indented dots and dashes from the canvas stretcher. Mace also managed to get a good close-up photograph of the code with Weed's cell phone camera.

-- -.-- ....-. . ... - .. -. --. ....--. .-.. .- -.-. . ...-.
. ...- . .- .-.. ... .- .-.. .-..

Mace then found the code conversion app on the phone and entered in the sequence. Within a few seconds we saw the dots and dashes converted into English text. *"My resting place reveals all."*

"I have a feeling we're getting closer," Mace said. "Now, we need to do some research into where Samuel Morse is buried."

I nodded my agreement. "I can't imagine Morse going to all of the trouble to leave clues if there isn't something really worthwhile to find. Let's go online and find out more about his, uh, resting place. We should let Lucretia know, too. We wouldn't be where we are now if it weren't for Drew and her."

I called Lucretia but was surprised when she didn't immediately answer her phone. I left a message and asked her to call us back. Next I called Maggie to see how things are at home.

"I'm concerned, Clay," were her opening words.

"Are you feeling all right?" I asked with genuine concern. "Is it the baby?!"

"No, I think the baby's fine," she related "It's Tori, Clay. I'm really concerned about how depressed she is with Weed's murder."

"I was afraid of that," I said. "She and Weed were about as close as two siblings could be. Although Weed was always sensitive about giving his blind sister space to deal with her world of darkness, he watched her dutifully. Now with him gone, it's understandable that she'd feel lost and scared."

"I know," Maggie replied, "but she's not herself. Rennie and I have spent a lot of time with her while you and Mace are in New Haven. Rennie's been staying at the farmhouse with her, and we share all of our meals together, but she's not eating or sleeping well. She's not even crying much. She mostly sits on the front porch, rocking in Weed's favorite chair, staring into the dark distance humming a sorrowful tune."

"Do you want us to come home?" I asked sincerely.

"I know how excited you are about following Samuel Morse's clues, but I think it would be a good idea if you and Mace did."

"I briefly told Maggie about Mace finding the latest clue from the *Dying Hercules,* but I didn't say anything about our breaking into Gilbert Throckmorton's office, and I definitely didn't say anything about Mace zapping the security guard with a weapon he and Weed had made.

"I'll get us a charter flight, and we should be home tomorrow afternoon," I said. "I'm sorry for all of the sadness, Maggie, I promise you our home is usually a place of peace and tranquility," I said to assuage her concerns.

"I know that, Clay, and I'm fine being with her as much as she needs. Rennie is being so good and patient, and we're forging a solid friendship in our own right, but we're both concerned about Tori's mental state."

We talked a little bit longer, and then I felt my phone vibrate, and I saw that Lucretia was returning my earlier call. Maggie and I hung up, and I quickly told Mace I'd fill him in on Tori after taking Lucretia's call.

"Good evening, Clay, and how're you and Mace enjoying New Haven? Was Gilbert Throckmorton helpful to you?"

"Uh, New Haven's fine, but our pal, Dr. Throckmorton, was a pain in the ass," I said frankly.

"Oh!" Lucretia replied. "What happened?"

I spent the next couple of minutes sharing with Lucretia how the gallery director had lied to us about the location of *Dying Hercules,* and that Mace had managed to see the hidden painting while Throckmorton and I talked about the Mathew Brady photograph.

"There's more," I said, "but I'm not sure how much more you really want to know."

"In for a penny, in for a pound," Lucretia said, and I told her about Mace and me breaking into the director's office, finding another clue about Morse's resting place revealing all, and zapping the security guard.

"You guys certainly don't mind taking risks, do you?" she said with more than just a little levity in her voice. Then, she got serious. "What a son of a bitch!" Lucretia uncharacteristically cursed. "That jerk, Throckmorton, promised me he'd be very attentive to you and Mace. I wonder what changed his mind."

"My guess is your charming brother has something to do with this," I said sarcastically.

"But how would he know that you were even in New Haven?" Lucretia asked.

"They're clearly getting their information from somewhere, and I doubt that you and Drew are the informants," I said.

"Maybe not directly, Clay, but I wonder if Malcolm has been able to intercept the e-mails between Drew and me."

"Maybe," I agreed. "Perhaps we should employ a little misdirection from our end and flush them out."

"What do you have in mind?" she asked.

"Why don't you e-mail Drew and tell him that Mace and I weren't successful in finding another clue, and that we're heading home to the brewery complex. Let's see what happens next. I doubt that Samuel Morse or his resting place are going anywhere anytime soon."

Lucretia agreed to the plan, and we hung up. Then I told Mace about Maggie's concern about Tori. We both knew that going back home was what we needed to do, and I called the charter service that we used to fly to New Haven and booked a flight back to Indy the next day.

"Ah, there you are, Mr. Titus," Malcolm Land said matter-of-factly when he answered his phone. "And, what do you have for me?"

"Good evening, Mr. Land, I just saw an e-mail come through from your sister to Drew Thomas," the security chief reported.

"And?" Malcolm urged. "What did dear Lucretia have to say?"

"Apparently, Clay Arnold and his friend, Mace Davis, weren't able to find any clues during their trip to Yale's art gallery, so they're returning home to Indiana."

"Excellent!" Malcolm declared. "It would seem that my 'friendly encouragement' to Gilbert Throckmorton worked. I had a feeling that appealing to his sense of greed with the, uh, gift of the Bierstadt painting would produce the results I wanted. So, they're going home, huh?! Thank you for letting me know, Mr. Titus. You're earning your keep, and I'm sure you'll continue to keep me informed, won't you?" he said with a veiled threat.

"Of course, Mr. Land," he replied, and then they ended their call.

Next, Malcolm contacted Ernst Kline and reported the new developments. "Clay and his pal struck out at the Yale gallery like I expected. They're heading back to their home just north of

Indianapolis. I want you to book a flight to Indy, and watch their place in case they try to pull a fast one on us and continue their search for whatever it is that Samuel Morse has them so excited about. Understand?"

"Yes, Malcolm, I understand," Ernst replied. "I still think my chasing around after these guys is a waste of time, but you hold all of the cards, don't you?"

"And don't ever forget it!" Malcolm replied with menace in his voice.

The two men hung up, and Ernst Kline shook his head in profound annoyance. "This insanity can't last forever. I see an end point coming, Malcolm Land," he muttered out loud. "One way or the other."

Chapter 23

OUR FLIGHT FROM New Haven to Indy went smoothly. It was great having chartered a small jet instead of dealing with the nuisance of crowds boarding a commercial flight. Besides, it was helpful to our going through security with our Demon cameras. The TSA agent looked quizzically at our antique detective cameras and seemed satisfied when I told him Mace and I had acquired the rare cameras for our museum.

I had left my Tacoma in long-term parking since we really didn't know how long our trip to the east coast would be. Twenty minutes after we landed in Indy we climbed in my silver truck and

headed for the brewery complex. Mace and I were both very concerned about Tori and nervous about what awaited us when we got home. Forty minutes later we pulled into the courtyard of the brewery complex.

Rennie and Lex greeted us in front of the farmhouse as we climbed out of the Tacoma, and Maggie joined them a moment later. Tori hadn't come out yet which Mace and I both recognized as unusual behavior from our typically outgoing friend.

"Is Tori inside?" Mace asked Rennie.

Rennie nodded his head affirmatively. "She's just been moping about ever since you left for Yale," Rennie said sadly. "I asked her if she wanted to go for a walk with Lex and me by the White River, but she just wants to stay indoors and sit in the kitchen."

Maggie and I stood arm-in-arm trying to decide how best to help our friend when Tori finally stepped out on the porch to welcome us home.

"Hey Mace. Hey Clay," she said in a weary monotone. "Sure glad you guys are back home safely."

Mace and I both went up to the porch and gave her warm hugs which seemed to brighten her spirits a bit.

"How was your trip?" she asked with a little more lift in her voice.

"Pluses and minuses," Mace replied honestly. "Being on the road with Clay was one of the pluses, of course, and seeing some of the Yale art gallery was a highlight. Unfortunately, the director said he couldn't locate the painting by Samuel Morse that we went to see which was a total bummer."

"I thought you said that Lucretia Land had helped arrange an appointment with the director for you," Tori replied.

"Oh, we had the appointment," I stated, "but the doofus director said he couldn't find the painting and hadn't written down my telephone number accurately to tell us."

"You're kidding, right?" Tori exclaimed.

"No, he's not," Mace said. "Needless to say we weren't amused."

"So what'd you do? Just come home?" Tori asked.

I looked over at Mace, and asked him, "Should we tell her?"

"Tell me what? And hey, I'm standing right here!" she said with some irritation.

Mace nodded and said, "Yeah, tell her, and besides Maggie and Rennie ought to know, too."

And so I did. "Gilbert Throckmorton took a phone call while we were in his office and suggested that we look around at the framed letters and photographs on his walls. While I was admiring a photo by Mathew Brady, Mace noticed a large, draped painting leaning against a wall. Sneaky guy that he is, Mace got a good look at the concealed painting, and lo and behold, it was *Dying Hercules* by Samuel Morse, the painting we had come to see."

"Did you say anything to the director when he got off the phone?" Maggie asked.

"I thought about it," Mace replied, "but this Throckmorton guy had made such a point about not being able to locate it, that I saw no point in calling him a liar to his face."

"So, what'd you do?" Rennie asked.

"After the art gallery closed, we broke in," I confessed.

"Sweet!" Rennie laughed with youthful enthusiasm.

"You did what?!" Maggie asked excitedly. "You broke into the Yale University art gallery and the director's office?"

"Well, we were already inside the art gallery's library so technically we didn't really break into the gallery, but yeah, we did break into the director's office."

"Oh swell!" Maggie replied sarcastically. "Thanks for the clarification, darling. I look forward to telling our child someday about his father, the charming criminal."

Tori stood there listening to our banter about breaking and entering, and for the first time since

Weed's murder, an approving smile formed on her face.

"So, what happened when you got inside that guy's office?" Rennie asked.

Mace and I immediately made subtle eye contact, and he noticed me ever-so-slightly nodding my head indicating not to say too much.

"Well," Mace began, "while Clay played lookout for any signs of a security guard, I found the Morse painting and located the coded message that Samuel Morse had imprinted in the canvas stretcher."

Now Maggie's posture turned from one of concern and apprehension to one of curiosity and anticipation. "What happened next?" she asked.

"We got the hell out of there as fast as we could!" I fibbed. I didn't see anything positive to be gained by telling them that Mace had zapped the crap out of a security guard. "We ran to our car, with the art gallery's security alarms blaring, and didn't look back until we got to our motel room."

Rennie was enjoying all of the drama we described, and even Maggie lightened up and playfully chastised Tori for not telling her that her world-famous fiancee was a burglar. All things considered the conversation went about as well as it could've, especially since it brought some entertaining relief to Tori.

We all chatted for a few moments longer, and Mace and I returned to my truck to collect our gear. Then, Mace and Rennie went to the power plant to stow Mace's belongings, and Maggie took my duffel to our bedroom. I didn't feel ready to leave Tori yet.

"You know, Tori," I said, "we haven't had a chance to talk much alone ever since Weed's death, and if there are some things you want to discuss, I promise to try to be a good listener."

"Oh Clay, I don't even know where to begin other than talking about the heavy sadness I feel. I miss Weed so much, and I worry some about how I'll be able to cope with life without my brother's watchful eyes and his caring heart."

We sat down on the front porch of the farmhouse and listened to the wind in the pine trees. "I can't believe he's gone, either," I said. "I wish I could find the right words to help you feel better, Tori, but I don't think there's much of anything that any of us can say to ease the grief we all feel."

"I know I'm not the only one of us affected by Weed's murder, it's just that for the first time in a very long time my blindness has me feeling insecure."

"I understand, even though I know it's impossible for me to fully comprehend your physical limitation. There are two things that I do know for sure," I said. "First, that we all love you to the moon and back, and that we'll never stop being caring friends to you. And, of course, financially, I don't want you to ever fret about money. I've got you covered. Second, I believe in my heart that Weed would want you to recall all of his bodacious, fun-loving attitudes about life and not be felled by grief. I know that's hard to accept right now because his murder is so fresh in our minds, and honestly after Jennifer was murdered four years ago, I never thought I'd be the same. I felt angry and alone, and despite everything that you and Weed and Rennie and Mace did to help me, my full recovery didn't occur until enough grieving had passed. Obviously, Maggie's love was, and is, a calming balm for me."

"I know you're right, Clay," Maggie replied, "and I can't thank you all enough for circling the wagons around me. I promise not to be a grieving mess forever."

I pulled Tori into a brotherly hug and whispered to her, "We stick together, and nothing will ever change that."

At that point Rennie came jogging back to the farmhouse from the power plant to spend the night, and I returned home to the brew house, the woman I love, and our baby who will arrive in four months.

Meanwhile back at the Indianapolis airport, Ernst Kline exited his flight from New Haven and walked through the concourse leading to the car rentals. He was weary from his travels, and even wearier from the weight of his brutal attacks on good people, and weariest still from doing the bidding of that worm of a man that he detested, Malcolm Land.

"I just arrived in Indianapolis," Ernst said to Malcolm on the phone after he got his rental car. "What instructions do you have for me?"

"Ah Ernst, it's so lovely to hear your voice," Malcolm chirped insincerely. "I believe you know where Clay Arnold and his friends live. Even though it appears that Mr. Arnold and his pal won't be searching for clues anymore, I'd still like to teach them a lesson for joining forces with Lucretia and Drew Thomas. I want you to keep an eye on them, and if the opportunity presents itself, I want you to send another, uh, message that we haven't forgotten them, and that we can reach out and touch their lives in ways most unpleasant. How's that sound, Ernst?"

"It sounds damn unnecessary, Malcolm, but I know you hold all of the cards." They hung up, and Ernst put his car in gear. "At least for now," he murmured to himself.

Chapter 24

"OH MAGGIE, it feels so good to hold you," I murmured into her cheek. "After the craziness of our trip to the Yale art gallery, I can't tell you how great it is to be home with you. How're you holding up?"

"I'm doing fine, Clay. Very relieved to have you home safe and sound, though. I think the baby is doing okay too, but I've been very concerned about Tori. She's so sad about Weed. It's really good that you and Mace are back."

We walked out onto our rooftop deck and let the last remnants of the day's sun warm our faces. We held each other and just enjoyed the alone time

together. We scanned the horizon and watched a small flock of Canada geese flying in formation to their night's resting ground. We listened to the wind in the pine trees and became one with our surroundings.

"Oh, I've missed this," I said.

"Me, too," Maggie whispered. "Do you think you're going to stay home for a while?"

"Probably, I've told my agent, Lily, that I didn't want to take on any more photographic assignments until after the baby is born, maybe longer, you know, depending on how things go."

Maggie leaned against me, and we listened to the voices of the pines calming our spirits.

"So, what do you want to do about the search for Samuel Morse's hidden treasure trove?" she asked.

"I'm not quite sure," I confessed. "On the one hand, there may be something terrific to find. On the other hand, the price we've paid with Weed's murder is more than enough. I'm more concerned about your health and Tori's regaining her emotional equilibrium."

"C'mon," she urged. "Let's climb in bed. We do some of our very best thinking there."

"Sounds divine. We do some of our very best nonthinking there, too, isn't that right, Sputnik?!" I said as I gently patted Maggie's swelling belly.

The next morning brought a crystal clarity to the new December day. We had everyone join us at the brew house for breakfast, and for the first time since Weed had been killed, it felt like we were starting to see some signs of emotional rebirth within our family.

Tori was initially subdued as Mace and Rennie began telling amusing stories of stuff they'd seen or heard Weed do, and before too long a smile crept across her face. She knew she wasn't alone in her grief, and that she had great company in recounting various episodes with Weed.

"How about you, Clay, what do you remember the most?" Rennie asked.

"Oh golly, so many different things," I said. "You have to remember Rennie that Weed, Tori, and I have been friends since we were what, Tori, about four years old? So, there are a lot of stories I could tell you."

"What're the last fun things that you remember, Clay?" Rennie persisted.

Sadly, the first thoughts in my mind were not fun things. I flashed on being covered in Weed's blood as I held him during his last moments alive. Obviously, I didn't want to bring that up, and then I laughed out loud when I thought about something else.

"What?" Rennie asked again. "What were you just thinking about?"

"I was thinking about Weed's appreciation of the female form," I replied using the most appropriate words I could muster.

"What do you mean?" Rennie asked.

I looked over at Mace and rolled my eyes. "Weed liked looking at women's figures, Rennie!" Mace said removing any confusion in Rennie's thinking.

"Oh," was about all Rennie could think to say at first. Then he added uncharitably, "I didn't think old men thought about stuff like that."

"Hey! Watch the 'old men' talk," I returned. "Weed and I were the same age." We all laughed.

After breakfast Tori stayed at our place with Maggie and me while Rennie and Mace went off to handle some maintenance chores around the brewery complex. I washed the dishes and put things away while Maggie and Tori went outside on the deck to enjoy the last vestiges of warmth from the morning sun before three long months of midwestern winter set in. I was glad to think that we were still keeping Maggie's home in Santa Fe for warm midwinter getaways.

After several minutes, Tori heard the sound of a car pull into the courtyard below. "We have company!" she called out.

"Are you expecting anyone, Clay?" Maggie asked as the two women came back inside.

"No, I'm not. It's probably someone wanting to visit the camera museum. I'll go check."

I took the elevator down to ground level, expecting to see Mace in the museum, but apparently he and Rennie were elsewhere.

I walked outside and saw an unfamiliar car and a solitary man whom I didn't recognize.

"Help you?!" I said amicably. "The museum's not open until ten o'clock, but I can let you in early if you want."

The man just stared at me without speaking at first, and I had a feeling that something wasn't quite right.

"Like I said, I'll be happy to show you around," I repeated but with some concern creeping along my spine.

"You're Clay Arnold, right?" the man asked with no expression of warmth.

"Yeah, I'm Clay, but you have me at a disadvantage, sir. What's your name?"

"The name's Kline," the man replied. "Ernst Kline."

"Have we met before, Mr. Kline?" I asked cautiously.

"You could say that," the lone man said.

I didn't feel comfortable with the direction this conversation was going, and I quickly scanned the area to see if Mace and Rennie were nearby.

I heard Lex bark, and I figured they were inside their power plant.

"Again, sir, you have me at a disadvantage. I don't recall our ever meeting," I replied as graciously as my increasing anxiety would allow.

Ernst Kline then pulled a small revolver from his coat pocket and said, "We met first at the Snow auction house in Chicago and then again outside of the National Gallery of Art in Washington."

And then I knew that this was the man who had been tailing us as we sought Morse's clues. Worst of all, I realized that this is the man who shot at Lucretia and me and the son of a bitch who murdered Weed.

I froze when I saw his gun. "What do you want?" I said seriously.

"Well, it's not so much what I want. It's what my boss wants," he declared. "Where's your pal? The old black man."

I didn't answer him.

From inside the power plant Rennie looked out a window and saw me talking with the stranger. At first he thought nothing of it, just another early museum visitor. Then he saw the gun trained on my torso, and his blood turned cold. He called over to Mace, "Hey Mace, come here!"

Mace walked over, and he looked where Rennie was pointing. He stopped midstride and knew we had a serious problem. He gave Rennie his cell phone and told him to call 911. Rennie didn't need to be told twice.

"All right, Mr. Arnold, let's go inside and have a little, uh, chat," Ernst Kline said. I hesitated knowing that Tori and Maggie were inside, but he cocked his revolver to emphasize his point. We walked toward the entrance to my home.

"What's this all about, anyway?" I asked over my shoulder. "Is our running around the country looking at artwork really that important to you?"

"I could care less, but a nasty individual who holds my life in his hands does seem to care, and I'm compelled to do his bidding," Ernst openly admitted.

"Even if it means committing murder?!" I challenged. "You killed my friend and shot at me and Lucretia Land."

"Yes, even murder," he responded evenly. "I'm in too deep now."

We went inside and walked the flight of steps into my living room. Maggie and Tori heard us enter and walked down from the bedroom to see who the guest was. Maggie stopped short when she saw the stranger's gun pointed at me, and she grabbed Tori's arm to halt her stride. Tori instantly knew we had a serious problem with this man.

"Oh, how nice!" Ernst Kline said. "Looks like we have even more reason now for you to do exactly as I say, Mr. Arnold. Hello ladies, please have a seat."

Back in the power plant Mace said to Rennie, "You stay here and wait for the police to come."

"Where are you going, Mace?" Rennie asked urgently. "That guy's got a gun, and all we have is that Demon camera you carry and that old revolver you keep in your bedroom."

Mace grabbed the Demon camera, and gave Rennie specific instructions, "Remember, you wait here for the police. I'm going to see if I can defuse this situation. I can't walk directly across the courtyard or I'll be seen, so I'm going to take the hidden passageway under the courtyard."

The passageway was actually a tunnel that the Block brothers had built during the days of alcohol prohibition in the 1920s. It was used to channel guests to a private speakeasy where they served their guests beer and hard spirits. Mace had been aware of it for years and had used it to sneak up on Clement Hacker when he threatened to kill Tori and Clay a couple of years earlier. He saved our lives then, and now he hoped to sneak up on this perpetrator as well.

Mace went to the rear of the farmhouse and into the potting shed behind the house. He moved a workbench that revealed a trap door in the floor. He disappeared under the floor and descended a ladder that dropped some twenty feet down to the tunnel. He flipped a light switch and moved quickly through the forty-foot long tunnel under the courtyard until he came to another door leading to the brew house's subterranean work room. It was here that he and Weed had weaponized and tested Clay's antique detective cameras. Their favorite one was the Demon camera.

"What do you want?" Tori demanded from the intruder. "Surely we can resolve this. It's only a silly hunt for something that probably doesn't even exist."

"I could care less about some trove of junk that Samuel Morse may have squirreled away over a century ago. When I shot and killed that buddy of yours, Clay, in Washington, I knew my life was never going to be the same again. I really have nothing to lose now."

It was then that Tori and Maggie realized that they were being held at gunpoint by the man who had killed Weed.

"You murdered my brother, you goddamn bastard!" Tori spewed venomously at Ernst Kline. She started to go after him, but Maggie pulled her back.

"Now what?" Clay challenged. "Are you going to shoot us all? You'll never get away with this."

"Oh, I've been pretty lucky so far," Ernst replied. "Now just sit tight and maybe you'll live. Now tell me what you really expect to find from this little Samuel Morse adventure you're on, Mr. Arnold."

"There's nothing to be found," I said. "We came away from the Yale art gallery with nothing to show for our efforts. Perhaps your employer had something to do with that?!" I challenged.

"Perhaps," Ernst allowed.

Two floors below where we stood, Mace had exited the tunnel under the courtyard and entered the subterranean workshop. He stealthily traversed the room and began to quietly climb the steps up toward the living room. He knew he couldn't use the elevator because the whir of its motor would give his position away. Step by step he climbed the stairs until he stood just outside of Clay's living room. He paused and listened.

"That's not the answer I was looking for, Mr. Arnold," Kline said. "Maybe you need a little more convincing about how serious I am," and pointed the gun toward Tori.

Maggie instinctively stepped in front of Tori, and I stepped in front of both of them. "Just give it up, Kline, you're a real big man threatening blind and pregnant women," I said.

"You're a brave guy, Clay Arnold, challenging me. I used to have a great career. I was respected by my colleagues and my legal services were in demand. Then, I met that turd of a human being, Malcolm Land, and made the error of giving him supreme leverage over me. Now, it doesn't make much difference what I do. My life is basically over." He kept the gun pointed at the three of us.

Just then, Satchmo entered the living room and hissed loudly at the intruder. "He's a good judge of character, Kline. Just give it up, okay?"

"I don't think so," Ernst replied, and just as he was about to shoot, Mace quietly entered the room with the Demon camera in his hand. I was very surprised to see Mace, and unfortunately Ernst Kline saw my eyes move to where Mace was standing. Kline wheeled around and pulled the trigger when he saw our big friend standing in the doorway. Mace hadn't been ready enough to push the Demon's release button, and the bullet ripped into his right shoulder. He fell to the floor in a heap and lost his grip on the Demon. Kline kicked it away.

When Rennie heard the gunshot from the power plant he ran into Mace's bedroom, grabbed his loaded revolver, and risked a sprint across the courtyard.

"Nice try, old man," Ernst hurled at Mace. Maggie and Tori heard him wince in agony as the bullet tore into his shoulder, and they ran across the room to render aid. Ernst Kline and I stood still staring at each other.

"Like I said, you're a real brave man, Kline. Threatening pregnant and blind women and shooting an older man. I bet you sleep really well at night," I scoffed at him.

"Shut up, Arnold, you don't know when your luck is about to run out, do you?" He raised his gun from pointing at my torso and directed it toward my face. Maggie screamed in fear, and then a gun discharged with a sound that echoed off the walls and penetrated our hopes and dreams.

I instantly knew that I hadn't been hit and looked at Tori, Mace, and Maggie to see who the victim was. I saw Ernst Kline stagger a few paces, and when he finally fell face first onto the floor, I saw Rennie standing behind where he'd been with Mace's smoking gun in his shaking hand. Ernst Kline was dead.

"Evening comes," I said solemnly.

I rushed across the room and took the gun from Rennie, and we both went to check on Mace. There was a lot of blood, but Tori and Maggie managed to stem the flow a little. A few seconds later we heard a wail of sirens as police cars and a life squad rushed into the courtyard below. Rennie ran outside to direct them to my living room.

The EMTs immediately treated Mace's bullet wound which they said had gone straight through his muscle tissue without hitting the bone. They said Mace should be all right, but they loaded him onto a gurney and into the life squad. Rennie and I jumped in also to escort our friend to Conner Prairie Hospital a few miles away. Even though Mace had not been able to dodge Kline's bullet, I couldn't help but feel like we had all dodged a super huge one. We'd stuck together, and all lived to talk about it.

Mace was patched up in the hospital's ER and admitted for observation overnight. Fortunately, it was a clean wound, and he didn't require reparative surgery. While at the hospital the police interviewed Rennie and me about what had occurred and agreed to release Rennie to my recognizance. I knew they'd have more questions later. Before leaving the hospital, my long-time friend, Trent Reynolds, assistant superintendent for the Indiana State Police, came to see us.

"I heard the police radio chatter about gunfire at your place and figured you might need someone to vouch for you," Trent said. "How's Mace?"

"The EMTs and doctors seem to think he'll be okay, but he lost a lot of blood, and he is seventy-two, after all."

Rennie insisted on staying the night in Mace's hospital room, and the hospital personnel were okay with that. Trent gave me a ride back to the brewery complex, and I told him about Malcolm Land and all of the turmoil Lucretia Land and our family had suffered because of his greed.

"You might want to contact Detective Christopher Cioffi with the Chicago PD. They've been looking for this Malcolm Land prick, and Cioffi can fill you in."

"I'll do that. Thanks," Trent said.

When I got home, the police were gone, as was Ernst Kline's lifeless body. Maggie and Tori were on their hands and knees scrubbing his and Mace's bloodstains from our living room floor. It had been a day none of us would ever forget.

I swept them both up in a big hug and felt so thankful that they'd been spared. That we'd all been spared. "Mace's gonna be fine. Rennie's staying at the hospital with him, and Trent Reynolds is going to make some calls on our behalf. Anytime someone gets shot and killed, the authorities get pretty animated, especially if a juvenile is involved."

"Anyway, I've had enough excitement for one day. I'm ready to hit the hay. Tori, you're more than welcome to stay in our guest room, or if you prefer to go to your place that's fine, too."

"Thanks, Clay, I do think I'd like to stay here tonight. I'll sleep a lot easier knowing that you guys are close by."

We said goodnight, and Maggie and I climbed the steps to our bedroom. She looked over at me with a wry smile and said, "Never a dull moment, huh?!"

I nodded my head in agreement. "Apparently not."

Chapter 25

THE NEXT MORNING I woke up before Maggie and Tori and made two telephone calls. The first one was to the nurses' station at Conner Prairie Hospital to see how Mace was doing. He had been given pain medication and slept fairly well through the night. Rennie had experienced a nightmare, and the hospital offered him an over-the-counter sleep aid which helped. The head nurse reported that the doctor had examined Mace an hour earlier and had signed his discharge order for noon today. I planned to pick them up around that time.

My second call was to Lucretia Land. "I hope I'm not calling you too early, Lucretia, but I have some news to report to you and Drew."

"That's okay, Clay, I've been awake thinking about my deceased parents, my jerk of a brother, and what I want to do with the rest of my life. You know, small insignificant stuff!" she deadpanned. "I've also looked at my father's will that Benton Pettengill sent me before he was murdered. That handwritten note that father scrawled on the will still has me baffled. It read, 'LL cedarsleba.' I still don't know what that means. Anyway, so, what's new on your end?"

I proceeded to tell Lucretia about our visit from Ernst Kline yesterday and how close he came to killing Maggie, Tori, and me at our home. "Had it not been for Mace and Rennie, I doubt we'd be alive today."

Lucretia was stunned by what I told her and felt a great sadness that her brother's evil actions had spilled over to our lives as well. "I'm so sorry about Mace, and despite young Rennie's heroic intervention, he'll remember shooting Kline the rest of his life. It was necessary, but it'll be a burden he'll probably need some help coping with emotionally."

I agreed. "The good news is that we all managed to survive."

"I know you may not have an answer for this question right now, Clay, but have you given any more thought to continuing your search for Samuel Morse's treasure trove?" Lucretia asked.

"You're right. Given everything that's happened in the last twenty-four hours, chasing after Morse's clues has not been at the top of my list. I'm picking Mace and Rennie up at the hospital around noon, and frankly I want to get our family together again before I start making any plans. Besides, I doubt that Mace is going to be in any condition to go traipsing off on another, uh, adventure anytime soon. Now, having said that, I really don't like unfinished business. Give me a couple of days, and I'll let you know for sure, okay?"

"I understand, Clay," Lucretia replied. "If you decide on visiting Morse's final resting place and want some company, I'm willing to join you."

"I appreciate that, Lucretia. You know that we're still not out of danger as long as your brother is on the loose. I'll let you know, okay?"

We hung up a few moments later, and I went back to our bedroom to check on Maggie.

"G'morning sweetheart," I whispered to her as I sat on her side of the bed. "Are you ready for some breakfast?"

Maggie yawned and stretched and then bolted upright in bed when she remembered yesterday's turmoil.

"It's okay," I said. "We're all safe."

She relaxed a little and moved closer to me. "Did that really happen here yesterday?" she asked rhetorically. She shivered and reached her arms around my waist. I nodded affirmatively and then told her I had already spoken with the hospital staff and that Mace seemed to be recovering well. "I'll get Rennie and him in a few hours. Do you want to sleep some more?"

"No, I'm awake now and Tori may need a little help navigating around your place. I'll go check on her."

———————

"Where is that son of a bitch?" Malcolm Land muttered out loud to himself. "I haven't heard back from Ernst Kline with his latest report on Clay Arnold and his pal."

Just then his cell phone vibrated, and he saw that he had a call from his security chief, George Titus. "What's up, George?" Malcolm asked. "I thought it was Ernst Kline calling me."

"Uh, that's not likely to happen," Titus replied. "I scanned the Indianapolis police reports earlier today and read where a man named Ernst Kline had been shot and killed during a home intrusion."

"What!" Malcolm bellowed. "I never did much care for him, but he was an effective agent for me. Damn! Did the police report say who killed him?"

"Not really," George said. "The report mentioned something about a juvenile being involved but didn't release his name because he's a minor."

"No matter," Malcolm said. "Dead is dead. It appears that I may need you to pick up the slack, George."

George Titus gulped. "I don't know what that means, Mr. Land, but I have a feeling I'm not going to like it."

"Whatever," Malcolm replied. "Just stay available to me, and you may be rewarded even more handsomely than you already are."

George didn't know if that was the good news or the bad news. They hung up, and Malcolm Land stared out his window at Lake Michigan. He decided to accelerate his plans to sell more artwork owned by the Land Foundation and to relocate to the south of France.

At about noon I pulled up to the front circle at Conner Prairie Hospital to retrieve Mace and Rennie.

I couldn't help but flash back on the attack on the hospital a couple of years earlier by Clement Hacker and his nut-job twin sons, Newt and Twit. It was a horrible experience. Twit Hacker had driven his bomb-laden truck into the main lobby, and Weed had been shot through his hand trying to avert the explosion. I felt a pang of deep sadness knowing that Weed was now gone to us forever compliments of another nut-job, Ernst Kline. Too much death. Too much destruction. I missed my buddy, Weed, and knew I always would.

Mace was sitting in a wheelchair with Rennie by his side when I walked into the lobby. Their faces lit up when they saw me.

"Are you gents about ready to go home?" I asked.

They nodded their affirmation, and Rennie began wheeling Mace out the door toward my Tacoma.

"How're you feeling, Mace?" I asked.

"Well, I think they still have me pretty doped up on painkillers, and I have a feeling it's going to hurt like a son of a gun when the stuff wears off."

"Well, you'll just have to let us all baby you for a few days when we get you home," I asserted. "And you, Rennie, how're you doing?"

"Fine," came his one word reply, but from his flat affect, I could tell that he really wasn't. Mace and I both knew Rennie had been traumatized by killing Ernst Kline.

We all got situated in the truck, with Mace in the front passenger's seat and Rennie in back. I started the truck, and we headed back home to the brewery complex.

I looked in the rearview mirror at Rennie and saw him staring vacantly at the floor. He was uncharacteristically very quiet.

"Hey Rennie!" I said. "How're you holding up back there?"

"I killed a man, Clay. Shot him dead."

Mace attempted to turn around in his seat to look at Rennie, but even with the painkillers, he winced in discomfort.

"Do you want to talk about it now, or do you want to wait until we get home?" I asked Rennie.

"I dunno," he replied. "I killed a man," he said again.

I saw a park entrance and pulled my truck into an empty lot. I turned the engine off, and Mace and I made eye contact. We knew we needed to address Rennie's emotional trauma.

"So, can you tell Mace and me how you're feeling?" I asked.

"I dunno," he replied. "It's just so final. One second that man was there with a gun pointed at you guys and the next he was dead on the ground with a lot of blood. And I did that, and I don't like it that I did that."

"Rennie, what do you think would've happened if I hadn't shot Clement Hacker on the front porch three years ago?" Mace asked.

"Tori and Clay'd be dead," he replied solemnly.

"That's right," I said. "Thanks again, Mace," I added.

"So, what do you think would've happened if Rennie Cotton hadn't been there yesterday when that man broke into our home, shot me, and threatened to kill everyone?" Mace queried.

"I don't want to even think about it," Rennie said softly.

"Rennie, there are a lot of bad people out in the world," Mace consoled. "You already know that. And, as horrible and scary as violence is, there are times when it's the only recourse to protecting those you love. I, for one, am damn glad you were there with my revolver, and especially glad that you didn't hesitate to use it when you saw no other choice."

"I didn't want to kill him," Rennie pleaded. "Just hurt him or scare him. Anything for him to put his gun down. I didn't mean to kill him."

"As painful as it is, you did the right thing," I said. "I know you don't want to be called a hero, but what you did was truly heroic, and we're all grateful for your good judgment … and your good aim!"

"I still feel awful about it," Rennie whispered.

"That's not a bad thing," I said. "Feeling good about killing someone is not a good thing. Someday when you're older remind me to tell you a few stories," I added evasively. "Try not to be too hard on yourself. Your actions yesterday shouldn't be praised or derided. You did what you had to do, and you kept us safe."

Rennie looked at Mace and me with an adult understanding. "Thank you," he said. "I appreciate everything you're both saying. I just want you all to be proud of me, is all."

I started the truck, and looked at Rennie in the rearview mirror. We made eye contact, and I asked him, "So, should we get this old guy back home before his pain meds wear off? He'll probably get real grumpy if we don't."

Mace made a sound like a loud growl, and Rennie smiled and said, "Floor it, Clay! Otherwise we may not make it in time!"

Chapter 26

WE GOT MACE HOME to his power plant residence, and Rennie and Tori helped him get settled while Maggie and I prepared some easy meals for him to make once he felt up to it. Right now all Mace wanted to do was rest. Rennie was pretty bushed, too, from his lethal confrontation with Ernst Kline and his restless night at the hospital. Our three-legged Labrador, Lex, kept a watchful eye on both of them.

Tori joined Maggie and me as we were cleaning up the kitchen, and then she also decided it was a good time for a brief nap. That meant Maggie and I were left to our own devices which is a polite way

of saying we crawled back in bed and enjoyed each other's company which is another polite way of saying that we made love. Man, do I enjoy this woman!

By the time our feet hit the floor, it was late afternoon, and everyone including Mace was beginning to show signs of activity around the brewery complex. I went to check on Mace and found him in the antique camera museum puttering around the displays.

"There you are," I said when I entered the museum. "I shouldn't ask you if you're overdoing it, should I?"

"Naw," Mace drawled. "It was just a flesh wound," he understated.

"So, do you think our little conversation with Rennie helped him feel any better about shooting Ernst Kline?"

"Probably a little. This is something that he's just going to have to come to grips with on his own. I think our words helped, but it's our simply caring about him that'll help even more. Love heals all wounds."

Mace continued, "Have you given any more thought about Morse's coded message we retrieved from the *Dying Hercules* painting?"

"Some," I said. "My main concern is making sure you're okay and that all of us feel safe and secure in our own home."

"How's Maggie dealing with all of this violence?" Mace asked.

I sighed and said, "She hasn't gone running away kicking and screaming … yet, for which I am eternally grateful, but she may be thinking that the man she loves has a totally crazy life."

"I don't know that I could blame her," Mace added.

"Me, either," I confessed. "But the good news is that she's still here."

"So," Mace started again. "What do you want to do about the search for Morse's treasure trove? You'll recall that the last clue read, '*My resting place reveals all.*'"

"I really don't like any unfinished business, but the price has been enormous for us with Weed's murder and all of us getting damn near killed. Plus, I don't think you're in great shape to go rooting around Samuel Morse's resting place."

"I'm definitely not in great shape, Clay, but there's no way I'm not seeing this through to the end with you," Mace declared. "I'm ready when you say the word."

"Are you sure about this Mace?" I asked with real concern. "You know first hand how dangerous this can be."

"Yeah, I'm sure. As incredible as it would be to actually find a treasure, I want us to finish what you and Weed started. Besides, like you said, it's dangerous, and that's why I don't want you doing it alone."

"All right, then," I relented.

"Have you been in touch with Lucretia?" Mace asked.

"Yeah, I called her yesterday morning to tell her about our visit from Ernst Kline. She was very upset that you got shot. She also offered to join me in finishing the hunt for good ol' Sammy's stuff. I told her I'd get back to her and let her know what I'd decided."

"You should let her join us, Clay," Mace said. "She's got as much skin in this game as any of us."

I considered Mace's suggestion about Lucretia joining us and began to allow thoughts of finding Morse's resting place creep back in my mind. "I'll call her again in a little while, but first I want to make certain that Maggie is comfortable if I leave again."

In between talking with Mace in the camera museum and finding Maggie with Tori at the farmhouse, I went online to see where Samuel Morse is buried. I wasn't surprised to learn that his tomb is in the historic Green-Wood cemetery.

"Brooklyn!" Maggie exclaimed. "You want to go to a cemetery in Brooklyn?!"

"It'll only be for a couple of days, I promise, and then the search should be over. Morse's message said that his resting place would reveal all."

"And, Mace is going with you, too? Are you guys nuts? He got shot two days ago." Maggie said incredulously.

"He wants to come, and I can't say no. It's important to us," I said fervently.

Maggie sighed her understanding and acceptance. "Clay, don't you think that if his burial site would reveal something valuable, it would've been found by now?" Maggie asked skeptically.

"I don't know," I admitted. "Maybe people weren't looking in the right place. There's really only one way to find out, and that's why I want to go."

"Mace isn't in any condition to travel with you," she stated, "but I don't feel comfortable with you going alone."

"I want to do this for Weed as much as anything. We owe it to him. And, Lucretia needs to join us for her parents' sake and for her murdered attorney. I'll be fine, and like I said, it'll only be for a couple of days."

Maggie and I talked some more about my leaving, and in the end she knew that this was a trip I needed to make.

"When will you leave?" she asked in resignation.

"I need to speak with Lucretia about her schedule first, but my guess is we'll meet in New York the day after tomorrow."

Lucretia answered my phone call with anticipation in her voice.

"Hi Clay, how're things at home? Are you all holding up under the strain?"

"We're hanging in there, Lucretia, although each of us is wrestling with the horror of loved ones and other people getting killed. I shudder when I think of it."

"Believe me, I understand, Clay," Lucretia said. "The thought that my brother would have someone slowly murder our father and kill poor Benton Pettengill is something I'll never get past. I take it you've had some time to think about Samuel Morse's final resting place. Do you want to continue the search at this point?"

"Yes, I do, and Mace insists on coming, too," I replied.

"You're kidding! The poor guy just got shot. Is he in any condition to travel let alone risk getting hurt again?'

"Mace is one tough old bird," I said. "We talked about the dangers, and I don't think wild horses could keep him from coming along. In fact, he convinced me that you should definitely join us, so yeah, we're ready when you are. I went online a little while ago, and read about Morse being buried at Green-Wood cemetery in Brooklyn. Do you know much about it?"

"While waiting for you to get back to me, I risked e-mailing Drew, and we learned quite a bit about the place. I also seem to remember my parents taking Malcolm and me there once when we were children. It was probably during a little side trip from one of our parents' art buying adventures."

"I was surprised by how little I knew about Green-Wood cemetery until I went online," I admitted.

"It's really quite a historic place," Lucretia began. "Green-Wood was founded in 1838 and was one of the first rural cemeteries in America. By the early 1860s, it had earned an international reputation for its magnificent beauty and became the prestigious place to be buried, attracting 500,000 visitors a year, second only to Niagara Falls as the nation's greatest tourist attraction. Crowds flocked there to enjoy family outings, carriage rides, and sculpture viewing. The marvelous landscapes enhanced Green-Wood's popularity and helped inspire the creation of public parks, including New York City's Central and Prospect Parks."

"Wow!" I exclaimed. "So, I guess we shouldn't be surprised that a famous figure like Morse would choose Green-Wood as the site of his resting place."

"Right!" she replied. "So, when do you want to go and where shall we meet?"

We spent the next few minutes discussing our itineraries, and we agreed that we'd meet in the lobby of the Plaza Hotel the day after tomorrow. From there, we'd firm up plans to renew our search.

Chapter 27

THAT EVENING WE ALL gathered at our home for dinner and a time to reconnect and reflect. Maggie, Tori, and Rennie pirouetted around the kitchen, each with responsibility for a course. Rennie opted to keep a close eye on the salmon while it grilled, while Tori and Maggie took on the salad, side dishes, and dessert. And Mace, well, he made certain everyone's wine glass was full, including Rennie's. I, of course, dutifully did whatever task someone needed help with.

Within thirty minutes we were ready to sit down as a family. Tori sat down next to Rennie, and Maggie and I sat opposite them. Mace was

comfortable at the head of the table, and Lex came and laid down next to him, no doubt looking to be the beneficiary of Mace's generosity. Satchmo was nowhere to be seen but that could change in an instant. And sadly, we left an empty chair at the other end of the table for Weed.

I look around the table at each face and felt deeply moved by the emotions their individual features bring to me. This is my family. My parents have been gone for years. I never had a sibling and only the most distant of cousins. And, I don't know how I could feel any closer to anyone than I do to these people. Maggie looks in my direction and gives me one of her quintessential smiles. I'm a lucky guy.

I lean against her a little and say, "Why don't you say a few words so we can dive in to the vittles?!"

She asked us to join hands which at first struck me as a little hokey, but, in reality, given all of the ugliness that we've experienced together, a little hokeyness was warmly welcome.

"In some ways," she began, "this is the Thanksgiving dinner that I've been waiting for. Despite all that has happened in recent days, I am so very thankful to have each of you in my life and for the love and friendship you've shown Clay over the years. We'll all process what has happened in our own ways. In the end, we've got each other to lean on and to give to. We stick together!"

Maggie raised her wine glass. "A toast to Weed and to each of us!"

"Cheers!" Mace confirmed. "To Weed!"

The rest of the dinner was modulated by the tone and rhythm of our voices ... side conversations, stories, the occasional joke at someone's expense. Familial banter ... a return to some normalcy. I held Maggie's hand and gently touched her tummy. I was flooded with thoughts about soon being a father.

Mace told Rennie and Tori that he and I would be flying to New York tomorrow and then meeting with Lucretia Land the next afternoon to resume our search.

"If you need me, Clay, I can go, too," Rennie declared.

"I know you can, Rennie, but we need you to be here with Tori and Maggie making sure all is safe and well. Mace and I have this one covered, my friend."

"Do you have any idea what you'll do when you get to Green-Wood cemetery and locate Morse's gravesite?" Tori asked.

"Look for clues and keep our fingers crossed that Samuel F. B. Morse isn't up there looking down at us and laughing his ass off."

We spent the next hour or so just hanging out listening to music, drinking, and telling stories.

Mace got up to call it a night, and I walked him home to the power plant.

"You holding up okay, Mace?" I asked. "You can still change your mind about going, you know."

"I'm okay enough, Clay," he replied. "We can do this."

"All right then, why don't you get a good night's sleep and then let's meet in the subbasement workroom around eight o'clock. I have something for you that I think you'll remember."

"Sounds good," Mace said. "I'll see you then."

I left Mace and returned to my place. Maggie and Tori were clearing away the dinner dishes, and Rennie was wrapping up food for leftovers. And finally, Satchmo deigned to show up and entertain his humans. Fortunately for once, he hadn't brought a dead rodent with him.

I motioned for Rennie to come outside with me for a moment. "I want to make sure that you're feeling okay, Rennie, about the shooting."

"You and Mace helped yesterday, but man, I still cringe when I think about it."

"You probably always will," I said sympathetically. "But, I need to know if you're feeling well enough for us to leave for a few days."

"I'm all right, I guess," he said. "I have our end covered here while you're off looking for treasure.

I mean, who would want to do that, right?!" he laughed.

"Next time, I promise," I replied.

"Yeah, well, I just want you and Mace to come home in one piece so there'll be a next time. Fair enough!?"

"Definitely fair enough," I said.

As we were going back inside, Tori walked out the door. She and Rennie went over to check on Mace before retiring to the farmhouse. I walked back inside and finally Maggie and I were alone. Well, Satchmo was there, too, but he seemed more fascinated in a ladybug than my brilliant wit and repartee.

"Whew. All done!" Maggie said about putting the evening dishes away. She came over to me, and we walked upstairs to the bedroom and then outside onto our rooftop deck. It was definitely chilly. December had arrived, and we huddled together under a woolen afghan and listened to the night's sounds.

"You'll be careful, won't you?" she asked. "And you'll look after Mace and Lucretia?"

I nodded yes to each question. "And, I'll call you every night. We won't be gone long ... and who knows what treasures we'll find," I laughed.

We stayed out for no more than another three minutes and decided that the warmth of our bodies under the bed covers would be far more appealing than being outside in the cold. And that's what we did.

I awoke the next morning with a feeling of peacefulness I hadn't felt since Weed's murder. I wondered if it was the calm before the storm. I nestled closer to Maggie and gently put my hand on her tummy. She stirred a little and drifted back fully to sleep. I quietly slipped out of bed so as not to wake her, got dressed, and went downstairs to the kitchen to make coffee. At eight o'clock I went into the camera museum and found the object I was looking for. I then descended two flights down to the subbasement workshop and saw Mace reviewing diagrams for weapons that he and Weed had worked on together.

"G'morning, Mace, how'd you sleep last night?"

"Oh okay, I suppose, I didn't take any pain medication last night and I was a little uncomfortable, but it's bearable. What do you have there?"

"Surely, you remember my 1903 Ben Akiba Cane Handle Camera," I said.

"Oh yes," Mace recalled. "If I'm not mistaken Weed and I weaponized it so you could shoot .22 caliber bullets from the cane's handle. Didn't you tell us you used that on some deserving jerk in San Diego who was abusing a Hispanic restaurant owner and his wife?"

"Yeah," came my one word reply. "I thought you might like to take it with you on our trip, you know, to help steady yourself and for self-defense if the need arises."

"Good thinking, Clay, I'm also bringing along Weed's backpack with his cell phone and that antique telegraph key and the coil of copper wire that came with Morse's camera. It's my way of keeping Weed's spirit in the hunt."

I nodded my understanding. "I've reserved another private jet for us. We should leave for the airport pretty soon. This should be a very memorable trip for us, don't you think?!"

Mace gave me a wry smile. "Gee, Clay, I can't imagine anyone ever taking a trip with you that didn't end up, uh, memorable."

Malcolm Land sat near his picture window overlooking the Chicago River reviewing a lengthy list of paintings that the Land Foundation owned in its collection. He was deciding on which paintings to keep and which to sell.

"Well, let's see," he murmured to himself. "I already sold an Albert Bierstadt, a Winslow Homer, and a Georgia O'Keeffe at Snow's auction, plus that old camera. Perhaps it's time to sell the

Mary Cassatt and a Grant Wood. Hmmm." He was deep in thought but got jolted back to the present by the ring of his phone.

"Ah, hello George, and what information does my security chief have for me?" Malcolm inquired.

"Hello, Mr. Land, I just intercepted another series of e-mails between your sister and Drew Thomas."

"Oh, do tell, and what did she share with good ol' Uncle Drew?"

"Apparently, they are interested in finding Samuel Morse's burial site at the Green-Wood cemetery in Brooklyn," George reported.

"Hmm, I seem to recall going to that cemetery as a little boy with my family. I wonder what she and Clay Arnold are up to now."

"I dunno," George Titus replied. "I just thought you'd want to know. Is there anything else you require of me, sir?"

"Yes, Mr. Titus, with my devoted attorney, Ernst Kline, uh, out of the picture, I need you to pack a bag and charter a flight for the two of us to New York. Oh, and two rooms at the Stuyvesant Hotel would be good, too."

"But, sir, wouldn't my services be best employed here at the foundation office?" George tried.

"Now now, George, your services are best employed wherever I say they are. Is that understood?"

"Of course, Mr. Land, I'll let you know when our flight and lodging arrangements are made. Is there anything else, sir?"

"Yes, one last thing, George. Bring a gun. Hell, bring two!"

Chapter 28

MAGGIE, TORI, AND RENNIE stood on the farmhouse porch and waved goodbye to Mace and me as I steered the Tacoma out of the courtyard and headed south along the White River. Both Mace and I packed light for our trip. We each carried a duffel bag, and Mace carried Weed's backpack. As we approached Indianapolis, I entered the ramp for I-70 West and followed the signs for the airport.

Mace shifted in his seat to get more comfortable, and I shot him a quick glance of concern. He must've sensed my watching because he said, "I'm fine, Clay, just getting settled."

I smiled to myself and wondered if I'd be anywhere nearly as fit and tough as my friend when I'm his age. We drove on, and twenty minutes later we pulled into the long-term parking lot and walked toward the terminal where our pilot and a private jet awaited our arrival.

Thirty minutes later we were wheels up and soaring easterly over the dormant Indiana farmland. Neither of us felt a need to speak much. We knew what price we'd paid in this search so far, and we weren't sure what we'd be facing once we got to Brooklyn. We each gazed out our windows at the anonymous world passing below and tried to divine what the future might hold.

At some point, amid the steady drone of the engines, I fell asleep with my head resting on the window. I succumbed to a deep state of sleep and found myself in a familiar realm with an old white-haired man. He looked at me with a knowing smile on his face. He nodded his approval of my presence and beckoned me to follow him. In the past when I've had similar dreams, I resisted following him but was swept along by some unknown current. This time I walked toward him and followed him toward a hidden crypt with flashes of electricity dancing at its entrance.

"Are you Samuel Morse?" I asked the apparition. "Are we on the right path to your trove?"

The white-haired man looked deeply into my being, and I felt as if I was, at once, joined with the land of the living and a realm for those who've passed. His features began to grow dimmer, and I called out, "Wait. Please wait. I have so many questions!" And, then I heard a distant voice and realized it was the pilot announcing that we'd be landing soon. All visions were gone, and my questions went unanswered.

"Are you okay?" Mace asked. "You look like you've just seen a ghost."

"I think I just did," I confessed. "Very strange dream."

Flying into New York City is always an exciting experience. The concrete and steel canyons, along with bridges and large bodies of water, always make me take notice of a city that changed the world. I thought of the irony of possibly finding a treasure near here and how that might change our world.

"Hey Mace, are you ready to give up our mundane life at the brewery complex for an existence of loud noises, flashing lights, and pollution?" I teased.

"Not in a million years. I think I'd rather be shot again!"

Our pilot expertly put our aircraft down on the runway and taxied to a hangar away from the large commercial airlines. Mace and I deplaned, and I called Uber to give us a ride to the Plaza Hotel.

"How're you holding up?" I asked.

"Pretty stiff from sitting for so long, and I'm feeling some pain still. I'll take a pill when I get to our room. But don't worry, my friend, I'm hanging in there."

The drive from the airport into the city was visually stimulating but cacophonous. Like Mace, I don't quite get why millions of people want to live on top of one another. True, New York is a city that never sleeps, but c'mon guys, take a nap every once in a while. Before too long we rode past the Metropolitan Art Museum, and I flashed back on Weed's and my visit with Clifton Maguire. I cringed at the thought of his brutal murder at the hands of Ernst Kline. Next up was the Plaza Hotel and our driver deposited us at curbside. We waived off a valet's attempt to assist with our bags and walked through the hotel's stunning lobby to the front desk. Mace whistled when he saw the ornateness of the lobby's fixtures.

"Ah, good day, Mr. Arnold, I see that you stayed with us very recently. Do you wish to stay in the same suite as before?" the desk clerk inquired.

I politely declined since it would be too fresh of a reminder of Weed's and my visit. "It was a delightful suite, but do you have something else with a different view of the city?"

"Let me see," the desk clerk said. "How about our Manhattan suite? It'll provide you with a different view of Central Park."

"That'll be fine," I acknowledged. I handed her my credit card for room charges, and then Mace and I rode the gilded elevator to our suite.

Mace whistled again when he saw the plushness of our room and asked me the same question Weed had asked two weeks ago. "Do you always stay at places like this when you travel?"

"No, I usually stay at far grander places!" I fibbed. "Do you want me to see if they have something better?"

Mace chose not to dignify my snarky comment with a reply. Instead he walked over to his side of the suite and spread his battered body onto his bed. "Just forty winks is all I need," he declared and promptly fell asleep.

I stretched out on my bed as well and phoned down to the receptionist desk to see if Lucretia had checked in yet. She hadn't, and I asked the clerk to please leave a message for her that we'd arrived and to please call us when she was ready to meet. I then made a dinner reservation for the three of us in the Peacock restaurant for eight o'clock.

An hour later Mace was still sawing logs when my phone rang and Lucretia was on the line.

"Good afternoon, Clay, I just arrived," Lucretia said. "How's Mace doing?"

"I think he's okay, tired but okay," I reported. "I've made a dinner reservation for the three of us at eight o'clock. If that works for you, we'll meet you in the lobby a few minutes before then."

She said that would be perfect, and we hung up.

I laid in bed staring at the ceiling, and my mind was flooded with all sorts of thoughts. I still couldn't believe that Weed was gone, or that my friend, Mace, was recovering from a gunshot wound, all as a result of my trip to Chicago to buy Samuel Morse's daguerreotype camera. Next, I thought about Lucretia and all of the turmoil that her deranged brother had caused, and that led me to think about our upcoming visit to the Green-Wood cemetery and hopefully some closure to this adventure.

Finally, I thought about how much I was missing Maggie and how excited I was that we'd be parents before too long. I began to think of baby names, and soon I drifted off to sleep, perchance to dream again of a man who'd been dead for nearly one hundred and fifty years and a treasure trove that might really exist.

At about seven thirty, I felt a gentle tug on my sleeve and saw Mace standing next to my bed. "It's time to get up, sleepy head. We're meeting Lucretia in thirty minutes."

Meanwhile several blocks away, Malcolm Land and his security chief, George Titus, exited a taxi at the entrance to the Stuyvesant Hotel. "Let's get checked in, George, and then I want us to go over to the Plaza Hotel and watch for signs of my sister and those upstarts from Indiana. I want to know when they're heading over to Morse's burial site."

"Are you sure you really want to do this?" George lamented. "I don't see why any of this is necessary. Plus, the police are looking for you. I say you take all of your millions and skip the country while you still can."

"George!" Malcolm said as genteelly as he could. "Why don't you keep your unsolicited opinions to yourself. Now, let's get situated and then head over to the Plaza and stake out the front entrance."

Mace and I took the gilded elevator again to the Plaza's lobby to meet Lucretia. She arrived promptly at eight o'clock looking fresh and happy to see us.

"There you are!" she said warmly and gave both Mace and me an affectionate hug.

"Let me look at you, Mace," our elegant friend said. "You look pretty darn good for a septuagenarian who just got shot a few days ago!"

"Thanks," Mace said. "I'm not sure what a septuagenerian is, but I'll take that as a compliment. It's great to see you again, Lucretia."

We walked to the entrance of the Peacock restaurant, and an attractive hostess greeted us and led us to our table. As she walked in front of us, I couldn't help but notice her lovely figure, including a shapely derriere that I knew Weed would be admiring if only he still could. It's funny what you remember.

We enjoyed a sumptuous meal in a stunning dining room, definitely unlike anything we have back home. I was pleased that Mace was able to experience this opulence and even more pleased that this was not a lifestyle that either of us craved.

"You know," Lucretia commented during our dessert. "It's still early yet. How do you guys feel about our taking a cab over to Green-Wood cemetery to get a feel for the lay of the land. It's dark outside, and I can't imagine that it's still open to the public at this hour, but it sure beats sitting in our hotel rooms, and honestly I'm not in the mood to take in a Broadway show."

"Are you game for that, Mace?" I asked.

"Sure," he replied. "My little nap did me some good. Let's settle up with the bill and head over to Brooklyn. We can always come back tomorrow if the cemetery's closed."

We decided to run up to our rooms briefly and change our clothes and then meet again in the lobby in twenty minutes. Mace grabbed Weed's backpack which contained two headlamps and other accoutrement. We both carried our Demon cameras with us, fully charged, and Mace used the Ben Akiba cane camera for stability. Not knowing how late we might be out, I called Maggie to see how things are going at home.

"It's quiet for a change," she laughed. "No gunfire. That's always a good sign. How're you guys doing?"

"We're doing fine. Mace and I both got naps before meeting Lucretia for dinner, and I think he's holding up remarkably well. I also think it's really good that Lucretia is here. She's endured so much heartache with her father dying, actually being murdered, all at the behest of her greedy brother. It's only right that she be present if we, indeed, find Samuel Morse's treasure."

"You're a good man, Clay Arnold, just come back in one piece for me and Sputnik, okay?!"

"You've got a deal. Look, I have to run, Darlin'. Lucretia's probably down in the lobby waiting for us. We're going to take a little excursion over to the Green-Wood cemetery."

"Oh my!" she quipped. "Try not to wake the dead!"

Little did she know …

Chapter 29

MACE AND I MET Lucretia in the hotel lobby, and the concierge arranged for a driver to take us to Brooklyn. What we were going to do once we got there was anyone's guess at this point.

From their perch across the street from the Plaza hotel, Malcolm Land and George Titus watched as an SUV pulled up to the curb and Mace, Lucretia, and I climbed inside. Malcolm quickly hailed a cab, and once he and his indentured servant, George, got in, he instructed the driver to follow that car up ahead, but to maintain a safe distance.

George tried to reason with his boss again, "Are you really sure you want to be doing this? We're

in enough trouble as it is. If I were in your shoes, I'd be trying to get out of the country as quickly as possible."

"Well, you're not in my shoes, are you?!" Malcolm replied snidely. "Just do as I say, and we'll be able to foil whatever plans my sister is making. Then, perhaps I'll be ready to run for it, but not until I know what she and this photographer and the old black man are up to."

"It's your life," George muttered to himself. "I'm screwed no matter what."

Our driver, whose name was Joachim, turned on to the FDR East River Drive from W. 59th Street, and we got a good view of Brooklyn as we headed south.

"I don't know if the Green-Wood cemetery is open at this time of day," Joachim noted. "What do you want me to do when we get there?"

"We'll pay you two thousand dollars for your services for the rest of the night, so if you don't mind being flexible with your time, we'll make it worth your while."

"That'll work," he acknowledged in heavily accented English. "Take all the time you need!"

Traffic is never light in New York City, but it could've been far worse. We followed the FDR Drive south toward Battery Park and entered the ramp for I-478. In a couple of minutes we crossed the East

River into Brooklyn and took exit 26 for Hamilton Avenue. We had no idea we were being followed.

"Don't lose that car!" Malcolm chided their driver. George Titus bristled with anxiety. "And, don't let them see us!" Malcolm commanded.

Soon, we arrived at the impressive entrance to Green-Wood cemetery and perhaps the final destination of our search.

"Wait here for us," Clay instructed Joachim. "It may take us a while."

Lucretia, Mace, and I exited our car and approached the main entrance. We saw a sign that showed the hours of operation to be 8:00 a.m. to 5:00 p.m. The cemetery was definitely closed for the night. I spotted a holder containing maps of the cemetery and took one. An employee wearily approached us as we peered through the gate.

"Cemetery's closed for the day!" came his brusque declaration.

"We see that from the sign," I said matter-of-factly. "We're from out of town for a brief visit, and we hoped to see our Uncle Samuel's tomb." I pulled a fifty dollar bill out of my pocket and asked, "Any chance you'd let us in for a brief look around?"

"Naw, I don't think so," the groundskeeper replied. "I'd probably lose my job, and besides the cemetery's patrolled by Dobermans at night, and you sure don't want those beasties gnawing on you."

"I can't argue with that!" Mace said.

"Well, I guess we'll just have to try and come back tomorrow. Are you sure you can't let us in?" I flashed the cash at him again.

"Naw," he repeated. "I'd get in a lot of trouble if I did, and I need the job." He walked off into the night.

"Now what?" Lucretia asked. "Should we just call it a night and come back in the morning?"

"Well, we're here now," Mace said. "What's your pleasure, Clay?" my friend asked.

"You know, if it were just you and me, Mace, I'd say 'screw it, let's just jump the fence,' but with Lucretia here maybe we should view this trip as a little recon visit and come back."

"I certainly appreciate your concern about my well-being, guys, but there's no time like the present. I doubt that either Mace or I are in any shape for climbing walls, but the map shows that Green-Wood has four entrances. Maybe we can sneak into one of them."

"The lady's got moxie!" Mace said with a grin. We went back to Joachim, and exchanged cell phone numbers with him in case we needed him to meet us at a different place.

"You're not going to do anything illegal, are you?" Joachim asked with concern. "I'm only in

America on a temporary work visa, and I don't want to risk deportation."

"Who us?!" Lucretia responded with her most convincing voice. "Now do we look like the sort of people that would do anything illegal?"

"Just wait here, Joachim," I said. "Nobody's going to kick you out of the country for sitting in a car outside of an old cemetery."

Mace retrieved Weed's backpack from the vehicle, and the three of us began walking down Fifth Avenue to another entrance. "This place is amazing!" Mace said as he spied one impressive monument after another.

"According to the literature that Drew forwarded to me prior to my flight, there are well over a half million people buried here, some of whom are true American legends."

"Like who besides Samuel Morse?" Mace asked.

"Oh, how about Louis Comfort Tiffany, or Horace Greeley, or Leonard Bernstein to name a few?" she added.

We walked on for a few minutes until we came to the next entrance which was fortuitous because, according to the map, it was not terribly far from Morse's tomb situated between Thorn Path and High Wood Path. What was not fortuitous was the large lock and chain sealing the entrance.

"Now what?" Lucretia asked. "No way we're getting inside this gate."

"Well, Lucretia, do you mind getting a little dirty?" I asked like the ever recalcitrant adult delinquent that I really am. I pointed to where the border wall was only about six feet tall. "What do you say, Mace, do you think your bones and a little bullet wound can handle scaling the wall?"

"I'm game, Clay, give me a hand, will ya?"

I laced my fingers together and formed a cup for Mace to place his foot in. Then, I lofted him up a foot or so, and Mace scrabbled his way on top of the wall. He sat there grinning like a Cheshire cat.

"Easy peasy," he declared triumphantly. "Not bad for a shot-up septuagenarian, huh, Lucretia?" he quipped.

"Not bad at all!" she replied. "Now how am I going to get up there?" she inquired.

"Same way!" I informed her. I cupped my hands again, and she stepped a foot into them but had some trouble getting her balance.

"I'm not sure I can do this," Lucretia said in frustration. "You guys may have to go on without me."

"No way!" I said. "Let's try it again." I cupped my hands, and she placed a shoe in them. She started unsteadily swaying side to side, and I held her lower leg to help secure her. I raised her up about six inches and she started teetering off balance again. "Just hang on, Lucretia!" I urged, and I grabbed her butt and gave her a good solid push up to Mace's arms. She arrived on top of the wall rather ungracefully, and her unbalanced weight caused a little problem. Next thing I knew she and Mace were tumbling ass-over-elbows to the ground inside the cemetery. I immediately leaped up to the top of the wall to see if they were hurt and saw Lucretia laying on top of Mace. They were both laughing at the glorious indignity of their prone postures.

"Are you guys okay?" I asked.

Lucretia looked at Mace's grinning face and said, "Hey, big fella, you sure know how to show a girl a good time!"

I leaped down to their position and helped them get on their feet again. "I have a feeling you're never going to let me forget this, are you, Clay?" Mace stated with feigned concern.

"Oh, maybe in a million years. Just wait until I tell Tori and Rennie."

Lucretia dusted herself off, and we checked to see if the fall had reopened Mace's bullet wound. He reported that he was fine. Mace reached inside Weed's backpack and found the two headlamps he had brought. We both took one, and turned on the red beams.

I looked at the map and said, "C'mon, this way."

We had walked about a hundred yards along Sylvan Avenue, and then I heard Mace say a word that sent a shiver down my spine. "Dogs!" We quickened our pace and ran for a large sandstone mausoleum. Just in time we ran up its steps and closed its wrought-iron gate behind us. Two ill-humored Dobermans appeared, and we were trapped.

Meanwhile back near the main entrance, Joachim sat in the SUV reading his cell phone and listening to salsa music. George Titus silently approached the vehicle and rapped his knuckles sharply on the driver's window. Joachim jumped in his seat at the unwelcome intrusion.

Through his closed window, Joachim asked anxiously, "What do you want?"

George Titus responded by pointing the muzzle of his gun at the hapless driver's face. "Lower your window," he commanded. Joachim complied.

"Where are the three people you drove here?" George inquired with his gun still pointed at Joachim.

"They walked down the street to try and find an open entrance," Joachim answered. "They may be inside. I don't know for sure."

"Get out of here," George demanded. "And, don't come back!"

Joachim didn't need to be told twice. He started the car and mentally said *adios* to the money Clay had offered to him.

George Titus then walked up to the main gate and looked though the ornate ironwork to see if he could observe any sign of their three targets. The same cemetery groundskeeper that had talked with Clay earlier approached him and brusquely declared, "The cemetery's closed. Come back tomorrow!"

George Titus was about to speak, when Malcolm Land appeared at his side. "Open the damn gate, you illiterate cur!" he hurled at the hapless employee. He pointed his revolver at the man's face.

It was all the poor groundskeeper could do to hold his keys steady. "No need for the gun, mister, just ease up, will ya?! I don't have a key for the car gate, but I can open this one for visitors on foot."

The pedestrian gate finally swung open, and Malcolm said, "We need you to direct us to Samuel Morse's grave site … now!"

"Well, heck, it's clear on the other side of the cemetery, and the dogs are on the loose. You'll need to be careful!"

"No," Malcolm replied. "You're the one who needs to be careful. We have guns and you have a, uh, rake. Lead on!"

Chapter 30

THE DOGS HAD NOT seen us, but they definitely picked up our scent. They were sleek, serious-looking animals who worked the area around the mausoleum like a precision hunting team. Back and forth, noses low to the ground, they crisscrossed the terrain around us and then stopped to sniff the air.

Mace, Lucretia, and I remained hidden behind a limestone angel and waited for the dogs to leave. The alpha dog of the pair trotted in front of the mausoleum and ascended the half dozen steps leading to the crypt's gate. The Dobermans weren't going anywhere anytime soon.

The three of us stayed as still as we could, but we knew that before too long either the dog or we had to move. I picked up a pebble and chucked it to the left of the dog. He immediately bounded in that direction and was joined by his canine partner.

"This is nuts," I said. "We can't stay like this forever. I'm going out there."

"I wouldn't do that if I were you," Mace said with alarm.

I stepped out from behind the guardian angel and hoarsely whispered, "Hey Dobie, wanna play fetch?!"

Immediately, like prehistoric velociraptors, the two dogs charged the gate snarling, spitting slobber, and generally being downright rude.

"Nice puppies," I tried calmly. "Nice friendly doggies!" There was no way that I honestly expected either of those endearing epithets to charm these savage beasts, but I thought I'd give it a try.

"Say, Lucretia, do you have anything to eat in your bag?" I asked.

"Let me look," she replied. And, by that time the dogs realized that there were two additional intruders in their realm. "All I have are some peanut M&Ms. Will that work?" She walked up and handed them to me.

To say that the Dobermans were excited would be putting it mildly. I threw a couple of M&Ms

between the iron gate onto the ground, and the dogs sniffed and then consumed them in a nanosecond. I walked up to the gate, and the alpha male snarled in a way that sent chills down my spine.

"Easy, big guy," I said. "Easy now." I reached out my hand, palm up, filled with M&Ms, and brought it up to the gate. The Doberman lunged forward and grabbed on to the sleeve of my leather coat and managed to tear a piece of leather loose. Mace and Lucretia cringed.

"All right, tough guy, I tried to be nice, but now you've gone and ruined my favorite coat. Hey, Mace, can you set your Demon on stun?"

"Yeah, it already is." Mace reported.

"Stun! What do you mean stun?!" Lucretia asked incredulously.

Mace and Lucretia stood on either side of me, and Mace pulled out his Demon camera.

"What's that?" Lucretia asked when she saw the strange, antique-looking device in Mace's large hand.

"Oh, it's just a little something that Weed and Clay and I cooked up to help even the score for the good guys."

Lucretia had no idea what that meant, and didn't have much of an opportunity to ask more questions.

The Dobermans continued to carry on like the crazed guard dogs that they are, and Mace asked me if I wanted to do the honors.

"Go for it, Mace. You know the power levels on that Demon better than I do."

The alpha male made another attempt to grab my sleeve, and I saw an electric blue charge of electricity shoot out from the Demon and engulf the dog three feet away from me. The alpha male fell to the ground in a twitching heap. He emitted an ever so delicate aroma of singed fur. The other dog turned tail and ran away.

"Is he dead?" Lucretia asked. "If so, please don't ever tell my friends at the Chicago Animal Shelter. They'll drum me off the board!" she managed to say with a small smile.

"Don't worry," Mace said. "I did actually have the Demon set on stun, so our sleeping friend here should be fine when he wakes up in a couple of hours."

"C'mon," I said. "Let's keep moving before Dobie's friend decides to get brave again." We exited the mausoleum and quietly set forth along the path.

The nighttime walk through Green-Wood cemetery was actually an incredibly vivid experience. I was so taken by the artistry of the tombstones and large burial crypts. It was clear that many an immigrant artisan made a living for his family carving ornate memorials for the wealthy. I made a mental note to sometime do a nighttime photo shoot in a similar setting.

"How're you holding up, Mace?" I asked my good friend.

"Hanging in there, Clay. Sure could use a couple of M&Ms, though," he quipped.

I looked over at Lucretia to gauge how she was doing, and aside from a few moments of her feeling extreme terror, she actually appeared to be having the time of her life.

"Man, I wish Weed was with us, Mace!" I intoned.

"Amen, brother," came his short but heartfelt reply.

We walked on, but every hundred feet or so we stopped to listen to the night's sounds, and to admire the stone structures and the eerie shadows that they cast.

"According to the map," Mace said, "we should turn left here onto Oak Avenue, then right on Hillock Avenue. That'll get us close to a circle formed by Thorn Path and Highwood Path. Samuel Morse's tomb should be in the middle of that circle. We should be there in just a few more minutes."

We heard a dog bark in the distance, and we quickened our pace lest the other Doberman find us without shelter. "I'm actually more concerned about two-legged adversaries at this point," Mace said. "You know the ones that carry guns rather than big teeth."

Eventually we came to a verdant circular path, and situated high on a grassy knoll, we saw a striking marble and limestone monument. We climbed the hillside to view it more closely. The tomb had a bronze placard that read "Samuel Finley Breese Morse Born 1791 – Died 1872." We had arrived.

"Now what?!" Lucretia asked.

"Now we look for another clue," I said.

"In the dark!?" Lucretia exclaimed.

"Yeah, unless you want to wait around until daybreak with the presence of early morning joggers and visitors," I offered.

"Uh, no thanks," she said. "Let's examine the outside of the monument as best we can, and take it from there."

Mace and I had the red lights of our headlamps turned on, and we began examining the front of the monument. We saw nothing at first, and then Lucretia touched the bronze placard like a blind person might do who was reading Braille. She felt some raised markings and called Mace and me over to shine some light on the spot. Sure enough, the markings were Morse code.

‒ .‒. ..‒ ... ‒ ‒.‒‒ ‒‒‒ ..‒ .‒. ‒... .‒ ... . .. ‒. ... ‒ .. ‒. ‒.‒. ‒ ...

Mace put Weed's backpack on the ground and pulled out Weed's phone with the code conversion app. He first took a picture of the dots and dashes to record them, and then he carefully entered the Morse code into the conversion app. A few seconds later the code converted into English text: *"Trust your base instincts."*

"Oh swell," I said sarcastically. "Another vague clue. Old Sammy boy isn't making this easy for us, is he?"

"Trust your base instincts?" Lucretia said. "That could mean anything, and unfortunately we don't have Drew with us to help solve the meaning."

"Well, let's step back a moment and see if we can figure this out," I said, lacking any other brilliant idea.

The three of us stood some six feet in front of the monument trying to comprehend the message that Morse had left hidden in plain view. It was obscure enough in its meaning that no one had thought to decipher it since Morse's burial in 1872.

Meanwhile, a half-mile away, Malcolm Land and George Titus followed the lead of their grounds-keeper hostage. "How much farther?" Malcolm barked.

"Oh, it's a little ways yet. Green-Wood's a big place," the groundskeeper said plaintively. "Wouldn't you prefer to wait for daylight?" he tried.

He received a rough shove from behind. "Keep moving," Malcolm commanded, "or you won't be seeing another daylight."

Chapter 31

"*T*RUST YOUR BASE *instincts*?" Mace murmured aloud. "So, wattya think, guys?" None of us had an immediate flash of insight.

Lucretia stared at Samuel Morse's resting place and tried to clear her mind of the flotsam swirling around her brain.

"When I studied art history in college, I took a course in classical and medieval architecture which included learning various elements of Greco-Roman design … you know, things like the three main types of column capitals and various pediments, friezes, atria, and the like."

"And?!" I asked in anticipation.

"And," Lucretia continued, "a structure's base was the foundation on which all else rested," she mused. "Perhaps Morse's clue is no more complicated than that … that we should trust our 'base instincts' and carefully examine the foundation of the monument … in its entirety."

With all due respect to our friend, Lucretia, I thought her suggestion was like grasping at straws, but I couldn't think of anything that made more sense, so we fanned out and began searching for anything that seemed unusual.

Off a little way we heard a loud dog bark, and I hoped that we wouldn't have to contend with the other Doberman. At that point my 'base instinct' was not to get chewed on again.

After the three of us looked for a couple of minutes, Mace spied a very old, green metal rod protruding from the rear of the monument's limestone base. It was partially hidden by grass and weeds, but it was firmly in place.

"Hey guys!" he called over to us. "Come take a look at this!"

The three of us knelt down in the dewy grass and saw the metal rod bearing nearly fifteen decades of copper verdigris. Mace pulled the tall grass away from the copper rod to expose it more fully. He shined his red head lamp on the rod and noticed something unusual about the limestone base just

above the rod. Engraved into the stone were more
dots and dashes ... yet another Morse code clue.

... . ⁻. ⁻.. ....⁻. .. .⁻. ... ⁻ .... ⁻⁻ . ...⁻ ⁻⁻. .

Mace whistled his surprise, and Lucretia and I
looked at each other in amused befuddlement. The
befuddlement quickly vanished, however, when
the second Doberman dashed into our space and
growled savagely from ten feet away.

"Oh shit! Not again!" I said. "Nice doggie ... go
away!" I tried pathetically.

This time the dog had the upper hand, I mean
paw, on us. He charged at Lucretia who was closest
to him and grabbed at her leather bag. He savagely
ripped it away from her and began circling her for
another attack. It came immediately, and Lucretia
was not prepared for the Doberman's viciousness. It
knocked her to the ground and was gnawing on the
collar of her coat, when a strong hand reached out
and grabbed the dog by the scruff of its neck. It was
Mace's hand. Even with his wounded shoulder, he
screamed like a samurai and hurled the Doberman
with almost super-human strength against Morse's
stone monument. It whimpered and limped awkwardly, then finally loped away to the safety of the
cemetery's shadows. I watched the episode unfold
with shock and awe.

Lucretia lay on the ground catching her breath and doing a fast mental inventory of her body parts.

Mace kneeled down in the grass beside her and helped her sit up. "Are you okay, Lucretia?" he asked with genuine concern. "Do you think you can stand up?"

She looked at Mace and nodded and then engulfed him in a huge hug. "Thank you, Mace, I've never been so scared." She held on to him to get her equilibrium, and he helped her to her feet. I joined them, and the three of us stood together wondering what other frightening ordeals we'd still encounter.

"Damn Dobermans!" I cursed. "That was close. Are you sure you're all right, Lucretia? We can bag this little adventure if you're not feeling up to it now."

"I'm a little shaken, but I don't want us to bag anything. Besides, I'll have a really great story to tell at the next animal shelter board meeting. Especially the part about Mace grabbing some seventy-pound Doberman and hurling it through the air. The animal rights folks in the group will get a huge kick out of that," Lucretia chortled sarcastically.

Mace said, "C'mon, let's take a closer look at the coded message on the limestone base."

We all bent down to look at the engraved dots and dashes.

"Now what?" Lucretia asked.

Mace placed Weed's backpack on the ground, and took out his cell phone and pulled up the code conversion app. "Now, we enter these markings exactly into the app, and we should get the English text translation."

It took Mace a minute or so to get the code entered properly, and then the message was revealed: "*Send first message.*"

"*Send first message*! What's that supposed to mean?" Lucretia asked with mild annoyance. "I sure wish Drew were here to help us with this clue. He was so helpful when it came to decoding the messages that lead you guys to the next painting and the next clue."

"He sure was," I agreed, "but this seems different. I don't think Morse is referring to a painting."

"First message," Mace said out loud. "You don't think Morse is referring to the original message you found inside the daguerreotype camera, do you, Clay?"

"I don't know, Mace. It seems like a very long message to send. And besides, how are we supposed to send any message, and to whom?"

The three of us sat in the chilly December air trying to figure out what to do next. I stared at the green metal rod. I touched the engraved dots and dashes in the limestone. I read and reread the translated code. Nothing immediately came to mind.

"Lucretia, do you have an emery board in your bag?" Mace asked.

"I believe so, Mace, but with all due respect, this hardly seems like the right time to be giving yourself a manicure," she replied in half jest.

She rooted around inside her leather bag, retrieved an emery board, and handed it to Mace.

"What are you thinking about, Mace?" I inquired.

"This!" he said. He began lightly rubbing the emery board along the green metal rod, and even in the red glow from our headlamps, we saw the brightness of fresh copper appear as the green verdigris was rubbed away.

"Well, the fresh copper sure is pretty," Lucretia deadpanned, "but I sure don't see how it gets us any closer to the promised land."

"That's the good news, too," Mace said, "because if it were too easy someone would've figured this clue out long ago."

"Well, how do we know that someone hasn't already done so?" I asked soberly.

"We don't," Mace agreed, "but we've come too far to stop before we know for sure."

He got no argument from either of us. We sat still in the grass behind the tomb of one of the brightest minds of the nineteenth century and tried to comprehend his meaning. *"Send first message ..."* I repeated aloud.

"You know, maybe we're going about this first message thing all wrong," I suggested. "Maybe Morse wasn't referring to the first message we found in the camera at all."

"What then?" Lucretia asked with rising curiosity.

"Well, from the reading I've done about the life and times of old Sammy boy, he perfected his telegraph in 1844 and sent his original message from the Supreme Court chamber in the basement of the U.S. Capitol building in Washington to the B&O Railroad's Mount Clare Station in Baltimore."

"So, you think that's the first message Morse was referring to?" Lucretia asked. "What was that first message, anyway?"

Mace picked up Weed's phone again and pulled up a search engine. He typed in, "What was Samuel Morse's first message?" He immediately got his answer: *"What hath God wrought?"*

"Oh yeah," I said. "I remember the quotation, but I couldn't remember who originally said it. Morse, huh?"

Mace then typed the quotation into the code conversion app on Weed's phone, and the following message appeared:

.-- .... .- - ....- - .... --. --- -.. ....-- .-. ---
..- --. .... - ..--..

"Okay," Lucretia said quizzically. "Even if that is the right message, how the heck do we send it?"

"I think I have an answer," Mace offered, and at that he emptied the rest of the contents in Weed's backpack onto the grass by our feet. In addition to Mace's Demon camera, the original telegraph key and the coil of copper wire that I had acquired when I won the camera auction lay in front of us.

Chapter 32

"STEP LIVELY NOW!" Malcolm ordered the cemetery groundskeeper. "I had no idea how big this darn place is. We need you to get us to Samuel Morse's tomb, now!"

Poor George Titus was tired of walking around this old cemetery in the dark, and the last person he was keen on spending any time with was his imperious boss, Malcolm Land.

"Uh, Mr. Land, don't you think this is all a little silly chasing around in the dark after your sister and her two buddies?"

"I'm holding a gun on this guy … do you think this is silliness, Mr. Titus? Now march! Both of you assholes!"

The hapless groundskeeper looked at Malcolm's gun and marched forward. They passed the grandeur of Louis Comfort Tiffany's monument and a crypt containing the remains of notorious political leader, Boss Tweed. "We're getting closer," he reported to his two abductors.

"So, what are you thinking, Mace?" I inquired.

"It's just a wild-assed guess on my part, Clay, but seeing the copper rod sticking out of the limestone makes me wonder if it's an electric terminal of some kind."

Instantly, I had an inkling of where Mace's mind was heading. "So, do you think that if we connect the copper wire to the copper rod, then connect it to the telegraph key, and tap in 'What hath God wrought?' that something is going to happen?"

Mace shrugged. "Nothing ventured, nothing gained," he stated. "Do you have any better ideas at this point?"

"Uh no," I admitted.

"Give it a try, Mace," Lucretia encouraged.

Mace uncurled the coil of copper wire and lightly ran the emery board against it to reveal the copper beneath its patinated surface. In the red glow from our headlamps, it gleamed like precious conduit, one that would hopefully connect us to a magnificent treasure. Then Mace took Morse's original telegraph key and securely wrapped one end of the copper wire to its terminal. Next, he attached the other end of the wire to the copper rod sticking out of the monument's limestone base.

"I can't believe we're actually going to try to send a Morse-coded message from an antique telegraph key to the tomb of a man who's been dead for a hundred and fifty years," I remarked.

Lucretia looked at both of us as if we had lost our minds. Honestly, I couldn't blame her.

"Mace, I have absolutely no familiarity with tapping out messages using a telegraph key. Do you want to do the honors?" I urged.

"It's not something I'm very comfortable with either, Clay, but Weed showed me how to do it a while back, and I'm game if you are."

"Give it a try, big guy! Like you said … nothing ventured," I encouraged.

Mace made certain that he had the connections secure between the copper rod and the telegraph key and began tapping the Morse-coded dots and dashes for *What hath God wrought?* His first attempt was awkward at best and resulted in nothing happening when he was finished.

"I don't think I did that very well," Mace confessed. "Unless you do this a lot, it's not easy to precisely tap a message."

"Take your time, Mace," Lucretia said. "I think your idea is a good one. Now, just focus and relax."

Mace reviewed the sequence of dots and dashes again and gave it another try. His effort was better but not perfect. Again, nothing happened.

"Aaarrgghh!" Mace voiced in frustration. "You had to make it difficult, didn't you, Samuel?!"

With two failed attempts, the three of us were growing increasingly skeptical about our ever being able to conclude our treasure hunt.

"Damn!" I cursed as I shook my fist in the air. "We've done everything you've asked of us, Samuel Morse. We've traveled to different cities to see your paintings. We've found and followed your insipid clues. We lost our best friend. We've been shot and shot at. And, we've been attacked by Dobermans. What the hell else does it take?!" I was getting fed up and wished we were back home with Maggie and Tori and Rennie.

"We haven't come this far only to quit now," Lucretia said calmly. "Give it another try, Mace!"

Mace checked the connections of the copper wire again, and mentally practiced how he would tap the telegraph message. "Okay guys, here goes!"

he said, and he began tapping the sequence of dots and dashes.

At first nothing happened, and then we all heard the strangest of sounds. It was as if the bowels of the earth had suddenly come alive. There was a very deep rumbling sound and the muffled grind of mechanical gears. A few seconds later we saw the mortar along the seams of limestone at the base of Morse's resting place separate, and a man-made opening at the rear of the monument was revealed.

"Holy shit!" I blurted out. "Did that really just happen?!"

The three of us stared at each other with stupefaction etched on our faces. Then, we gazed in the direction of the three-foot-wide opening in the ground near the rear of Morse's tomb. We cautiously walked forward and peered into the dark chasm below. Stone steps led downward.

I shined my red headlamp into the open hole and could see that the steps descended some fifteen feet. Where it led from there, I couldn't tell. "C'mon!" I said. "Let's finally see if there really is any truth to Morse's promise: *My resting place reveals all …*"

I placed my foot cautiously on the top stone step, and Lucretia and Mace lined up to follow me. I went down another step and was greeted by the musty, dry odor of a crypt that has been sealed for decades. Five steps later, and my head was below ground level, and I could actually feel that the December temperature was warmer underground. I switched my red headlamp to its white light setting for greater illumination and saw rock walls with a wrought-iron handrail. Ancient-looking candles were situated in little niches in the wall, but I chose to use my headlamp instead. It was clear that someone, ostensibly Samuel Morse, had gone to a lot of effort to prepare an entry way for whatever was contained below.

"Are you guys up for this?" I called over my shoulder, but I knew the answer.

"Hell yes!" Lucretia cursed uncharacteristically. "If I can endure getting gnawed on by some big-ass Doberman, surely I can descend into an underground passageway in a pitch-black cemetery," she quipped. "How about you, Mace?"

"I've never liked being underground," he confided. "Good thing I've got a tough woman to protect me from spooks!" he joked.

Fact is, we were all "whistling past graveyards" to muster the guts to keep descending into the bowels of the earth. A few moments later, and the three of us stood on the passageway's dirt floor and looked up as if to confirm that the earth had not entombed us from above.

"This way," I said which was pretty ridiculous since there was really only one direction we could go. We carefully moved along the subterranean path, and after some twelve feet we were finally confronted by a massive iron door with designs of what looked like blue electrical charges etched into the door frame. They looked like a stylized version of the blue charges I had seen in my dreams with the bearded old man.

We knew we had finally found Samuel Morse's vault. What treasure lay beyond was anyone's guess.

Mace and I examined the door closely and were relieved that there were no more coded messages that we'd need to convert. The only other thing facing us now beside our apprehension was a two-foot long iron handle protruding from the heavy door. I tried to move the handle and found that it was frozen by the vagaries of time.

"Gimme me a hand here, Mace," I said. "This thing's gonna need more strength than I've got if it's going to budge."

Mace lined up next to me, and we placed our hands for the best leverage. We pulled upward on the handle with all of our strength, but it didn't move. We tried several more times without success. Another frustrating step in our journey to Morse's treasure trove.

"Any thoughts?!" I asked Lucretia.

"Well, you guys have tried pulling the handle up. See what happens if you push down," she suggested.

Mace and I were both a little skeptical, but we followed her advice. We leaned heavily on the handle and pushed down. We heard an audible click, and the massive vault door that had been sealed for nearly a hundred and fifty years opened a crack. What happened next would be forever seared into our collective memories.

Mace and I slipped our fingers inside the slightly opened door and gave it a coordinated tug. The sound of the old iron door screeching on its hinges was our initial reward. Buoyed by our success, Mace, Lucretia, and I jointly pulled on the iron door until it sung open revealing a dark vault measuring some fifteen by twenty feet. We shined our headlamps into the interior and saw what looked like a few dozen wooden crates of various sizes leaning against the vault's airtight walls. In the middle of the subterranean room was an old wooden table supporting a framed portrait of Samuel F. B. Morse and a white paper envelope bearing his monogram. Our search was finally over.

Chapter 33

W E EACH SPENT THE next few minutes examining the vault. Our moods alternated between awe and amusement. We even managed to temporarily allay any sadness we felt because of the violence that we'd experienced during our search.

Mace and I lifted a particularly large crate into the center of the room and leaned it against the table. He pulled his multitool from the leather sheath he wore on his belt, and asked me, "Do you want to do the honors, or shall I?"

Lucretia and I both encouraged him to begin dismantling the wooden crate. With some effort

Mace pried the old nails from the wood and lifted the cover off of the crate. The first thing that our headlamps shined on was a gleaming gold-leaf picture frame. Lucretia gasped when she saw the painting it held.

"My God!" she invoked. "I swear that looks like a Michelangelo!"

With a little more effort, we liberated the painting from its crate, and the three of us stood mesmerized staring at an unknown work of art by the Renaissance master.

"It's got to be worth tens of millions of dollars, maybe more." she appraised.

Mace whistled his surprise, and the three of us lifted another crate to open. Given the rarity of the painting we'd just revealed, Mace took great care in opening the crate on this one. Our patience was rewarded. It contained a DaVinci portrait of an upper-class Venetian woman. It wasn't a subject that Lucretia was familiar with. Next came a stunning Raphael, then another Michelangelo, followed by a Caravaggio, a Titian, a Botticelli, a Veronese, a van Eyck, and an Albrecht Dürer … the greatest artists of the Renaissance era. The last item we uncrated was a stunning two-foot tall marble sculpture of a wandering minstrel by Donatello. Within twenty minutes we had the majority of crates opened, each one containing a masterpiece that any museum in the world would be delighted to own. We couldn't believe our good fortune!

"It's like Morse wanted to assemble his own collection of the artists featured in his *Gallery of the Louvre*, I said.

"I think you're right, Clay," Lucretia began. "In his day Samuel Morse was inspired by the great Renaissance painters, and he played a prominent role in introducing Americans to European art."

I looked at Lucretia and noticed a tear silently slide down her cheek.

"Are you all right?" I asked her.

She smiled a wistful smile. "I was just thinking about my parents, and all of the wonderful paintings and sculptures they acquired over the years. And, I'm also very angry at my brother, Malcolm, for murdering our father and selling our paintings at the Snow auction where you bought the Morse camera."

"I know," I offered sympathetically. "Maybe some of these will help make up for the loss of those."

"They're all wonderful, Clay, but nothing will ever make up for the loss of the Georgia O'Keeffe paintings that my mother loved so much. My father bought them for her as a birthday gift. Malcolm auctioned off one, but neither Drew or I have been able to locate the other. I can only assume that Malcolm sold that one as well."

I squeezed her shoulder supportively, and we stood in front of the table bearing Morse's portrait and the white envelope.

"Look here!" I said. "This portrait of Morse was taken by Mathew Brady. Brady was an early photography student of Morse's when he returned to New York from Paris in 1839 and opened his photography salon. Brady went on to achieve great acclaim for his evocative photographs of the Civil War."

"That photo would go really great with Brady's camera that you own," Mace suggested.

"I'd love to add it to our museum's holdings, Mace, but I have a feeling that determining ownership of this portrait and all of these masterpieces could be held up in the courts for years to come. After all, we're basically trespassing on private property, and some might even accuse us of desecrating a gravesite."

"Yikes!" Mace said. "In all of the excitement, I hadn't even thought of that."

"Maybe this might assuage your concerns a little," Lucretia offered. She had opened the white envelope with Morse's monogram that had been resting on the table with the photograph.

"What does it say?" I asked eagerly.

"Arguably, it appears to be a bequest of sorts," she replied. "Essentially, Morse states that whosoever finds his treasure trove is entitled to all of its contents. It is signed by him and bears the signatures of two witnesses. It's dated 1871, the year before his death. It sure looks legit to me."

"That's helpful for sure, but I imagine it'll take some time to get a legal ruling on true ownership. I'd like to think the trove is ours, but we'll just have to wait and see."

"So, what do we do now?" Lucretia asked.

"What you do now, dear sister," a rough but familiar voice said, "is move your butt over there with your buddies and keep your mouth shut."

We all turned and looked at the entrance to the vault and saw Malcolm Land and two other men standing there. Malcolm had a menacing-looking revolver pointed in our direction. "Now move!" he commanded.

Mace, Lucretia, and I felt like we had just been gut punched by these intruders.

Lucretia glared at her brother. "How dare you, Malcolm, how dare you turn against your family for your own petty gain?!" She lunged at him, but he deftly pushed her aside, and Mace went to her defense.

"Now, now, big man!" Malcolm said as he pointed his gun at Mace's face. "Let's all stay, uh, civilized, shall we?"

Mace helped Lucretia to her feet, and they moved back to where I was standing.

"Oh, and I can assure you, Lucretia, there is nothing petty about the gain I've realized so far, with much more to come from what I see here. You and your friends have certainly found a nice little collection of paintings, haven't you? I'm sure the Land Foundation will be able to find good homes for them … at the right price, of course!"

"You killed our father, you bastard, and poor Benton Pettengill, too!" she spewed venomously at him.

"Well, I didn't do the actual killing. I had someone else do that for me, but I digress …" he added.

"So now what?" I said to him.

"I've just been wondering the same thing, Mr. Arnold. I can't just let you walk away, now can I?"

"Uh, sir!" George Titus finally said. "You actually could just walk away, sir. You've got plenty of dough. You probably don't need anything more, do you?"

"George, don't be a whiny employee. No one likes a whiner! For that matter, why don't you give me your gun?" he said as he turned and pointed his revolver at his security chief. "Nothing personal you understand."

George dropped his gun, and moved over by the three of us. Malcolm picked it up and slid it inside his pocket.

"And as for you, groundskeeper, you can join them, too," he said as he shoved him in our direction.

"Whatever you're planning, Malcolm, it doesn't have to be this way," I tried.

"I'm sure you're right, Mr. Arnold, but alas, 'in for a penny, in for a pound' as the expression goes."

Malcolm backed up to the vault's entrance and offered these parting words, "I imagine with the five of you locked in here your oxygen will run out in about twenty-four hours. That should give me ample time to arrange for clandestine retrieval of the artwork. As for your bodies, well, this is a cemetery, after all."

Malcolm quickly stepped backward outside the vault, and with his gun still aimed at us, he shoved the iron door shut and turned the handle. We were trapped inside Morse's vault with one of the finest collections of Renaissance paintings ever assembled. Our good fortune had crumbled before our very eyes.

George Titus and the groundskeeper rushed the vault door and tried to force it open. It wouldn't budge. They pounded on the door and shouted for Malcolm to let us out. Their pleas went unanswered.

Mace and I looked at each other with forlorn. Unless Malcolm Land had an unlikely change of heart, we knew we were screwed. Lucretia joined us, and we all slumped to the floor. Samuel Morse's portrait looked at us unemotionally from its position on the table.

There's something about knowing that you're going to die that brings a certain clarity to life. My immediate thoughts were of Maggie and our unborn child. Buried down here in this vault, Maggie would never know what happened to me and Mace, and our child would grow up never knowing how much I cared. I felt my heart breaking.

"Do any of you have any cell service?" I asked hopefully.

No one did. I asked the groundskeeper, "Do you have any thoughts about how we can get out of here before our oxygen runs out?"

He shook his head no.

"Any thoughts?" I asked Mace.

"Only that I'd rather be anywhere in the world other than down here," he offered somberly.

I looked at the trove of incredible paintings with disinterest. I viewed Brady's portrait of Morse and said, "You know it's all just stuff, don't you, Samuel? Perhaps very rare and valuable stuff, but it's rather meaningless now, isn't it?" I asked him rhetorically.

Lucretia sat on the ground in between Mace and me, and I couldn't help but think that we would be spending eternity together.

Time passed. It could've been minutes or an hour. I wasn't sure. I looked at my watch and figured it would be getting light outside soon. I wondered how long our headlamp batteries would last before we were cast into perpetual darkness. Not happy thoughts. Mace turned his headlamp off to conserve our battery supply for as long as we could. We both knew we were likely putting off the inevitable. We were royally screwed.

No one spoke for a while. It seemed rather pointless. Then, George Titus said, "Ms. Land, I'm very sorry that I played any role in Malcolm's sinister plans. I never meant to hurt you or anyone."

"Well, you did, George, and that's something you're going to have to live with for whatever time we have left," she said unapologetically.

"What's your name?" I asked the groundskeeper. "If I'm going to die down here, I might as well meet the neighbors."

"Vernon. My name's Vernon," he said absently. We nodded toward each other but said no more.

More time passed. I closed my eyes and tried not to think too much, but images kept flashing in my mind's eye. I thought about my wonderful parents who had been gone for many years now. I thought about Weed who Mace and I loved like a brother. I thought about Tori and Rennie and how much I missed their smiling faces. I thought about my career, and how I'd be willing to trade all of my accolades and wealth for just a few more minutes with Maggie. We had concluded our search for Samuel Morse's art trove, but the victory was as hollow as this tomb in which we were encased. More time passed …

I drifted somewhere in semiconsciousness not sure if I was awake or dreaming. It didn't seem to make much difference now. My batteries finally failed, and Mace turned his headlamp on. I flashed on an old biblical verse, "Tis better to light but one little candle than to curse the darkness." I figured I'd have ample time for cursing before too long.

"Did you hear that?" Lucretia asked with surprise.

"Hear what?" Mace asked. Our ears instinctively perked up, and we strained to hear any sound that carried hope. It was deathly quiet.

"There it is again!" Lucretia claimed. Neither Mace or I had heard anything. Then, all of a sudden we heard the screeching sound of the iron door handle being forced and the door flew open with Malcolm Land standing in the doorway.

Chapter 34

MACE AND I IMMEDIATELY leaped to our feet and charged where he was standing. We didn't care if he was armed. We didn't even care if we managed to subdue him. We just wanted to make damn sure that that life-ending door never closed on us again. I dove for the door, and Mace body slammed Malcolm Land into the dirt. Malcolm fell awkwardly with his hands restrained behind his back. When Mace and I looked next, we were face down in the dirt staring at a pair of nicely polished, dew-spattered shoes.

"Uncle Drew!" Lucretia shouted as she rushed to her long-time friend. Drew Thomas stepped into

the vault with a person that Lucretia recognized instantly. "Detective Cioffi! I can't believe you're both here."

Lucretia held on to Drew as if her life depended on it, and she sobbed tears of relief and joy. She then reached over and touched Christopher Cioffi's arm. "Thank you, Detective. Thank you from the bottom of my heart."

George Titus attempted to casually slip past all of us during our reverie, but Detective Cioffi grabbed him by the collar and placed handcuffs on him. "My friends in the New York and Brooklyn police departments are going to have a new home for you, Titus."

"That's fine with me," George said. "As long as I don't have to spend another minute underground, or have to take another order from this prick." He kicked Malcolm Land in the ribs to emphasize his point.

"But Uncle Drew, how did you even know where to find us?" Lucretia asked quizzically.

"Well, before your father died, he asked me to always look after you, which I think you know I've been happy to do ever since you were a little girl. Naturally, our communications about the search for Morse's treasure kept me in the loop about your location, and I had a feeling that you and Clay and Mace would venture to Morse's resting place."

"And how did you decide to get Detective Cioffi involved?" she asked.

"Well, given the fact that Malcolm was the main suspect in your father's and Benton Pettengill's deaths, and that you might be trespassing in the Green-Wood cemetery with our friends here, I thought it would be a good idea to inform the authorities," Drew stated.

"My colleagues in the local police departments thought our idea of running around the cemetery after dark sounded a little wonky, so they were more than happy to let Drew and me have at it," Christopher Cioffi remarked. "As we approached Morse's monument, we saw Malcolm sneaking away, and we were able to surprise and subdue him. He tried pulling a gun on us, but that earned him a well-deserved knee to the nuts from your Uncle Drew. That took the fight out of tough guy Malcolm!"

"Damn good thing you're very clever men!" Mace said. "We owe you our lives, that's for sure!"

The detective led both Malcolm Land and George Titus out of the vault and up the stone steps to ground level where they awaited Brooklyn's finest. Vernon, the groundskeeper, was thrilled to be alive and promised to cooperate to the fullest. Lucretia, Mace, and I were eager to get the hell out of Morse's vault, but first we wanted to show Drew what we'd found. Drew was amazed by the bounty of Morse's trove.

"Detective Cioffi will have the local police department and the cemetery management post guards at the entrance to the vault," Drew stated. "Then, we'll have to go about the business of sorting things out regarding ownership and where to store the artwork."

"Let's get out of here," I finally said. I gave Samuel Morse's portrait a final nod, and we all exited the underground vault.

The sun was just beginning to rise as we ascended again to the land of the living. Mace was beginning to feel the effects of his gunshot wound and our late night close call with death. He leaned on me and Lucretia, and we were happy to be there for him.

Three Brooklyn police officers arrived shortly thereafter and secured the scene. They were originally going to take Mace, Lucretia, and me in for questioning and possibly charge us with trespassing, but Detective Cioffi convinced them of our character, and they were willing to release us to Cioffi's supervision.

We said adios to our new friend, Vernon, and told him we'd make his harrowing near-death experience up to him. An hour later, Drew, Lucretia, Mace, and I were back at our suite at the Plaza Hotel wondering if what we'd just experienced wasn't

a very bad dream but with a very happy ending.
I called Maggie to tell her how much I love her …

———————

The next day that followed was a bit of a blur. Mace
and I flew back to Indianapolis, and Drew and
Lucretia returned to her home along the Gold Coast
in Chicago. Detective Cioffi remained in New York
for a few extra days to firm up the case against
Malcolm Land for murder and attempted murder.
George Titus was charged as an accessory, but he
didn't much care. He was just happy to be alive.

Mace and I climbed into my Tacoma at the
Indy airport's long-term parking lot. "Ready to go
home?" I asked my friend.

"Oh yeah!" he said without any equivocation.
"And, I don't think I'm ever leaving home again!"
he said only in half-jest.

"Amen, brother!" I replied, and then I asked
him, "Mace, do you mind if we don't mention anything to Maggie and Tori and Rennie about almost
dying in the treasure vault? I just don't see how it
would do any of us any good."

"I agree with you, Clay," Mace replied frankly.
"Maybe someday, but not for a very long time. Let's
go home!"

I called Maggie to tell her we were on our way,
and that we had some fascinating news to share. She

and Rennie and Tori, along with Lex and Satchmo, of course, were waiting for us as we pulled into the courtyard of our brewery complex. Our home and family of friends never looked so good.

Maggie and I suggested that we all meet at our place for dinner, and then we walked across the courtyard and took the elevator up to our bedroom. "You seem different, Clay," Maggie remarked. "Are you sure you're okay?"

I was tempted to blurt out the full truth about everything that had transpired at Green-Wood cemetery, but I controlled the impulse. "Just tired, is all," I said. "Right now all I want is to be with you and Sputnik."

A couple of weeks passed, during which time both Mace and I were very happy to stay fairly close to home. We'd had breakfast a few days earlier at Stella's Diner with our good friend, Trent Reynolds of the Indiana State Police. We shared all of the details about our finding Samuel Morse's art trove and how close we came to being buried alive. Trent promised to contact Christopher Cioffi in Chicago and the colleagues he knew at the New York police departments. Both his and Detective Cioffi's character references went a long way in keeping Lucretia, Mace, and me out of legal trouble.

I wandered downstairs to our antique camera museum and stopped to admire the Morse daguerreotype camera. I heard a door open and close and Mace joined me.

"It's hard to comprehend everything that occurred after you and Weed went to Chicago for the auction," Mace said.

I nodded my agreement. "I'd give it all up to have Weed back, Mace."

"I know, Clay. We all would," Mace consoled softly.

Just then my cell phone rang, and I noticed it was Lucretia calling. "Good morning, Clay, I hope I'm not catching you at a bad time."

"It's never a bad time to talk with you, Lucretia," I said. "Mace and I are in the camera museum looking at the Morse camera and talking about stuff."

Lucretia didn't have to use much of her imagination to consider the "stuff" we might be talking about.

"I've got good news to report," she started. "We received an early ruling from the New York probate court, and after much deliberation they feel certain that the three of us do a have a strong legal claim to all of Samuel Morse's art treasures."

"Seriously?!" I said. "You mean it's ours?!"

"Well, we're still awaiting the final decision, but yes, I think we have legal rights to everything."

Mace had his ear close to my phone and heard everything Lucretia had just said.

"I have a suggestion for you guys on how we might divide up the artwork," Lucretia said.

"Please go on," I encouraged. "I have my phone on speaker now so Mace can hear everything you say."

"It seems like the State of New York feels some entitlement to what we found. They've requested that two paintings, of our choosing, go to the main public libraries in Brooklyn and Manhattan, and another painting goes to the Metropolitan Art Museum. I'm comfortable with that, if you are," she said.

Mace and I looked at each other affirmatively, and I replied, "Works for us! Do you want to make a recommendation to us about which ones they should receive?"

"Sure, I can do that," she said, "but first I wanted to see which paintings you and Mace want."

"Well, Mace and I have discussed it a little, well maybe more than a little. It's hard not to get excited at the prospect of owning Renaissance masterpieces," I said frankly.

We spent several more minutes talking about the artwork, and Mace said he'd love to have one of the paintings by Michelangelo. I commented on having the painting by Da Vinci and the stunning painting by Botticelli for Maggie and the baby. I also asked for the Mathew Brady portrait of Samuel Morse.

Then I said, "You know, Lucretia, there's really only one place where all of the rest of the paintings should go."

"Where's that?" she asked.

"The Land Foundation collection," I said.

"But," she began. "You guys deserve so much more! We wouldn't have found anything if it weren't for you and Mace ... and Weed."

"And you and Drew!" I replied. "Besides, the majority of these paintings really belong to the world, and the Land Foundation's program of loaning works of art to various museums is a perfect way to share the wealth."

Lucretia felt humbled by my suggestion and knew that it made a lot of sense. "I'll talk with our new attorney about this, but I'm confident we can make that happen."

"I have one final request about the artwork though," I said.

"Just name it!" Lucretia said.

"The Donatello sculpture of the musician," I began. "Since Tori is blind, I thought she might appreciate having something tangible that she can touch and feel, especially since Weed was a gifted musician himself. Oh, and Mace just nodded affirmatively. He says he likes the idea, too!"

"Wonderful suggestion! I agree 100 percent!" Lucretia declared.

We spoke for a few minutes longer, promised to keep in touch, and hung up for now.

I was finally beginning to feel a sense of closure on this life-altering experience. So much had occurred in such a short period of time. Sweet high notes and heartbreaking low ones. I knew it would take a while to process all of it. Thank goodness I had Maggie, and our baby-to-be, and our close family of friends to help me navigate the future.

Mace and I cast an admiring glance at the wonderful camera Louis Daguerre gave to Samuel Morse in 1839. The memory of Morse's first message came streaming back to me, *"What hath God wrought?"* "Indeed," I murmured to myself.

"Any other thoughts about our adventure with Samuel Morse?" I asked Mace as we departed the camera museum.

He looked at me pensively. "I do," my wise friend said, "but for the life of me, Clay, I don't have a clue where to begin."

Epilogue

LUCRETIA STARED OUT at the gray expanse of Lake Michigan from her living room and pondered her past, present, and future. She marveled at the turn of events that had occurred. Happily, her brother had taken up permanent residence in Cicero's prison courtesy of the State of Illinois. Malcolm Land would never taste freedom again.

Her doorbell chimed, and Lucretia welcomed Drew Thomas into her foyer.

"I have more good news for you, Lucretia," he beamed. "The board of trustees of the Land Foundation has unanimously elected you as president and restored all of your financial holdings."

"Oh, that's wonderful, Uncle Drew, I'm sure you may have had something to do with that."

"Maybe a little," he smiled, "but everyone is relieved that your brother is out of the picture, and that your parents' artwork is no longer being sold off."

They walked over to Lucretia's desk, and she said, "There's still one mystery that keeps nagging at me, though."

"What's that?" Lucretia.

"It's my father will. The notation that he had scribbled in pen as he was in the throes of dying."

"Let's take a look," he said.

Lucretia pulled the legal document out that Ernst Kline had prepared at her brother's direction. Ralston Land's scrawl was readable but made little sense: "LL cedarsleba."

"That is stupefying," Drew agreed. "Maybe it was the effects of the arsenic poison that caused him to write that. I don't know."

"We may never know," Lucretia admitted. "Believe me I've wracked my brain over this. I just can't imagine why writing this was so important to Father as he was dying, but apparently it was. That's why I really want to know."

"I understand," Drew said. "I'll give it some more thought, too. But, hey, look at the bright side, you've been reinstated and even elevated in your personal and professional standing. With Clay and Mace, you found one of the greatest collections of Renaissance art ever … and you live in this magnificent house. Not too shabby, my dear Lucretia."

"I know, and believe me I don't take it for granted. That's something that facing death will do to you!"

She looked around the interior of her family's home. "We've owned this place for a long time now, Drew. Growing up here was a very special experience. Lots of places to explore and use our imaginations. When I was little, Father and I would often play up in the attic ... you know, pirates and robbers ... that sort of thing."

"We particularly liked the large closet that had a bunch of old trunks and grandmother's furs. Father liked its aromatic wood-paneled interior. He called the closet the Cedars of Lebanon, because of the cedar paneling ..." Lucretia stopped midsentence. "Could that be it?" she asked herself as well as Drew. "Did Father's note refer to the cedar closet where we used to play. And LL, did he use my initials?"

Drew looked again at Ralston Land's hand-written scrawl on the will and thought about what Lucretia had just said. "C'mon!" he said. "I'll grab a flashlight. Let's go up to the attic."

A minute later, they had climbed the two tall stories in the old Victorian mansion and entered the musty atmosphere of the dimly lit Land family attic.

"It's over here," Lucretia pointed. "Wow, it's been a while since I ventured up here, and longer still since I've been inside the cedar closet."

Even after Drew flipped on the switch for the closet light, it's single bulb barely carried enough light to the corners of the paneled room. Drew flipped on the flashlight and began looking for anything that looked oddly out of place. He saw nothing especially curious. Together, they looked through old trunks and boxes for thirty minutes, but found nothing that they thought that Lucretia's father would deem special.

They stood together at the rear wall of the paneled closet trying to figure where else they might look. Lucretia turned to exit the "Cedars of Lebanon" when she spotted something she and Drew had missed before. Part of the wall paneling had a rectangular wooden molding measuring some four by five feet. It was made of cedar as well, and its finish matched that of the rest of the paneling. With Drew's flashlight, she examined the molding and saw the initials LL stamped into the wood. Next to it was a black button.

"Look at this, Drew! This is odd. My initials are engraved here next to that button."

"I'll be darned, Lucretia! That's very odd, indeed. Let's push the button and see what happens, shall we?"

Lucretia did as Uncle Drew suggested, and the wood panel quietly slid aside revealing a concealed niche. It contained something that immediately brought tears of joy to Lucretia's eyes. A framed canvas of a large white Moonflower occupied the illuminated space. It was her mother's other painting by Georgia O'Keeffe.

~ The End ~

About the Author
Stuart Fabe

OVER THE LAST FOUR decades, Stuart Fabe has directed his creative energies to three artistic media: photography, weaving, and writing. He has published several books showcasing his fine-art photography and his intricate weavings. He has exhibited artwork at numerous art shows and galleries, and his work is widely collected.

Evening Code is Stuart's fourth novel and is the third story in the Clay Arnold series. He enjoys the role of storyteller and in examining the human conflicts inherent to good-versus-evil. His writing is intended solely as entertainment.

Stuart lives in the bucolic countryside near Greencastle, Indiana, with his partner, Marla Helton, two dogs, two cats, and ten hens.